ENCHANTING SARAH

Morgan Fitzsimons

A Fitztown book

I0631680

Enchanting Sarah by Morgan Fitzsimons

PUBLISHING HISTORY

Published 2012 by Fitztown

Cover art © 2012 by Ariane Soares

ISBN

ISBN 10:   0-9816401-8-4

ISBN 13:   978-0-9816401-8-1

Printed in the United States of America

www.fitztown.biz

Enchanting Sarah by Morgan Fitzsimons

Acknowledgements

My thanks go to my teenage granddaughter Sarah who inspired the   Sarah character in this book. She is small, delicate, highly intelligent and elfin in appearance, yet has the resilience of youth. She is one of 14 grandchildren all of whom are talented and inspiring.   Sarah was the inspiration for the paintings and concept art work for the book and gave me a look into the life of teenagers today. I am also very grateful to Diego, one of the Fitztown team of artists who allowed me to use him as the inspiration for Arin, the hero of the book. And Ariane for her wonderful cover. These three people are from totally different backgrounds and different parts of the world, yet demonstrate the energy, talent and inspiring nature of the young everywhere. It is a privilege to be part of a team of young talented people from all these countries and one cannot fail to stay ever young. Thank you.

Morgan 2012

Contents

Enchanting Sarah by Morgan Fitzsimons

Enchanting Sarah by Morgan Fitzsimons

Chapter One

Who is Sarah?

Sarah sighed as she sorted the pile of comics. Her mother was insistent she cleared out all this old stuff in the attic. Dad had wanted to have the loft converted into a usable room for some time. She threw a whole pile of comics into the big cardboard box that was already overflowing with discarded items. Something told her it was all a waste of time anyway and dad would probably never get the project started. She could think of far more interesting things to do with her day. She turned her head to listen as her mother's voice floated up from below.

"Chrissie's here. I'll send her up."

Enchanting Sarah by Morgan Fitzsimons

They had been inseparable friends since they had been five year olds starting school.

A few minutes later Chrissie's head peered round the old attic door.

"Want a hand?" she said

"I don't want to be up here at all," said a disgruntled Sarah, "but if you don't mind the dust and crawlies, I guess it would be much better with you here."

Chrissie grinned and threw herself into the task with enthusiasm. The girls carried quite a few things down stairs to the ever growing pile for the garbage. They surveyed a considerably clear area of floorboards with great mutual satisfaction.

"I don't think we can do anymore today," said Sarah. "We might as well clean ourselves up for supper. I take it you are staying the night,"

"Yes, I already cleared it with mum," said Chrissie still picking away at things.

Enchanting Sarah by Morgan Fitzsimons

Tucked away in a dusty corner Chrissie spotted a large and very old wooden chest.

"What could there be in that old thing?" she said. It was covered in cobwebs and looked quite mysterious.

"Well I didn't put it there, so I don't know. It doesn't look like anything you would stuff with old toys or clothes does it?"

"Perhaps it's something valuable that's been hidden away for years, or maybe it could have a body in it or something equally scary."

"I hardly think so," said Sarah. "I know we have had some shady characters in the family tree, but I don't think we had any murderers. I don't think the term 'skeleton in the family closet,' is quite meant to be taken literally. "

"You never know, we should approach with caution."

So cautiously Sarah lifted the wooden planks lying across the chest, raising a whole dust cloud making her cough.

Enchanting Sarah by Morgan Fitzsimons

The top of the chest was very dusty but the wood looked quite solid and relatively undamaged. The clasps were not locked and she raised them peeling back the leather straps and slowly she raised the lid. The old hinges on the back creaked a bit. They peeped inside. There were lots of old newspapers. How disappointing.

Chrissie started to lift them out.

"You know, some of these date before the war," said Chrissie. "There's a picture of Winston Churchill with King George."

"Put them to one side, "said Sarah," Maybe the history teacher would like to see them."

"There may be something underneath."

They lifted the rest of the papers out and put them in a neat pile, careful not to tear them. They weren't all newspapers. There was a whole pile of Harpers Bazaar ladies fashion magazines from around 1860 to the turn of the century. They were originally black ink on white newspaper but the paper had over time, turned brown at the edges and a lighter colour overall. They were really fascinating with all sorts of adverts that made them laugh and pages of dressmaking tips and similar things Sarah's fingers caught in the cobwebs and she pulled a face. Yuck, they were nasty and sticky. There was an assortment of bits and pieces, including an old cricket bat and an ancient looking lamp full of dust.

Chrissie laughed and rubbed it. "Hard luck! No genie! "

"Pity, I could do with three wishes, well at least one anyway."

"What would you wish for, let me guess, you would like a certain person to disappear, "said Chrissie.

"You must admit the world would be a better place without Bradley James in it!" Sarah thumped at the battered old Teddy by the chest as though it were Brad and stopped hastily as dust clouds rose again.

They lifted the various items out, quite intrigued.

Enchanting Sarah by Morgan Fitzsimons

"I bet if they could speak they would have quite a tale to tell," remarked Chrissie.

Underneath an old piece of linen at the bottom of the chest was a very old much smaller box. Chrissie helped Sarah lift it out. It had two handles on the sides and was rather like a chest in shape with drawers in it but there was a metal band down the front of the box which seemed to curve down from the lid and it was locked.

Sarah frowned, her curiosity aroused and she wondered how she could open it. The metal seemed to be carved or inscribed but it was so dirty it was hard to tell. She reached over and grabbed an old cushion and took off the cover. She used it like a duster and began rubbing at the metal. To the astonishment of the girls, the more she rubbed at it the more beautiful it got, it wasn't a cheap metal but glowed with the gleam of silver. It really was quite beautiful and the patterns were so fine and delicate.

"It looks as though it could be quite a valuable find," said Chrissie.

Enchanting Sarah by Morgan Fitzsimons

The lock was quite small but there was no key. Sarah scrabbled about in the bottom of the crate and triumphantly emerged with a key that looked as old as the box. She put the key in the lock and turned it. The silver band separated and she was able to lift the lid. Inside were several books. She lifted them out to find they were very very old. One was really ancient, made of leather tooled with silver and gold.

"What on earth is such a thing doing in your loft? " Chrissie asked.

"Mum said there was an old box belonging to my great gran, maybe this old chest is it. Mum surely couldn't have looked under the newspapers or she would have found this stuff and had it on display somewhere."

She shifted on the floor and realised how uncomfortable she was.

"I don't know about you but it hurts on these floorboards so I vote we carry this downstairs to my room and look at it in comfort."

Enchanting Sarah by Morgan Fitzsimons

"I'm for that!" agreed Chrissie.

Sarah put the books back in the box and they each took hold of a handle and carried it down from the attic. They put it in Sarah's room and went down to the kitchen.

"We are done for today mum. Can we take our chocolate and biscuits to my room? We found an old box with some books in and we want to check them out."

"OK," said Sarah's mother. "Just make sure you bring the mugs and plates back down here."

They got their snacks and went to examine their find.

Once there they took out the books again, Chrissie sitting on the bed and Sarah cross legged on the carpet. The larger book appeared to be a story about an ancient time. There were paintings in it and a lot of copper plate style writing which was in a strange language. The pages were discoloured in places and looked to be extremely old indeed. Sarah loved books and researching stuff and she was familiar with one or two from a collection in the museum. This looked even older. The other two books were journals, diaries kept by two people centuries apart. These, they could read some of the entries, and they read bits out to each other, describing their gifts and talents which were exceptional They also contained herbal remedies which they claimed had been passed on orally and they had written them down to preserve them. She looked again at the very ancient book and right at the beginning was a little painting of a very young face, with fair hair and pointed ears and a mark just like the one on Sarah's forehead.

"Sarah this is weird," said Chrissie, "but this looks so like you."

Sarah swept back her hair revealing those all too pointed Elf ears and she went to the mirror and using a piece of tissue, she removed the makeup covering the birth mark in the centre of her forehead just above where her eyebrows began.

"It is similar," she said.

Enchanting Sarah by Morgan Fitzsimons

"Do you suppose they are ancestors of yours," asked Chrissie.

"Anything and everything is possible," Sarah replied.

"There is a picture here of a beautiful star-like necklace. Is there anything else in that box?"

Sarah reached out to it and opened the drawers. There were several pieces of delicate jewellery in the tray like drawers but she couldn't see anything else. She pressed some of the intricately carved flowers and noticed a small star carved on the side. She touched it and a small drawer popped up at the back. Inside was a small bag covered with cobwebs. Chrissie was really excited as Sarah slowly opened it and out fell a piece of what seemed to be stone. It was dull and lifeless and suspended on a chain. The setting was quite beautiful in itself.

"It's lovely, said Chrissie in   Do you suppose it could be the one in the painting."

Enchanting Sarah by Morgan Fitzsimons

""Look, "said Sarah "I can see something inside it."

"It looks like flowery meadows and trees," whispered Chrissie looking over her shoulder.

"I think we had better consult mum," said Sarah.

She raced down stairs with it in her hand. Her mum had just relaxed with a glass of wine and Sarah's burst into the room was quite unexpected and the glass slipped from her grasp sending a flow of red wine down to the white rug.

"What's the panic," she said crossly. "Look what you made me do."

"Sorry mum" she grabbed a cloth and hastily scrubbed at the liquid.

"Why can't you move that fast in the morning when it matters, and you can stop scrubbing, that won't shift it."

Sarah stopped and stood up and the rug looked quite white and sparkly.

Enchanting Sarah by Morgan Fitzsimons

Her mum frowned. "That's odd, it was red wine. Maybe I should get you cleaning up more often."

"We found this mum, in the box."

She held it out and it still sparkled as the light caught it.

"I wondered where that was," said Mum.

"Your great grandmother left it to your gran to give to the first granddaughter she had. That was you so she passed it to me together with a bunch of stuff. We packed it away somewhere. Apparently it had been in the family some years. Where did you find it?"

"It was in n a small chest, inside the big one. So it's mine then. Can I wear it," said Sarah.

"It's an antique of sorts, but you are old enough to wear it now if you want to, so why not."

Her mother went to the kitchen to fill her glass again and Sarah and Chrissie went back upstairs. Sarah put on the necklace and the sparkling jewel felt quite warm under her shirt. Back in her room she examined it again.

"It doesn't look much like a star," declared Chrissie.

Sarah gave it a rub and as she touched it, a beam of light radiated from it.

They gasped with shock and Sarah continued to polish it until the whole thing shone like a diamond star, the light so brilliant it was dazzling. It had a life of its own. Even as they looked they were conscious of an eye staring back at them. Sarah dropped it with a gasp. It rolled under the bed. They got on their hands and knees scrabbling to retrieve it. Sarah came up with it in her hand. She stayed on her knees looking into it. The eye had retreated and she could actually see a whole person. They just stared at each other, Sarah being mesmerised into silence, suspended in the moment.

The person moved and the Twilight Star sent forth a beam of light that lit up the bedroom wall and she saw whoever it was inside it, move forward to stand on their carpet. They were speechless and in such shock they were totally struck dumb and couldn't have shouted for help if they tried. It was a young looking male with long pale silvery hair much like Sarah's. He was dressed in leather and wore a silver grey sleeveless coat that almost swept the ground. Over his shoulder he carried a bow but he also had the pointed ears that said Elf. He said something to her, but in such a strange language she hadn't a clue what he was talking about.

Her tongues came unstuck from the roof of her mouth. "I don't understand you," she said, "Stupid of me! You probably don't understand me either."

He spoke again and it sounded a cross between ancient welsh and Anglo Saxon. I need help here!" she said and the moment she spoke, her mind began to unravel his speech.

"I believe I am once more in the world of men," he said in a rich deep voice. He reached out and touched Sarah's hair. She was still rigid and speechless. "You look just like Lilia the Golden," he said.

Sarah found her voice which came out almost in a squeak. "Who is Lilia the Golden," she asked. "And who are you, for that matter," she added. "I didn't know what you were saying, and then I did. How could that be?"

"It would have to the dragons," he said. "They understand all things."

"The what?" said Sarah, "who *are* you?"

"I am Sorrel, an Elf of the Golden Tribe," he smiled. "Lilia was once my aunt and my queen."

He looked about curiously. "It has been a long time since I was last here. Things are very different." He saw the ancient book on the table. He opened it and showed her a painting. It was of himself. She looked at it and looked at him.

"Is that an ancestor of yours," Chrissie asked him.

"That is a portrait of me," said Sorrel. "I am Elf. We live a great deal longer than men. In your terms, I have lived for several millennia, but we age so slowly, time means nothing to me, the past, present and future is all one."

He reached out and touched the mark on Sarah's forehead.

"It is the mark of the Enchanters of the Dulcamara." He traced it with his finger tip. "It is strong, but not as Blackthorn's is. It explains the connection with dragon."

He touched the book again and it fell open at a painting of black haired young Elf who also had the same mark. She gasped as she looked at it, her eyes meeting Sorrel's.

"It's possible, you could be descended from Blackthorn," declared Sorrel. "He married a human female, Princess Rowan. They left a son here and grandchildren who were all definitely not Elf, or so we thought, yet here you are."

"Do I look like this Blackthorn?"

"Not a bit, said Sorrel. "He is dark and you are fair, but you do look like his grandmother my aunt

Enchanting Sarah by Morgan Fitzsimons

Lilia. You have her hair and her eyes and that extraordinary mouth that curves into a smile all the time. The more I look at you the more you remind me of her."

"I would love to see her, said Sarah

"Alas her life was taken from her, but it is something that will remain with me always it was so terrible."

She didn't push it and he offered no more details.

"Where did you appear from? How did you actually get here," said Chrissie.

"I came through a doorway created by the Star. Blackthorn had to leave it behind in order to pass through it."

"I know what a portal is but portals into another world just don't exist," said Chrissie.

"Well he actually is here and he is quite solid and not an apparition." Sarah touched his arm.

"You *have* to be related in some way to the Enchanter Lords," he said.

Enchanting Sarah by Morgan Fitzsimons

"What do you mean, *Enchanter* Lords?" Sarah asked.

"You will have a great deal of time in which to find that out," he said. "What may I call you?"

"My name is Sarah," she said. "This is my best friend, Chrissie."

"I am delighted to make your acquaintance my Lady Sarah." He bowed and smiled at Chrissie. "Blackthorn was my greatest friend and still is, so I am happy to see you have a best friend too."

"You mean this Blackthorn is still living just like you?"

"He never leaves the Twilight kingdom now my lady. He will not be parted from Rowan who is there with him. She is not elf and can never return, so he will not."

"Kingdom? That implies he is a King. I don't understand any of this. What does it all mean?"

"He is a king and an Enchanter, the High Elf King if we are to be exact. Now that I know you are here, I will find ways to help you," He flicked through the book on the table. "I would suggest you read all that is written here, and you will understand something of our ways and what you must have inherited with that mark. It is not as Blackthorn's was, there will never be another like him, but it has some strength that must be guided."

"But I can't read it!"

"I think you will find you can now, since you can speak to me and understand me. I will come back, and help if I can. You will need your friend to support you as you find your way."

He turned to go but she grasped his arm. "You can't just go and leave me to make sense of this by myself. "

He turned back briefly, "all in good time, just don't forget to leave the portal open. The fact he may well have a part human, part elf descendant will make him curious enough I think, to want me to come back. "

Enchanting Sarah by Morgan Fitzsimons

"Wait a minute," said Sarah

He went back through the light to the place beyond, calling back as he went. "May I suggest you wear the Star at all times Lady Sarah."

"But I don't know how to open or close this portal, I don't know how it happened," but she was wasting her time.

She picked up the sparkling jewel and looped the chain over her head and concealed it under her t shirt.

"Did that really happen," said Chrissie," or did I dream it."

"If you did we both had the same dream," said Sarah.

Sarah grabbed the book and they curled up on their respective beds while Sarah read about The Twilight Star and Blackthorn, the Last Enchanter as it was written by his granddaughter long ago. When they reached the point of their eyes closing, Sarah put the book on the table and gave in to sleep.

Enchanting Sarah by Morgan Fitzsimons

"Sarah, Sarah you are going to be late for school,"

The voice penetrated Sarah's sleepy mind and her eyes partly opened, her hand snaked from under the bedclothes as she groped for her watch on the table next to her bed. Her grandfather was right. Her mother and father had already left for work. She rolled out of bed and hastily dashed to the bathroom, but the door was shut. She knew without asking who was in there. She banged on the door, "Come on Charlie! Give me a break. I am already late and I haven't had breakfast yet." Then she remembered Chrissie and dashed back to her room, but she wasn't there and neither were her school clothes. The book was there though and she realised the events of the night before hadn't been a dream, and the jewelled star nestled under her night attire as though it had found a home. She ran back to the bathroom and banged on the door again. The door opened and Charlie strolled out as if next week would do.

Enchanting Sarah by Morgan Fitzsimons

"Keep your hair on," he said, "I'm not leaving myself without some toast or something." He strolled down the stairs leaving Sarah to rush in. She raced back to her room and pulled on her uniform as fast as she could and was going through the door, bag in hand when she took in the state of the room. She cleaned her teeth and looked at her face in the mirror.

Sarah appeared to be a normal sixth former, apart from her size. Blue eyes under sweeping lashes stared back at her from a really pretty face. She had a fragile delicate quality which gave no hint of the strong and agile young lady she was. Her hair was long and very fair. She was everyone's idea of a fairy princess. On her forehead in the centre between her brows she could see that delicate blue birthmark. It was almost like a spider web in shape. She reached for the jar on the shelf containing a well-known brand of covering make up and gently applied some cover to the mark. It concealed it perfectly. She went back to put on her uniform and brushed her hair. She was much smaller than her friends and everyone had trouble relating her to the sixth form. The wall mirror over her desk reflected her image, revealing the pointed ears under that long hair. She brushed it this way and that, but she couldn't hide them completely whatever she did. Were they real elf ears? "Don't be daft Sarah; it was all your imagination." She said to herself. But the necklace was real. She could feel it against her skin. As usual she grabbed a hat and crammed it on her head running for the door. She looked back and realised she would be in trouble if her mother saw the mess. Impatiently she went back and threw her night clothes in the wash basket and straightened her bed. Now she really was running late. She rammed the book into her bag and raced down the stairs to find her three brothers ready to leave, and Chrissie chatting to her grandfather. He sympathetically passed her some toast which she ate on her way out to the car. Grandfather drove the older boys to the city college, and the girls to the sixth form academy, and Paul to the same school where he was in the first year. He often picked them up, though the two older boys,

Enchanting Sarah by Morgan Fitzsimons

Charlie and Mike, sometimes went on their bikes, particularly if they were meeting friends.

When she got to school, she and Chrissie ignored the boys scattered at the entrance, and chatted briefly agreeing to meet up later. They were both studying different subject mixes and levels inside the academy but they had quite a few of their lessons coincide She was still bemused over what had happened but she couldn't get her head round it, and she needed to concentrate on lessons. There would be time enough to think about it later, when she went home.

Chapter 2

Unreal events

Everything was fairly normal as she attended lessons, changing rooms for the appropriate one each time the sound of the bell penetrated. Meeting with Chrissie at break she discovered her group would be in the gym when Sarah's group was there. She put up with usual banter from the pushy boys and the girls who thought they called the shots. It was always about her ears. She got 'Pointy ears,' and Elf ears or 'Big Ears, "and a variety of comments some of which shouldn't be coming from the mouths of babes. Everything was the same until she went into the gym. The Twilight Star was still there under her gym shirt and she had more or less forgotten it. She changed into her shorts and trainers along with everyone else and tied her hair back out of the way, which couldn't be avoided but exposed the ears to a few more comments. Chrissie appeared, glaring at the tormentors and they joined the rest of the girls waiting to practise their athletic skills.

Suddenly she heard what Brad James said to his partner in crime Tom Murray, who was grinning like a cat with the cream.

"Watch out for some laughs, I stuffed a big spider under Claire's jacket and any minute now she's going to dance and scream and start ripping of her clothes to be rid of it."

Claire was a very shapely brunette who was absolutely terrified of spiders. Sarah didn't think about how she had heard the conversation, she just got mad.

"You idiot Brad," called Sarah and she marched up to Claire. "Don't panic Claire but that fool Bradley has stuffed something you don't like under your jacket and I am going to remove it Just stay still."

She slipped off Claire's sports jacket revealing the gym shirt and shorts and in the middle of her back was the spider. Sarah had it off and on her hand before they could start screaming and held it out to show the instructor. Without any problem, she touched the spider which then stayed uncannily still while she dropped it out of the window,

The boys just stared at her. "How could you possibly know, you couldn't have seen me," said Brad.

That was enough for the instructor who grabbed them by their collars.

"I heard you tell Tom," she was puzzled.

"You couldn't have done that either, he whispered it in my ear. Cliff couldn't hear him and he was next to me."

"True, "said Cliff "or I would have shopped him."

Enchanting Sarah by Morgan Fitzsimons

"The two of you, outside on the bench, I'll deal with you later. At your age you should be setting a good example, not behaving like kids."

"Maybe the ears are good for something," said Chrissie trying to make it into a joke, but she wondered as much as the rest how Sarah had managed to hear the words so clearly.

However the more the afternoon proceeded, the more odd things came to light. Sarah began to excel at everything she attempted. She wasn't too bad at athletics for one so small and fragile looking, but now her performance on the equipment was faultless whatever she did, and she raced up a rope and somersaulted down so fast your eyes blinked.

"Well well, "said Miss Forester, "You have been hiding your light under a bush somewhere Sarah. "All this time you have been pretending you were just average."

Outside was just the same, she ran faster than anyone there and went over the hurdles like a professional star. She sank on the grass barely out of breath

"Oh my, "said Chrissie, "Oh my oh my,"

"Will you stop saying that and help me figure this out."

"It must have something to do with the Elf ancestor bit of our encounter last night," said Chrissie, "I had almost convinced myself it didn't happen, but aren't elves supposed to be super athletic and able to outrun anything?"

"Elves are not supposed to do anything; they are just myth and legend from historical times. I suppose the legends imply they are thought to be super agile."

"Well the guy last night isn't a myth, he exists." said Chrissie. "You felt his arm remember."

"I couldn't do any of this before, so it just can't be any elf genes I may or may not have," said Sarah. "If it was genetic, I would have shown the skills long before now."

Enchanting Sarah by Morgan Fitzsimons

"But maybe the Star recognised the genes and kind of switched you on," said Chrissie.

"I don't know what is going on any more than you do," replied Sarah. "The most likely is this isn't real and I am not really here."

"Then we should go home and work it out."

"If I'm not here how can I go....oh never mind." Sarah jumped up and went to change. They made their way out of the gym towards the classroom lockers to get their bags and coats. On the way they passed the wretched Bradley who was busy annoying some first year boys and girls. Considering he was a sixth former, he didn't behave like one. He tossed the watch he and Tom had taken from William throwing it up to land in the gutter.

The boy was almost in tears. "My dad will kill me if I go home without it."

"Too bad," said Bradley, "You should have paid up your fees at break this morning."

Enchanting Sarah by Morgan Fitzsimons

They turned the corner each heading for their own cloakroom, William's friends offering sympathy as he went. Sarah looked up at the gutter, checked no one was looking but Chrissie, and raced up the wall grabbing the watch before somersaulting down again. They looked at each other.

"I just felt compelled to try it," she said.

"That's it," said Chrissie, "my mind's blown. I am going home now," and she walked away in a daze.

Sarah went to the boys cloakrooms and when William came out she handed him the watch and ran. He just stared at it, trying to figure out how she had managed to get it back so quickly. She changed swiftly and went out to the car but all the time conscious of the warmth of the necklace still there under her clothes and still in shock over the events of the day.

She walked in to the house still a bit dazed, her mind going over everything that had happened. Charlie was in the computer room engrossed in a game as usual. "Do you ever doing any work at college Charlie; you are always back here before I am?"

"I get by," he yelled back

She went out into the garden and sank into a chair and closed her eyes. A second later a ball whizzed past her head and made a strange sound as it hit the hedge. Her eyes opened and she turned her head to see a small hole, the size of a ball, right through the thick hedge. She turned her head the other way to see her bewildered younger brother Paul. He was a slim delicate looking boy with an engaging grin, but right now he was frowning at the hole.

"How did I do that, I mean I know I'm not as weedy as I look, but no way can I throw a ball that hard."

"You are as weedy as you look, and dad's going to kill you."

"Not if he doesn't see it!"

"And how do you plan on hiding it?"

He didn't answer immediately but stood in front of the plant trough from which a plant grew up a trellis stand. "If you give me a hand to move this a bit further over, he won't see it,"

He gave the stand a little push and in the twinkling of an eye, the stand and the trough had moved along a bit.

They both stared not at all sure what happened. The trough and stand were joined together by the twining plants and would need at least two people to ensure the plants were not damaged.

"There you see, you can't see it now, but how did it move so easily and perfectly. I haven't got a magic wand or anything." He grinned at his sister who was frowning.

She puzzled about it until the next day. Grandfather couldn't take them to school that morning so they had to catch the bus. Charlie was in the college and he didn't have to go in that day and Mike had already gone on his bike, so it was just Sarah and Paul. They had a few minutes to spare so Paul nipped into the little shop. The bus came and he hadn't come out. Sarah shouted him as she got on. The bus started to move off as Paul appeared and he ran to jump on. The bus was moving really fast but Paul had no trouble keeping up and he grabbed the rail and jumped on. Everyone who noticed sat open mouthed at the feat as Paul sat down breathing quite normally, unaware of what he had just done. Sarah looked hard at him her mind working overtime. She had never seen Paul run like that. He was so small for one thing and his legs were more on the short side. It was a repeat of her extraordinary behaviour yesterday, though albeit not so spectacular. Was it something in the breakfast cereal or the TV ads comes to life? Somehow she didn't think so. Maybe Paul did have a small birthmark on his forehead but it was barely a smudge and it only really showed if he got angry or stressed out. Could it be that if he was near the Star he had a reaction to it. Could he also have inherited something of the Elf gene? She stared at his ears which looked quite normal as far as she could see.

Enchanting Sarah by Morgan Fitzsimons

"Why are you staring at me Sarah, have I grown asses ears or something?

Maybe they were just a little pointed, maybe.

"Not exactly, "she replied. "We need to talk though you will never believe me!"

"Talk away," he grinned cheerfully.

"Not here, see you after lunch by the cricket pavilion."

"Ok but a date with my sister isn't going to do my image much good."

"What image," she laughed. "I'll bring Chrissie anyway, that should give you consequence sitting next to an attractive sixth former."

They went their separate ways and it seemed to Sarah forever before the lunch bell, but to Paul it came around pretty fast. He told his friends Sarah had some kind of desperate crisis and he would have to sort it or face his dad when he got home to which they were all sympathetic and couldn't really decide which was worse. He raced over the field to where he could see Sarah sat with Chrissie on the grass.

"Now what is this all about and make it quick," he said.

He threw his bag down and dropped down next to her as the bag caught Chrissie's fingers. The heavy book inside it really made an impact and she cradled her fingers.

"You nut Paul, I think you broke my finger." It was already swelling and looking bruised. Sarah reached out and grabbed her hand to inspect it and she winced but in seconds her finger glowed with a soft light and she let go Chrissie's hand as if she burned her fingers.

"What did you do," whispered Chrissie. It doesn't hurt anymore."

"It probably wasn't hurt in the first place," said Paul, but he was clearly disturbed.

Sarah told him the story of the box but when she got to the bit about Sorrel, he just looked at her as if she were daft though his face changed somewhat when she showed him the Twilight Star pendant. His finger touched it and he jerked back.

"There is someone inside it, "he said. "It's kind of scary."

"Too scary to talk about it," said Chrissie.

"I mean super powers are unreal. It's just Television and movies; no one really has any such thing." Paul talked as though trying to convince himself.

"I don't think its supposed to be super anything, I think it's just the normal attributes of Elf."

"Who do you know that can run up a wall and leap down again," asked Paul

"True. You did that I saw you," said Chrissie to Sarah.

"If anyone finds out they'll think we're nutcases," he muttered. "If it's true that is."

"Don't go anywhere tonight and we will see if this Sorrel bloke does come back," said Sarah.

Enchanting Sarah by Morgan Fitzsimons

All afternoon both Sarah and Paul, in their respective classes, were unusually silent. Paul's teacher thought he was coming down with some bug or other as his cheeky grin and amusing banter were missing from the lesson. Chrissie phoned her mum and got permission to go home with Sarah and the three of them boarded the bus and didn't say much until they reached Sarah's house.

Chapter 3

The Ryder

"Ok so let's review the situation," said Paul

"We do need to recap," agreed Chrissie.

They were sitting in the bottom garden which was bordered by apple trees on one side and a hedge of hawthorn on the other. It was quite secluded and not overlooked. To tell the truth it was a little neglected and overgrown but it was naturally beautiful in a way Sarah liked. She much preferred it to neat bordered lawns. There was an old oak tree you could sit under, and an ash not far from it and a couple of birch trees partially hidden behind. Beyond it was a small coppiced wood. Sarah pulled the necklace out into the light where it shone and glittered. She allowed the light to reflect through it unto the tall silver birch tree trunk and waited. The light grew as Paul watched in awe and Sorrel stepped into view. He smiled a greeting and laid his bow down on the grass before sitting at Sara's feet.

"Blackthorn and I have spoken together. It would seem likely you are in some way connected to him you are so like Lilia his grandmother and Blackthorn's small granddaughter when he last saw her. We will help you find yourself, and your place in the weave of life, though I can tell you things, much of it you must experience to understand."

"I am beginning to wonder," she said."Paul is also showing some small signs of the Elf heritage at least when he is close to this jewel you call the Twilight Star."

"If you are asking my opinion It perhaps is possible for humans to exhibit some small connection with any elf ancestor. Blackthorn's elder son was all Elf and clearly Dulcamara, though not Enchanter. His second son was human in appearance, and the linear time aging, but he was an exceptional leader as I recall."

"Why would this Blackthorn be so interested," asked Chrissie.

"Elves don't have many children despite their long lives. The fact he had two so quickly, was perhaps down to his wife being human. They are few and far between. He finds the idea of still having some connection in the world of men quite fascinating, as do I."

"Have you no children then?" Chrissie questioned.

"Alas no," he replied

"Are Elves so different from humans then," asked Sarah.

"We have two arms and legs and eyes and ears of course I suppose you can't miss those, but you have all of those too."

Sarah grinned at him.

Enchanting Sarah by Morgan Fitzsimons

"We have a heart that beats and we breathe the same air and as I remember Blackthorn and his human wife Rowan were very compatible, so I think we are not so very different."

"But Elven abilities are different and there must be other things that are," said Sarah.

"I can only speak for myself but on a good day I can outrun the fastest horse, in fact I can run all day and not tire. It is noticeable I have more physical abilities than men, but my enchantment abilities are very small, and I can't heal. I am not an Enchanter Elf you see. We have many things in common in our beliefs and way of life with men I once knew, but it may be different now."

"Why would you think that?" Sarah was curious.

"It feels very different, just standing here, even though I am surrounded by trees, my senses tell me beyond them, it is changed."

"I am not sure I want these abilities that make me different. I can run faster and jump and climb and not get tired ever since I found this," she held up the necklace "what else am I going to find and do I want to? Maybe I should put this back where I found it."

"I don't think it will change things," said Sorrel. "Finding it just awakened you to the possibilities of who you might be. It isn't a magic talisman in itself. It may be a portal but it isn't controlling you. Now you have touched your inner self you can't lose it again. I am afraid it is more likely to get tougher for you than easier. "

"What does that mean," asked Paul.

"Blackthorn found it hard to come to terms with what he could do and what he should do, and you no doubt will have the same problem though perhaps on a smaller scale." Sorrel replied.

"You mean you could misuse the abilities?" said Chrissie.

"It would be tempting," said Sorrel, but the fact Sarah was able to heal says it is highly likely she will have the enchantment of the Dulcamara also."

Enchanting Sarah by Morgan Fitzsimons

"You mean magic, like evil witch magic?"

"It would depend on what you were using it for, but the evil we had to contend with in those days perhaps does not touch you here."

"It might be peaceful in this garden at this moment in time, but the world is a very tough place for a lot of people. There is more wickedness out there than I would care to encounter," said Sarah

"If that is so then you will need our advice even more?" Sorrel said quietly.

"Why?" she asked.

"The evil will seek you out Sarah. It will want what you have, however small your gift is. Evil is greedy always for more."

"Now you are scaring me," she said

"Me too," echoed Chrissie and Paul

"You need to discover what you can and can't do for yourself and use the abilities wisely. I myself would like to see a little more of this place as it is now. Like most elves I am curious. How far do these woods stretch?" He waved at the tress around them in the garden.

"They don't," said Sarah. "It isn't a proper wood. It's a garden behind my home. I suppose it's a bit bigger than most, but there are no real woods of any size near us. The trees over the fence form a small coppice wood but it isn't much and there are a few larger old trees and lots of undergrowth. There are groups of trees at the roadside but it's quite a way to proper large woodland."

Sorrel frowned. "I see I will need to learn more myself. I will leave you again. Blackthorn intends to send you one of his companions. Through him he will be able to communicate directly to you. Such communication is something that must have limits put upon it. Sustaining any form of enchantment depletes the person doing it and the distance between you both is vast, so contact must be fairly short."

He looked around intently.

Enchanting Sarah by Morgan Fitzsimons

"I see you have an old oak tree here. It has sufficient foliage for Ryder to occupy it for the time being. He checked the small coppice wood area and the larger trees behind, and approved that too. He moved back to the silver birch tree and was gone. He popped his head back to speak briefly. "I will be back tomorrow before twilight with our friend," and he vanished again.

""Dont vanish again, I have more questions," her voice faded to a whisper. He had gone without hearing her.

"It's breathtaking. It's awesome," said Paul. "Wait till I tell my friends, they just won't believe it."

"Not a lot of people would believe it and anybody that did would lock us up somewhere and treat us like aliens or some sort of experiment," said Sarah

"They will lock us up if they *don't* believe it," said Chrissie.

"You can't tell anyone, not even mum and dad at this stage," said Sarah.

Enchanting Sarah by Morgan Fitzsimons

"I suppose you're right," said Paul, we would either be locked in a loony bin or Sarah mis-used by someone or other and probably locked up by them, not a very exciting prospect either way. We could even get stuck in some scientific facility somewhere and experimented on."

"You watch too much TV," said Chrissie.

"I wonder who this friend is," said Sarah.

"Maybe someone tall dark and handsome who isn't a relative or thousands of years old," laughed Chrissie.

"I wouldn't mind if it was a robot or something like it," enthused Paul.

"Don't be daft! He is from an ancient culture not a future one," said Sarah

"Well they could have had robots," said Paul.

"Maybe he will send you a dinosaur then Sarah or some sort of bug, that will please Lord Paul here no end,"

Enchanting Sarah by Morgan Fitzsimons

Laughing and arguing they went in to find the evening meal was ready and Sarah's mum was in shock as they didn't watch TV afterwards or play computer games but rushed upstairs to talk.

The following day was both funny and disastrous. It was Saturday so they went to the park, Paul; to play football and Sarah and Chrissie just to lounge about. The park bordered a wood, which was quite beautiful. It was a good way to pass the time until late afternoon. They sat under the trees while Paul ended up some distance away on the field with some mates kicking a football. Sarah carried a little sketch book in her pocket and Chrissie her camera and they made sketches and took snaps for one of their school projects. Sarah had a straw hat pulled over her ears which looked quite attractive with the sleeveless top and short skirt and patterned tights.

"Just sitting here in the quiet is quite refreshing," said Sarah, as she put the finishing touches to a sketch.

Enchanting Sarah by Morgan Fitzsimons

"I think I would be more refreshed if I had an ice cream," said Chrissie.

"The kiosk is just round the corner. Let's get one,"

They stood up, putting their bits and pieces in their pockets and started strolling down the path in the direction of the little kiosk selling ice cream and cups of tea.

"Walking under the tress is always awesome," said Sarah gazing up at the weaving branches.

They continued down the path in the direction of the ice cream. From nowhere a group of teenage boys appeared, young men really, each one looking tougher than the next and they were surrounded before they realised the threat. Sarah thought she recognised a couple of them. They were the age of her elder brother Charlie.

"The weirdo with the hat fetish," said one.

"She's not a bad looking weirdo," said another.

Enchanting Sarah by Morgan Fitzsimons

"A bit small maybe, but the other one is more my size,"

They were taller and bigger than Sarah and Chrissie and there were too many of them.

"What are you hiding under the hat," He pulled it off her head revealing her silvery blonde hair and the pointed ears.

"Elf ears," he laughed. "She's escaped from a movie set."

The ring leader reached out and grabbed Sarah by the throat to hold her still while he checked out the ears. She instantly kicked him hard in the shins. He let go and she ran. She was gone before anyone could blink but then she remembered Chrissie could not run that fast. She ran back to Chrissie. She hurtled at the one holding her and knocked him over. They were furious then and things looked very bad, just as Sarah broke free. Something flew low over her head with a displacement of cool air blowing through her thick hair lifting it to reveal the ears again. Her face was hidden for a moment beneath a dark shadow and the screech echoed through the trees. The youth screamed and grabbed his face. Blood was visible oozing through his fingers and dripping down on his shirt.

"The bloody thing clawed me," He ran howling from the scene rapidly followed by the rest of them, the creature zooming over them. It was so fast it almost hadn't happened.

"Did you see that," cried Chrissie. She was still shaking, her arm red where the youth had gripped her so cruelly.

"It was a bird, a huge golden creature with great claws that ripped at the guy holding me. It drew blood! I saw it on his face and hand."

Sorrel appeared through the trees. "I waited for you in the garden, but the Ryder took off so I ran after him."

As he was speaking, they heard the beating of wings and a huge bird, with what seemed to be at least a six foot wing span, drew close coming to rest on a tree branch. It was a hawk, but Sarah had never seen one so close and certainly not one as big as this for it was larger than any hawk species she had seen pictures of, or seen on any nature TV programme.

"It is one big bird," said Sarah.

"It's possible the species may have become smaller over the years," said Sorrel. "It has been a long time."

She was fascinated and moved closer to it. The huge hawk sat on a tree stump staring at her. The amber eyes seemed to have a light of their own, and she was drawn to them until their eyes were almost level, the blue staring into the golden amber. It was almost as though the hawk was trying to say something. She was completely captivated.

"Who are you," she whispered, "Where did you come from exactly?"

"From the beginning," was the answer.

"It spoke to me, I heard it!"

Enchanting Sarah by Morgan Fitzsimons

"Now this time you are nuts," said Chrissie, and she turned to Sorrel. "Now you, you look different and not quite so nuts," said Chrissie.

Sorrel was wearing a t shirt and jeans and all his hair including the traditional long locks at the side of his face and in front of the ears, was swept back and tied with a leather thong. He still only looked in his early twenties maybe and with no sign of aging. He did in fact have a lot of silver in it but he was so fair it wasn't noticeable, and the ears of course were still visible.

"I have left my bow and sword in your garden shed," he said with a grin.

"I think that was probably sensible, we don't use them so readily these days and definitely not to shoot people," Chrissie pointed out.

"What about this beautiful hawk," said Sarah, "Where did it actually come from?"

"He came to Blackthorn from his ancestor Ainarr Asveldur and is not at all as he appears to be. He is a hawk, yes, but he has been here since the beginning. He was with Blackthorn here for a while then went with him to the Twilight Star, and now he has come to you. He has much knowledge and is so bonded to Blackthorn it will be as though he were with you. If you look into the eyes you will hear Blackthorn."

She turned back to the bird, who was truly magnificent. The amber eyes were like molten golden pieces of the precious amber yet within them were depths of dark shadow that held you mesmerised. She could not take her eyes from him

"Who or what are you?"

She saw a dark shape of a beautiful male with long dark hair whirling in the breeze in the large golden orbs. It was so brief it was probably her imagination. She blinked. Two eyes within the eyes stared back just as briefly. It was fascinating but very quick. Was it real or her imagination but she was sure the figure had ears even more pointed than she had. It was so tantalising and frustrating. She shivered a little. It was all rather overwhelming.

Enchanting Sarah by Morgan Fitzsimons

"You fear the darkness within me Sarah, I too was once afraid of it."

She jumped for the voice inside her head was so clear. It was deep and yet the voice of a young man in his prime and did not equate with ancient and millennia.

"You are as beautiful as Lilia. Sorrel said it was so."

"It makes you sad I look like her."

"Not sad now, a little wistful maybe for what might have been. She is sadly missed and will never be forgotten by her people."

"I wish I could see you," she said.

"Maybe one day, but look through the eyes of Wind Ryder".

"Wind Ryder, it is an exciting name."

"If you call for The Ryder, he will come. I will loan him to you for a while."

"Thank you for rescuing us," she whispered.

Enchanting Sarah by Morgan Fitzsimons

"You could have rescued yourself," was the whispered reply and the last word echoed in her brain.

"But how, what am I really," she cried but this time there was no answer. She turned back to Chrissie who was talking to Sorrel.

"How did you know what to wear," demanded Chrissie.

"We used a little magic to find out more about this time. It is interesting though worrying at the same time."

"In what way," asked Sarah

"Your race now seems to take so much from the environment and use it for selfish purpose, yet put so little back. You have lost so much quality of life. How can you relate to nature when it is all gone."

"It hasn't all gone yet," she protested.

"Perhaps not yet, but it is our heartland. It is fast disappearing and when it is gone it will be gone forever."

"I know what you mean," said Sarah. "If you lie under the ancient oak or the yew or the willow tree, and see the branches and leaves touch the ground all around you, you feel safe. You look up at the silent green world and feel the enchantment as its weaves a spell around you connecting you with so much. It whispers to you words no one else can hear and you feel at one with the natural things."

"There speaks the eternal elf," he said with delight. "Now I know you. Even before the star, somewhere in your consciousness you touched who you really are."

She looked at the bird. "You are beautiful and I love you already but how am I going to hide you from my mother."

"I will hide myself," The Ryder conveyed, and rose on the air to lead the way back to Sarah's garden.

Enchanting Sarah by Morgan Fitzsimons

Sorrel talked as they walked "It pleases me you find creatures of nature beautiful"

"All nature is beautiful even though it can sometimes be cruel," Sarah said.

"It seems human kind has forgotten the bond with the land. "

"Not all of us," said Sarah.

"Maybe not, but once we all fed on the mystery of the land. It sustained us! We existed in natural harmony with it and that led to existing side by side with man, feeding that marvellous gift of imagination. It was an extension of the mind that led to greater things and creating beautiful things."

"It sounds an exciting time."

"It was a very difficult and dangerous time, fraught with its own dangers, but we had formed such strong bonds which brought us through great adversity. Whatever time and space you occupy, there will always be extreme danger, but the nature of some of it changes, though greed is always there, the evil heart is always evil. Despite it man had a tremendous destiny."

She laughed "You said had!"

"Did I, well maybe they won't self destruct after all."

"That seems very harsh,"she said.

"I can only say what I see, and I *have* looked now."

When they reached home Sorrel was no longer with them and the hawk as Sorrel said, found a place to hide in the old oak.

She awoke in the night and sat bolt upright. Her eyes flew open. She felt the call of the hawk and she was beside the trees at the bottom of the old garden.

"How did I get here," she gasped.

"Mind walking, where did that come from? What does it mean?" Sarah spoke aloud.

Enchanting Sarah by Morgan Fitzsimons

"It came from inside you," was the answer. Deep in those eyes again she could see a shadow, a hint of high ears and long hair.

"Tell me what this is all about," but there were no more answers

She drew back into the shadows. It was getting darker now and all the lights were on in the house, but they couldn't be seen from this bottom garden. She moved back into the darkness of the tall trees. She wasn't at all afraid. The shadows were welcoming the leaves rustled in the gentle breeze. There was an affinity, a sense of belonging to the natural realm around her. She shut her eyes and opened them onto a world she had not really looked at before. A little hedgehog stopped at her feet and she bent to touch it. She was allowed to pick it up and look at the little dark eyes before returning it to the grassy path. An owl flew down to talk to her and she saw its head turning this way and that as it searched for the hawk.

"Hawks and owls are not usually companions, but this one is different, this one I know well." The owl's words spoke to her innermost consciousness and she just accepted it, past surprise now.

Suddenly the hawk was there, its wing span breathtaking as it crossed her line of vision coming to rest on the tree stump next to the climbing roses. Her ears were picking up sounds with ease and she heard Ryder before she saw him. She confronted the beautiful creature staring into the golden orbs once more seeking some truth in the dark shadows in his eyes.

"Who am I what are you?"

"The truth is simple. I am Ryder you are Sarah."

"But I need more than that. You are more than my eyes can see and I think that is true of me also." She put her hands to her head. "There is something, something I can't quite grasp, shadows of the past, things I can't quite see."

"Don't try so hard to find it. It will come."

"What will come? What is hidden here in my mind, and what secrets hide behind those golden eyes?"

Enchanting Sarah by Morgan Fitzsimons

"A dream perhaps, shadows of what might be, some racial connection. You need to find answers yourself."

Did that come from the hawk or her? The idea took root, a racial connection, something in her genes crying out for recognition. The hawk suddenly took off rising up above the trees. It was a so wonderful to watch and Oh how she wished she could soar with him and she raised her arms without conscious thought or hesitation and found herself looking down on the tree tops, soaring up with Ryder and matching him move for move. The wind curved about her and flowed with her and she was at one with the elements but a rush of weariness claimed her and she was standing once more on the ground the hawk resting with her.

Did that really happen or was it the product of an over active imagination? If it was it was imagination fuelling a reality of some kind. Her weariness of body told her it did.

"That is mind walking, or flying as you will."

Mind walking! There was that term again.

Enchanting Sarah by Morgan Fitzsimons

"Sarah!"

She could hear the strong male compelling voice speaking to her as though the owner of it was beside her, which in a way he was for the hawk was a bridge between them.

"Blackthorn?"

"There is only one," was the answer with something of the arrogance of the King of High Elf Lords.

"You have shown some small ability to mind walk. Don't fear it, just absorb it. I will come and walk with you tomorrow."

"What exactly is mind walking?" Sarah asked.

"Ask Sorrel! Mind walking, healing whatever you use of the supernatural, consumes your energy, so you will need to rest now for tomorrow as will I."

She knew immediately she was alone and the hawk had disappeared into the oak tree. She really needed her sleep now, and she had barely thought it and she was in her bed relaxing on the pillows,

Chapter 4

Mind Walk

She ran down the garden the next morning to look for Sorrel. The star was swinging on its chain as she went. She found she didn't need to open a portal anymore. It had become a constant within the birch tree. He stepped from the tree without her doing anything.

"What is mind walking," she said urgently, "How does it work, he said you would tell me, and how could you walk from the tree without re oprning the way."

"Whoa there, just let me sit down."

"Why didn't he tell me anyway?"

"Because the contact with you seriously depletes his energy, so he isn't about to waste it doing something I can do in person," he replied.

"Logical!"

He smiled. "Logical isn't me. I am very impulsive,"

" We share that at least, she said."Tell me,"

"I think patience isn't your strength either, but it's a virtue cultivated in the Elf. We have a long time to be patient. First your question about the tree portal, trees are vital in many ways to the Elf as you will discover, and in this case they are a pathway to other places, particularly the birch tree, so it was an excellent choice to open the portal and I can now continue to use it."

"So what is mind walking."

"Mind walking, it is a difficult concept for many and involves the senses beyond the five humans use normally. The Enchanter has the ability to transcend natural laws and the spirit, the inner consciousness leaves the body and moves through space and time. It is still in the world but is able to move faster and see and hear many things without anyone knowing the Enchanter was ever there"

"Wow! That is seriously cool. Can I go through closed doors and walls?"

He laughed. "I believe Blackthorn could eventually, but from what he tells me, I don't think you should try, at least not yet anyway. Your brother Paul doesn't have the ability at all. I think possible he may have something of the Golden Elf natural skills. But Mind Walking manifests only in the Dulcamara Enchanters, even then some have it, some don't and some in varying degrees. You can enhance what you have by improving techniques sometimes."

"It sounds very useful," she said.

"It is but it's also intrusive and you must learn to use it only when there is great need, and definitely not for personal satisfaction. Misuse causes you to lose it. It corrupts "

Enchanting Sarah by Morgan Fitzsimons

"How can I practise and improve then?"

"By going to somewhere you could have gone to anyway in the flesh, where there is little danger, for it can be dangerous. If anything happens to your spirit or you encounter something dangerous, it can destroy the body."

"Then I'll go to the university library, It isn't somewhere I could go normally as I am not yet at university, but I have always wanted to see some of the special old book collection and it is a public place so I won't be harming anyone, and nothing is likely to harm me. Will Blackthorn come with me this first time?"

"Ask," said Sorrel.

"Will you come," she said.

"We share the mind of the Ryder, so I can choose to go where your consciousness goes." His voice was inside her mind. "Sorrel will watch over what remains. "

"What shall I do?" Sarah asked.

Enchanting Sarah by Morgan Fitzsimons

"Touch your fingertips to the mark and fix the image of this 'library'. Allow yourself to rise.'

She smiled at Sorrel then touched the mark and did as Blackthorn told her. She felt herself moving, floating yet she could see her form sitting on the seat, eyes looking at nothing. She sensed something moving with her. The hawk sat very still beside her, and together they formed a living sculpture down on the garden seat as their consciousness floated through space. Sorrel lay on the grass at their feet. She found she could move quite quickly and flashed through the streets to arrive at the library portals. She followed a student through the door and studied the list of departments before moving up stairs to the Old Books Collection. Some of them were quite rare and were wrapped against the light and in special cases. She was aware of Blackthorn's fascination with the size of the place and the rows upon rows of books. The ones she wanted to see were open in their cases of glass but lit with a special light to lessen aging and damage. There were only two people in the room whispering in a corner. She tried not to listen but those elf ears couldn't help it.

"The book isn't here but I know where to find it," said the short one.

"You are sure it's the book he wants?" the tall one asked.

"Of course I am," said the short one. "It's the one referred to in his old manuscript. My enquiries lead me this far to find it was here, but got auctioned off when funds were a bit low. The library needed money for restoration. Why does he want it so much?"

"The manuscript has been in his family for years and actually tells of a Black Book of Curithir and a charm of making used by some sorceress or other, name of Belladonna," replied the tall one. "It seems he wants to use the book for some purpose linked with divination."

Sarah felt the instant shock coursing through Blackthorn. She began to move away. "Be still child," said Blackthorn. "I must hear this". She felt the urgency and was compelled to stay still.

"He will pay anything for it but the guy who has it now isn't going to want to part with it," said the short one.

"When can we go and get it?"

"Meet me here this afternoon and I will be able to tell you where he is and if we can get it. I am still curious as to what your buyer will do with it," said the short one.

"If is not a word he will accept! All I can tell you is when I asked him that, he just said Tal-git needed it and he needed Tal-git who ever that is."

She could feel Blackthorn's turmoil and was conscious of a tremendous stress building within.

The two men parted and Blackthorn spoke "Follow the tall one."

She obeyed knowing he could probably override her anyway. The man went to the car park and got into a very expensive black car. She was amazed to find they could just follow with ease. The air rushed past and her vision blurred a little as she focussed on the car. He drove to a secluded house with extensive grounds well away from the city. The gates opened to him and he drove up to the imposing front door. Someone came out to park his car, and he went inside. Sarah was now flagging. The experience was totally new to her and her stress levels increased. From the open doorway came the most revolting overwhelming rush of darkness that was stifling, choking and terrifying all at the same time.

"Leave now Sarah," ordered Blackthorn.

When she didn't respond he wrapped himself around her consciousness and whirled her away and she found herself shivering in her garden seat the huge hawk's wings around her shoulders. Sorrel bent over her in concern and she clutched his arm she was so scared. She heard Blackthorn speaking in her head again.

Enchanting Sarah by Morgan Fitzsimons

"You are not strong enough yet to confront such evil. I had not expected it! Send Sorrel to me He will return to explain."

Paul was there with Sorrel.

"Blackthorn told me you would explain but you must go back to speak with him first."

Sorrel went immediately and Sarah lay back to rest in the long grass while Paul sat munching on some crisps. They were still there when Sorrel came back.

"I am to tell you of Tal-git," he told her. "Blackthorn will walk with you again, but he can't do this very often, the strain on his strength over the distance is too much even for him."

"What made him so concerned," she asked.

"It was there reference to Tal-git and Belladonna. Tal-git is a predator, a dragon and more evil and bestial than any creature that walked the earth. Belladonna wreaked havoc for a time by using Tal-git."

"What has that to do with our time," she said.

"I don't know. He was killed a long time ago, but these people can be up to no good if they talk of Tal-git. Blackthorn says we must find out what is going on, particularly as they mentioned the charm of the making. "

"Now you are scaring me."

"Tal-git scared *me*, I just didn't tell anybody. Back then Tal-git belonged to one of the most evil of Dragon Masters and did his bidding. It was Tal-git who killed Blackthorn's grandparents and his mother. Tal-git was eventually killed or so we thought, but Belladonna brought him back, and then he was killed again. It seems he just won't lie down."

"And this book they talked about?" Sarah asked.

"It was a Book of Black Runes containing necromantic characters relating to dead spirits. They are for connection with the dead."

"A bit like the Egyptian Book of the Dead,"

Enchanting Sarah by Morgan Fitzsimons

"Not exactly, The Dragon Master's Books of such runes contained chants used by spell weavers and spoken by Dragon Masters. They were used for evil purpose, even making the dead walk again."

"Why would this man want it?"

"I don't know, but it can't be for any good reason, unless it was to destroy it, and somehow I don't think so."

Sarah turned to greet Ryder who appeared on a tree branch.

"Will you watch over me Sorrel, while I go to the library again?"

"Paul and I will sit and talk while you are gone."

"Be careful Sarah," said Paul.

She grinned but she was a little nervous all the same. This was something she knew little about. It was like jumping of the edge of a cliff into the unknown, and therefore frightening and exhilarating at the same time.

Enchanting Sarah by Morgan Fitzsimons

She closed her eyes and looked into the shadows.

"Blackthorn are you ready?"

"I am here,"

She closed her eyes and experienced once more that strange feeling of being in a swirling mist. It cleared a little and she could see herself below and registered Sorrel and Paul talking and the hawk staring upward. She moved quickly to the library, comfortable in the knowledge he was with her. She arrived at the library just in time to see the two men enter a study booth and she followed behind them.

The tall one seemed angry with the short one.

"Never mind how hard it was, did you get it?"

"He wanted 5 million for it but I didn't have that kind of money, " replied the short one.

"But Jefferson Hemlock does you idiot. I thought I was coming to collect it," said the tall one.

"He wants cash. He doesn't trust my cheque."

Enchanting Sarah by Morgan Fitzsimons

"Well I suppose I wouldn't either," said the tall one. "I will get you the cash and meet you and this guy with it. Write down his address,"

"So you can cut me out of the loop? I will phone you with the meeting place, you just bring the money," the short one was angry now.

"You could have phoned the details in the first place, and saved me a wasted trip."

The short man scurried away and Sarah followed the tall one to his car.

She got in it with him. They went once more to that same house set in substantial grounds. The car passed through the gates where a security guard sat reading his newspaper. This time when they reached it, despite what she could only term as the stench of evil oozing through the door, she followed the tall man inside. It was quite an imposing place. The tall guy went into a large room with desk and armchairs and a man seated near the window. He was wearing a long coat with a hood that partially covered his face. What she could see looked stern and sinister. She noticed his hands covered with dark patterns and she felt Blackthorn's heavy breathing.

"The book," he demanded.

"I still haven't got it."

His master swore at him. "You said today, and I want to be gone by the end of the afternoon. I have arranged for the helicopter to fly me to the castle. You have ruined my schedule."

So this house wasn't home to this man. It was probably one of many business stopovers. How could she find where home was? She looked round the room while listening to them.

"I have to take five million in cash. I need you to authorise it sir, and I can guarantee the book will be in your hands tomorrow morning."

Angrily the man by the window stood up and the hood fell back revealing his face. It meant nothing to Sarah apart from seeing a pair of eyes that looked as black as pitch eyes in which you could suffocate and black tattoo like patterns on his face and forehead., but she felt a protest within

Enchanting Sarah by Morgan Fitzsimons

Blackthorn and the man 's eyes swivelled round the room.

"Who did you bring with you?" he demanded.

"Nobody," said the tall man a little bewildered.

"I can hold on no longer and if I try, I may put you in danger!" The words spun round in her head as she felt him let go. Now she was alone.

The man in the hood prowled about for a moment and then sat down at the table and made a phone call authorising the money to be brought to him. She looked around again. On the wall she saw a painting of a house and at the bottom was the name Mandrake. It was flanked with aerial pictures of an island There were other pictures, a castle among mountains and several other pictures. The man was clearly disturbed by something and it dawned on her it was her presence. He had definitely picked up on Blackthorn, but somehow now he was beginning to sense she was there. Terrified she willed herself out of the house and into the grounds and out through the gates where she read the name on the gateposts. Dark menacing evil threatened to crush her; she could no longer see where she was and willed herself to her garden. She was shaking visibly when Sorrel bent anxiously over her.

She told him what transpired.

"I know the name of the house and where it is but it isn't the guy's home it seems."

"It could be where he stays in England," said Paul. "It sounds like he can afford to live anywhere he likes."

"We need to find out what he is up to though," said Sarah.

"I think so too," said Sorrel.

"We need to actually go there, but I am not old enough to drive a car," said Sarah.

"What about Chrissie's boyfriend?" asked Paul. "He just passed his driving test and his daft dad bought him a car."

"Daft?" said Sarah raising her eyebrows.

Enchanting Sarah by Morgan Fitzsimons

"Well think about it, Darren's a nice lad but not altogether there when it comes to practical. His dad must be daft or loaded to trust him with a car. I am amazed he passed a driving test, but the fact that he isn't too bright about every day stuff, could be useful as he won't ask too many questions."

Sarah phoned Chrissie and in no time at all, she and Darren were sitting with them in the bottom garden. Darren was indeed a nice lad, not bad looking behind his glasses and besotted enough with Chrissie not to ask many questions. But Paul was actually wrong about his intelligence. He was actually very bright indeed and excelled in science subjects, and was fascinated with any form of plant and animal life, it was just he was a bit out of touch with everyday things, as people with his abilities often can be. The university considered him exceptional in the various disciplines he was studying and gave him a lot of space. He was always either at the university studying or following Chrissie, and even then he often had a book in his hand. He was as Paul said, besotted with Chrissie and obeyed her every request, which was perhaps not altogether wise. His attention was caught by the hawk. It was larger than any species he knew of and he was very excited and plied Sarah with questions. Sorrel was the icing on the cake. He was face to face with a flesh and blood elf. He agreed with the need to keep this within the group. He understood only too well what the powers that be would do with unexplained life forms. He cheerfully fell in with their plans which meant that he and he alone was close enough to study this phenomena. He checked he had his laptop in the car and that the batteries were fully charged.

"We don't know what will happen tomorrow or how far we will have to go so we may need to pool resources," said Sarah.

"Resources?" asked Sorrel.

"We will need petrol for the car and money for food and stuff like that."

"You mean transport. Why can we not run? An elf can out run anything, and I can hunt with my bow," Sorrel pointed out.

"Chrissie can't run and we can't run along a motor way. It's not so much I think you can't catch our supper, it's more you won't find a lot *to* catch and definitely not if we end up in the city somewhere."

"You know best, this is the world you are used to," said Sorrel.

"Cash is no problem," said Darren. "I have plastic," he held up a couple of bank cards. "I only use money to take Chrissie out, or buy her presents. My allowances are there from way back. My parents buy me books and equipment and stuff so I don't know why they give me as much as they do. Mother is forever buying me new clothes and half of them I don't wear."

"They work all the time, I suppose they think it will make up for their absence," said Chrissie.

"Well it does now," said Darren. "I have a full tank too. Dad gave me a card on his petrol account. Somewhere I have a bank card for emergencies too. Dad set it up when he gave me the car in case I should break down or have to stay in a hotel or something."

"We can't let you spend it all on this," protested Sarah.

"You can spend what you like. Do you know what a privilege it is to come face to face with Sorrel, and to know I am the only one to study the hawk? I will happily exchange *all* my allowances for that."

"Ok," laughed Sarah. "Paul, fetch a map of the area and we will see if we can pin point the house I went to. While we are on the subject of Hawk, his full name is The Wind Ryder and I can communicate with him"

That did it for Darren, he was awestruck and couldn't speak for a full ten minutes. Paul came back with the map and Sarah gave him the name of the lane leading to the house and the area it was in. They soon found it and worked out a way to go.

"But how will we get in," asked Chrissie.

"*We* won't," said Sarah. "Ryder and I can go in and check the place out then Sorrel and I can vault the wall."

"Makes sense," said Chrissie.

"Can he answer some questions," asked Darren.

They all turned to him.

"We don't want to actually let him know we are there," said Paul.

"I think you'll find he's still with Ryder," said Sarah. "Make a list and don't make it too long, and I will fit it in somewhere."

Darren beamed.

"Everyone needs to be back here early. We don't know how easy it will be to find this place."

"How early is early," asked Chrissie.

Enchanting Sarah by Morgan Fitzsimons

"About 7" said Sarah. "I'll make the cereal and the toast." Chrissie pulled a face and groaned.

"I will sleep here under the tree," said Sorrel."It's the easiest way to be on time."

Darren took Chrissie home and Sarah went indoors to come back with a blanket for Sorrel.

"Thank you but I don't really need it," he said.

"It can get cold at night," she protested.

He just grinned at her. "Something to eat would be more useful, "he said.

She ran back inside and came back with cheese and pork pies and bottled water and a cake tin.

"Not a lot different from home," he said.

"I brought water as I wasn't sure what you would want to drink."

"Water is good but how does this thing work."

He turned it upside down and no water came out. She laughed and showed him how to pull the top and put it to the mouth to drink.

Enchanting Sarah by Morgan Fitzsimons

"You can close it again to stop the water spilling until you are ready to drink it again."

It was a fairly simple thing but it brought it home to Sarah how much would seem strange to Sorrel. She opened the cake tin and cut a huge slice of Victoria sponge.

"Now that is different, "he said "but it looks good.

"I bake them for my gran but I don't think she will mind sharing with an elf."

He took a bite. "It is delicious,"

"I would usually eat the sweet food last," she said.

She grinned and went inside again.

Enchanting Sarah by Morgan Fitzsimons

Chapter 5

Meeting with strangers

Darren arrived early as promised with a half-asleep Chrissie in tow. He had already written his questions and put them on a USB data stick which Sarah put in her pocket for later. They took their breakfast out to share with Sorrel and talked over the map again. Sorrel's bow and arrows were put in the car boot after Darren had taken photos with his mobile phone.

Sorrel was fascinated with the mobile. "What kind of magic is this," he said

"Not magic as you understand it," said Darren. "It's what we call technology. Someone developed and designed it using a combination of elements. Unfortunately too much technology draws too much from natural elements and that is destroying the world around us."

"Sadly there are people, who are greedy and want too much or even it all, and we have people who had it first and those who didn't have it, now want it and the resources to supply it with are reducing. No one wants to have less to give some to those who haven't any, so expanding is rather a difficulty issue."

"I think I get the idea," said Sorrel.

He had tied his hair back again and was wearing a hat over the tops of his ears, and looked like any other young student and it was impossible to tell he was several millennia old. He accepted the technology and the transport quite easily even though he was unsure of how it worked. It wasn't any more frightening or unbelievable as the events he had experienced with the Dragon Masters. He was blessed with an adventurous and curious spirit that embraced new ways and ideas. Chrissie insisted on sitting in the back with Sorrel and Paul so Sarah could map read.

"Not likely," said Paul. "She'd have us lost in a minute. You need me to do that."

He sat next to Darren and off they went. Sorrel asked questions about the car and Darren did his best to answer, though Paul seemed to know more about it. They stopped at a garage to buy some bottles of water as they were thirsty and Sorrel got out of the car to feel the air, as he put it. He pulled off the hat and let the wind blow his long hair. Several people pointed at the ears and one woman looked quite worried.

"It's ok," said Sarah hastily."We are in a movie and we're taking a break. See I have false ears too."

"It's a good make up job," said the woman, "I can't see the join,"

"They do marvellous things these days, "Sarah agreed.

"Are you famous," said her son."I am sure I recognise you. Can I have your autograph?"

Enchanting Sarah by Morgan Fitzsimons

"I'm not famous," said Sarah "but I will ask him if he will sign one,"

She leaned into the car where Sorrel had quickly got back in.

"An autograph will get rid of them," she said "We are attracting attention."

Paul hastily grabbed the notepad in the glove compartment and scribbled across it without letting the boy see it was him, and not the tall one with the ears. He tore off the page and jumped out of the car passing it to the boy.

He jumped back in. "Let's go Darren."

And Darren promptly roared away.

"What did you write," asked Chrissie curiously.

"Best wishes, Orlando," he said

"You didn't," said Sarah.

"Ok I didn't," grinned Paul and they all thought it was funny but had to explain the joke to Sorrel.

They eventually reached the lane where the house was.

"We need to park under the trees and pretend we are examining plant life or something."

"That's easy," said Darren.

The hawk had flown ahead and was there waiting. Sarah told Ryder she was going to mind walk very briefly just to see what dangers there might be. She looked around outside first and saw a helicopter on the lawn. The same car she had followed was on the front drive. She was conscious of Ryder waiting as she entered the house. She moved quickly and heard voices. She saw the man, again wearing a long black leather coat with a hood, poring over the ancient book, his voice showing his excitement.

"It's worth every penny Mason," he said

"Now I must go to the castle and consider the next phase. I will set the expedition in motion to recover the bones of this Tal-git. Just think of it

Mason, with this book I can re create a black dragon, a living breathing black dragon."

Before she realised his intention, the man crossed to the long windows and went through them with this Mason following.

"I am delighted you are pleased Mr. Hemlock," he said. "It wasn't as easy as I thought it would be."

"What do you mean Mason."

"Put it this way, I still have the money. It's in the brief case. I put it by the desk. He didn't exactly need it anymore."

"Don't bother going back inside for the case Mason. The secretary will deal with it. Get in."

He pushed Mason into the helicopter. "You killed him I suppose."

"He was too nosey," said Mason.

She heard no more as the helicopter took off. She went back to the car and told them what happened.

Enchanting Sarah by Morgan Fitzsimons

"We need to go in for real and find where this castle is," she said.

Sorrel removed his coat to reveal a sword and he strapped on his quiver and picked up his bow. Darren watched in amazement as Sarah and Sorrel vaulted up high over the electric fence and came down on their feet at the other side. They raced to the house and entered by the windows. They were inside the study with the maps on the wall and Sarah looked through the desk and studied the maps and photographs.

"His name is Jefferson Hemlock," she said.

"There is a place he refers to called Mandrake which appears to be surrounded by water. There seem to be various different addresses on this paper work. If you look at this map it has some of the places marked. There is another map of something that looks to be an island. That seems to have a lot of places marked on it."

She held up a photograph of a castle with mountains behind it. On the back it just said Scotland 2008.

Enchanting Sarah by Morgan Fitzsimons

"Mandrake was the name of Kor-gat's personal stronghold. Curious," said Sorrel. "Is that the name of this castle?"

"I don't know but it doesn't sound right for Scotland," said Sarah. There isn't a name on the photograph."

Sarah found ledgers and other files but the most interesting find was on the wall by the door. It was a chart of these so called Dragon Masters. There were names familiar to Sorrel including that of Kor-gat and Monkshood, but there were more he didn't know. On the bottom line was the name Hemlock. It seemed rather like a member's roll or something similar.

"Now that is not good if he is connected to Monkshood," said Sorrel.

They heard movement out in the corridors and Sorrel stuck his head out to see two guards doing a check. He shot out and with a quick whirling movement knocked them both out.

"You didn't kill them did you?" asked Sarah.

Enchanting Sarah by Morgan Fitzsimons

"They might wake up with a headache, "he said.

"We need to follow this Hemlock's trail, "said Sarah. "He is up to no good. We need to take what information we can that will help us.

She took photos of the charts and maps on the wall with her phone.

"We should go," she said.

She turned to leave through the French windows and walked straight into a youth who was wearing dark glasses of a very expensive brand.

"Where is Hemlock," he asked, "I need to find him."

"You are too late, he just left," said Sarah.

He looked them up and down as they looked at him and everyone was in brief shock. The youth was tall with very thick black hair cut to a style that covered his ears and was longer at the back. He had a long plait from the left side. He wore a dark green sleeveless coat and black leather under it. What held Sorrel and Sarah's attention were the ears, pointed   a bit higher than Sarah's. The coat and leather jerkin were also familiar to Sorrel, and the dark green coat definitely was. The dark glasses made it a bit difficult to figure him out, but Sarah judged him to be about Charlie's age.

"You are elf," said Sorrel. "How is that possible?"

"How it is possible Golden Elves are with Hemlock?" The youth replied.

"It's a long story and this is not the place to tell it," said Sarah.

"I might ask you the same question. How does an Elf of the Dulcamara happen to be wandering about here?" said Sorrel.

"And you would get the same answer. There are quite a few security guards in this place. If Hemlock isn't here we should go. I would prefer not to kill any of them."

Sarah wasn't altogether sure of this youth. Elf he might be, but the only way he would be here would be in the service of Hemlock, and he obviously wasn't Golden Elf, so it was quite possible. She raced out and over to the fence with Sorrel behind her but the youth disappeared into the study. When he emerged they had already gone over, but he raced after them at great speed and was over the fence in a moment and came up to them in the car.

"I must talk with you," he said "I have to know how you came to be here."

"I am not sure we should tell you," said Sarah. "We need to know more about you before we trust you."

"I am a Dulcamara Warrior," he said arrogantly, "therefore Hemlock is my enemy. Surely that is enough."

"Not for me it isn't" said Sarah stubbornly.

"We will talk," he said and reached out to her hair. He pulled the pretty clip that held her hair back on one side and her hair fell forward in waves over her face.

Enchanting Sarah by Morgan Fitzsimons

"I can find you now," he said and turned to the trees. He called out in a strange tongue which Sorrel knew to be the language of the Dulcamara. He called Firedrake.

Darren was almost delirious as a huge dragon came forth to allow the youth to leap on his back and they took off together soaring high into the clouds. He was speechless and unable to drive for a few minutes. They were all speechless really, except Sorrel.

"Was that what I think it was," Darren managed to stutter,

"It was," said Sorrel.

"It's awesome," said Paul.

"But how can such a thing exist without anyone knowing about it?" said Sarah. "How did they come to be here? You told me Blackthorn was the last of the great Enchanter Lords.

"Exactly what I was thinking," said Sorrel. "There were not so many of them, I told you they had few children. There were many family groups of

Dulcamara elves, The Enchanter group all died and what were left of the rest, returned home with us."

"Maybe this wealthy Mr. Hemlock knows about the dragon," said Chrissie.

"It is possible if the Masters survived through time, they may also have had one or two dragons," said Darren. "After all there have been so called sightings through the years of such creatures, which granted people are very sceptical about, but in the circumstances maybe they are not so improbable as we thought."

"That is what I would worry about," said Paul, "and he was wearing designer shades, which suggest access to money."

"Shades?" asked Sorrel.

"They are to protect the eyes from the sun. You see Sorrel doesn't even know what they are. It isn't something you would expect an Elf to wear," said Paul.

Enchanting Sarah by Morgan Fitzsimons

"Let's go home and worry," said Sarah. "We need to look at this stuff and see where we need to buy travel tickets to, and don't forget, to be fair, I wear sunglasses too. He seems to have been here well before Sorrel came."

"What about mum and dad?" Paul said.

"It's almost the holidays. My assignments are all in so I won't be missed, sixth form is so flexible. You could say you are studying with Darren for a few days as you need to use his stuff."

 I will tell mum I am with Chrissie and she can say she is with me. It is the truth but they will assume more than we say. Let's hope the parents don't start ringing each other up."

"Mine won't anyway, they won't even be there. Dad is leaving for a two week conference and mother is already on her new world tour."

His mother was a renowned musician.

"A quick call now and then from our mobiles should sort it," said Sarah "but I really don't like doing it.

"Brilliant," said Paul. "It's so brilliant I might have thought of it myself."

They drove home, stopping on the way to introduce Sorrel to a fast food cafe. It was fun getting him to try burgers and fries and milk shakes. They spread the charts out one at a time and pored over them. Sorrel told them all about Monkshood.

"He was a dark and devious sorcerer who excelled at mixing poisons. The Masters used poisons to enhance their abilities and also to control others. He was also skilled at producing new and terrifying life forms."

"Could he have developed an elf life form," asked Sarah.

"I suppose it's possible though I have only ever seen gross and aggressive creatures."

He knew what she was thinking and it could explain the presence of a dragon and the youth, but Sorrel thought it very unlikely.

Enchanting Sarah by Morgan Fitzsimons

"I am getting stressed with the whole thing," said Sarah. "Let's go home and you can tell Blackthorn and tomorrow we can plot a way to Jefferson Hemlock and find out about the bones of Tal-git."

"Lets do that," said Sorrel. They piled into the car and Darren drove them home.

"If that dragon turns up again, you will call me straight away?"

"Don't worry Darren. It's not going to turn up before you come back tomorrow with your toothbrush. It's a shame though your dad didn't buy you a bigger car."

"I could ask him?" he replied seriously.

"It was a joke Darren," said Paul

Chapter 6

Arin

There was still some light and Sarah sat under the oak tree looking up at the hawk watching over her. Sorrel had gone for now and Paul was off doing something. She thought about the strange encounter earlier. She had no answers but maybe Sorrel might get some from Blackthorn. Her head lifted sharply and she looked around but saw nothing untoward. Yet she felt quite uneasy as though someone was looking at her.

"Don't be daft Sarah," she said to herself. It was just the excitement of the day, and the sensation left her as quickly as it had come. She closed her eyes, but the face of the youth impinged upon her thoughts. Her eyes flew open to see a vague shape there by the ash tree.

"Hello," said the youth. "I came to see who you really were. You have the look of someone I met when I was an elfling."

He didn't look like any youth of her acquaintance. Although from the look of him, he couldn't be any more than twenty, he had an air of self assurance about him.

"I am Sarah. I don't know who I really am," she said. "I am still trying to work that out."

"But isn't it obvious. You are of the Golden tribe."

"Until last week I was just a human being with pointed ears and a birthmark."

"A birthmark?

She brushed back her hair and the youth's expression changed.

"The mark of the Dulcamara, how can that be?"

Enchanting Sarah by Morgan Fitzsimons

He removed the dark glasses and blinked a little but the light was less strong under the trees and it was fading anyway. He put them in his pocket. He pushed the hair back to reveal a mark much stronger and more clearly defined than Sarah's. Its shape was that of a symmetrical spider's web forming a diamond shape in the middle. Now he had come closer he was taller than she thought. He had a good posture and broad shoulders, with gave him stature, but he still fitted into Charlie's age group. Sarah was astonished when she saw the mark. Sorrel had declared all Enchanters to be dead. Had he been born out of time as she was?

"Sorrel says my ancestors were Lilia the Golden and her grandson Blackthorn who was the Last Enchanter War lord of the Dulcamara. Does that mean anything to you?"Sarah asked him.

"Do you know the names of his parents and grandparents? It would help me to place him?" the youth asked. "I do not know the name."

Enchanting Sarah by Morgan Fitzsimons

"His grandfather was Asphodel son of Asoril, his grandmother Lilia the Golden Queen so I am told."

"Do you know where they are? His tone was eager. "I did know Lilia, I saw her several times with my Lord Asoril and her husband Asphodel," he said. "Of course! It is she you remind me of."

"You ask a lot of questions without telling me anything much," she said.

"What do you want to know," he asked

"Who you are and how you came here?"

"My name is Arin. I am an Enchanter Warrior of the Dulcamara." He refused to say was. He could not bear to think he would never be so again.

"You are too young surely to be a warrior," she said.

"I admit I am still learning from my father. He is training me to follow him as Elf War Lord of Drake Ridge."

"But I don't understand?"

Enchanting Sarah by Morgan Fitzsimons

"You want to know how I came here. I suppose I can tell you that but I will not tell you anymore. Too many people are looking for me."

He came closer and she saw the gleam of a sword beneath his coat.

"My father serves Asoril. He sent my father and I to deal with the Dragon Master, Aorcha who managed to trap me with my companions."

"Companions?" Sarah asked. "Are there more of you?"

"Not elves," he said" My dragon Firedrake and my eagle Yulir. You have already seen Firedrake. I was foolish enough to fly in daylight, but I was so close to finding Hemlock. I don't know what happened with Aorcha exactly, some form of sorcery. He just came from nowhere to destroy my father."

His expression changed as he spoke.

"He shouted ancient rune words cursing him to a living death, and threw something at my father. I flew down Firedrake between them. I knew

111

nothing more until I awoke to men digging in the place where the sorcerer had sent me. I discovered much later it was an excavation funded by this Jefferson Hemlock. They saw me escaping on Firedrake and he and some officials he has in his pocket, have tried to find me and catch me ever since. I am looking for a way home, but so far haven't found one. I thought maybe you would know how to reach Asoril."

"I understood from Sorrel all Elves chose to go with Blackthorn to the Land of the Twilight Star," Sarah told him.

"Then they are no longer in this world of men at all. I had hoped when I found Dragon Masters, my people would still be here too. But when the enchantment failed to tell me anything, I suppose I knew really."

"I don't understand how someone could send you through time and space like that, but if it is true, you must find it very difficult to adjust?"

"An understatement, "he said "And I never lie."

"That must be just as difficult. I didn't know until a week ago that Elves existed, and I am finding it very hard to adjust to being one," replied Sarah.

"Explain!"

 The eyes were so deep and compelling she found herself doing just that.

"Perhaps we can be of use to each other. Would you like to meet Firedrake?" He said when she had finished talking.

"He is here with you?"

"*She* is here with me. The dragon is female."

He called quietly and from the little wood behind the trees, came a creature she had never thought to be so close to. She lowered her head to the nervous Sarah and gently blew in her hair.

"She likes you," he said. "She too is lonely and misses her companions."

"Your eagle, where is he?"

Enchanting Sarah by Morgan Fitzsimons

"Yulir is out searching, I don't know what for but he will tell me in good time. He is a free creature, I don't own him. To tell the truth he probably thinks he owns me."

She felt the hawk's presence rather than saw him.

"My guardian is curious about you and your dragon, Arin."

"Your guardian, you mean the hawk who sits in the oak tree," he answered.

"How did you know?"

"I am Enchanter. "

"You sound as arrogant as Blackthorn."

"You have been able to speak with him," he sounded very excited. "Could I talk to him? It may be my father is with him"

"I don't know but I will find out. He has far greater enchantment than I could ever have. Sorrel tells me it comes from his grandfather, his grandmother and his mother all of whom died together in a massacre of all Enchanter Lords.

Blackthorn was a boy, an elfling at the time and the only one left living."

He looked suddenly a little pale and sank down again on the grass.

"It is how Blackthorn became known as the Last Enchanter War Lord of the Dulcamara. He was the only survivor."

"My father was an Enchanter lord, a warrior who served Asoril. If he was still living he would have been there with Asphodel."

She looked at him in horror realising what he was thinking. His father would have been with his Lord or dead already.

"I am so sorry to be the one to tell you that. Maybe Sorrel will know more when he comes back tomorrow." Her distrust was temporarily overcome by her sorrow for him. How awful to be in a strange place with no friends and to have your hope destroyed in a moment.   .

"Will you come back tomorrow?" she asked.

Enchanting Sarah by Morgan Fitzsimons

"I am not going away," he said firmly. "I will wait here until he comes."

She hadn't noticed but the daylight was going. It was that misty hour of twilight when things are not quite normal. Familiar things take on another persona and all around there is an air of mystery and enchantment. The hawk stirred restlessly and the dragon drew nearer. It was a magnificent creature. The patterns on her skin were similar to tree bark and the greens blended with the leaves.

"She seems close to you, why is she with you anyway?"

"We are bonded," he said simply. "I am not a dragon guardian, though it's dragon guardians who usually bond with the dragon. Enchanters were bonded with black and white dragons once and for all through Ainarr Asveldur. We have the blood of the dragon in our substance."

"You mean I have that too?"

"I imagine you must. If you touch her you will know for sure. She will talk with you."

Enchanting Sarah by Morgan Fitzsimons

"That must be what Sorrel meant, "she said.

She reached out a hand and touched the dragon. It was rough hard leathery skin.

"Can I talk with you?"

She felt the answer. "You are an Elf of Light and Shadow. I would expect it."

She turned startled eyes to Arin and he smiled.

"I was very young when Firedrake saved me. I was left for dead in a Darg attack and was too young to self heal. I had terrible wounds and she allowed her blood to mix with mine and we were bonded. She has been with me ever since."

He removed the leather from his forearm and pushed back his sleeve and she could see his arms were patterned with dark green intermingled with the blue of the Enchanters, in places shading much paler.

"You can see the blue grey I was born with, but the rest are Firedrake."

Enchanting Sarah by Morgan Fitzsimons

She bent over his arm to see more, quite fascinated with this youth who looked just a little older than she did, maybe as old as Charlie. She didn't distrust him quite so much, though she still had this feeling of danger and mystery. The fact he had been sleeping for thousands of years didn't seem to matter. He was disturbed by her. She looked so ethereal and vulnerable, reminding him of things gone forever now. She looked up at him and he caught his breath as she smiled her enchanting elfin smile.

"I don't have blue grey patterns like these. Should I have them?"

"It is perhaps all those humans in between you and your heritage. But I expect you will have something somewhere. It could be they develop as you become more aware of the dragon. This wasn't instant but grew stronger over time." He pointed to his own patterns.

She sighed, "I suppose it will take time to know all the things I should, and to be able to handle it."

"Probably about the same time it will take me to get used to where I am. I may be trapped here forever, who knows."

"Why have you suddenly accepted me," she said.

"The hawk trusts you. He would not do so if you were one of Hemlock's traps."

"How can I know you are not one yourself?"

"Ask your hawk," he answered.

She turned to Ryder and looked deep into his eyes.

"I once belonged to Asvaldur, so too did Yulir," was the response.

"You mean Yulir would not be with him if he were not as he seems. We haven't seen this ancient eagle. How do we know he exists?"

"I know, he will come when he is ready," responded Ryder

"Now that's over would you like to ride Firedrake?" Arin asked her.

Enchanting Sarah by Morgan Fitzsimons

She turned back to him swiftly."Are you serious?"

"I am always serious. I have to be to survive this strange world. Will you trust me now?"

"Oh I would dearly love to ride her, if you are sure I can."

"I will have to ride with you," he warned but she was not listening, her eyes on the dragon. Arin politely stood beside her and reached out his hands to hold her.

"You will permit me Lady Sarah," he said and she nodded as he tossed her up onto the back of the dragon. He was behind her in an instant and the dragon rose at his touch. It was the most exciting thing ever and it wasn't mind walking. It was real. He communicated his needs to the dragon. There were no reigns such as used to ride a horse, the bond was such they were not needed.

"What is she swerves or something, will you fall?"

"She would not allow that. When I ride her we are as one"

Enchanting Sarah by Morgan Fitzsimons

"But what about me," she said, "we are not bonded."

"We can find out," and she gasped with fright as the dragon curved over sideways but instantly Arin put his arms around her and pulled her back against him.

"You are quite safe," he said.

Ryder soared up beside them and kept pace with Firedrake. They flew over treetops swirling with the clouds. It was real, yet unreal. She turned her head and looked up at Arin's face. He wasn't quite so tall and far away.

"It's breathtaking and you can do this whenever you please," she said.

"Not so much in the light of day as I would like," was his reply.

They flew over the city and it was dark enough now for the lights to be dazzling down below and although there were people about and traffic on the roads, no one looked up to witness their passing. On they went over hilltops and towns alike until Firedrake spotted a large expanse of woodland below and down she came. She was looking for a stream and she had found one. They came down from her back allowing her to drink her fill. Arin caught Sarah and placed her on her feet. The hawk flew down to wait beside them.

"That was so beautiful and exhilarating and I have it all to do again going back," said Sarah, her delight apparent.

"Don't get too used to it," he warned. "I will not give her to you."

She grinned. "Well maybe not, but I could borrow her maybe."

"Not that either, but maybe I will share her with you and take you up from time to time."

"That's good enough," she said "I will hold you to it."

They had wandered away from the dragon as they talked, but Arin was always alert. He stopped her and put his finger over her lips to convey silence. He was ready for the attack when it came and his sword was in his hand when he bounded to meet the creatures lying in wait. They were smaller versions of Dargs, but she just saw beasts standing on hind legs with dragon like heads. Arin showed his skill as a warrior. He had no difficulty disposing of them even though he was outnumbered. As they fell, they seemed to fade into the earth beneath them. He was scarcely out of breath. He had a small cut on his hand which she exclaimed over.

"What were they?"

"They were Darg Trackers, creatures created by Dragon Masters. I believe Hemlock's organisation has groups of them searching for me. They follow unseen, any trail they can get and sometimes they find me. None have survived to go back and tell him."

She was decidedly nervous, never having seen anything killed before, evil or otherwise.

"We will go now just in case more come," he reassured her.

Enchanting Sarah by Morgan Fitzsimons

"Does that happen often?"

"It's of no account, I do not dwell on it," he said

Firedrake was refreshed and they climbed on her back again and Sarah's magical ride was repeated, this time there was some concern for her companion. He had not noticed his hand was now bleeding profusely. She put her hand over the wound and it was gone without trace.

"You do have Dulcamara enchantment, "he said. "I thank you, but don't so that too often or you will become very weak trying to sustain it."

Once back in the garden she realised how late it was.

"I will never wake up early," she said.

"I will make sure you do," said Arin.

"How will you do that?" she said as she walked away.

"Wait and see," he called after her and she disappeared up the path.

Enchanting Sarah by Morgan Fitzsimons

Arin curled up under the oak tree and Firedrake disappeared into the clump of trees over the fence. The hawk didn't fly away but stayed vigilant above them in the treetops. Soon there was no sound, nothing moving, only the glowing watchful eyes of the hawk as Ryder continued his vigil until dawn's first light.

Chapter 7

Best laid plans

It was first light which was the time of rising for elves. Theirs was an inner clock that always stirred when it was light. Arin opened his eyes and remembered. He was quiet for a moment as he put on the glasses and sought the room where Sarah was sleeping. He softly whispered to Firedrake and she moved down the path into the garden behind the house. She crossed over the neatly trimmed lawns and stood beneath the window Arin pointed out. She pressed her face against the glass.

"Sarah," whispered Arin and it echoed around her room and she stirred.

Firedrake tapped a claw on the window pane. The tap tapping penetrated her sleepy head and she opened her eyes to meet the gaze of a dragon. The eyes were large and menacing, which was after all how dragon's usually looked. The huge jaws were open displaying fearsome teeth, and she sat bolt upright absolutely scared out of her wits. She clutched where her heart was rapidly racing and then she remembered, stopping herself just in time from screaming

She leapt out of bed and dashed to the bathroom where she hastily washed dashing back to pull on jeans and a top and hastily ran the brush through her hair. She glanced in the mirror.

"I look a mess," she thought, more like a street urchin than a female." Shrugging her shoulders she went for the door.

"It doesn't really matter anyway," but she knew that wasn't quite the truth.

Once she reached the bottom garden she went straight for Arin who smiled a welcome, the smile turning to shock as she kicked his shin.

Enchanting Sarah by Morgan Fitzsimons

"You beast, "she said "I was scared to death when I saw that face peering at me."

"Scared of Firedrake?" he was bewildered, "Why?"

"It was so unexpected and it took a few moments to remember yesterday and that was enough time for my heart to almost stop."

"I am so sorry Sarah. I thought you would be amused."

"It was lucky I didn't scream or mum would have come running, we would be in a mess. She really wouldn't understand all this and it will take time to find the right moment to tell her."

"I hadn't considered that."

"Well I suppose if I could have seen myself, it would have been funny." Her lips curved in a smile and when she smiled she looked her most Elfin. She was at her most engaging with the timeless quality of Elf.

He warily grinned back and rubbed his shin.

"Did I kick too hard? I forgot I was wearing boots."

"I'll walk again but I will remember not to get too close to those boots in future," he was laughing when the others arrived.

"I told you they would be early. You will have to be kind to Darren he will want to know all about you and Firedrake for his studies, but hopefully he will be so overawed by her, he will shut up for a while."

Chrissie was stunned to see Arin.

"What's he doing here, how did he find us," she hissed in a whisper, which was pointless as Arin could hear quite easily just as Sarah did.

"I found you with this," he said and held out his hand to show the hairclip resting on his palm with a few golden hairs twisted round the clasp. "I held it and drew an image of Sarah from it and mind walked to this house. Once I knew where it was I came in person."

Enchanting Sarah by Morgan Fitzsimons

"How did you get here without a car? You couldn't have walked," said Paul.

"Good you're up at last," said Sarah to Paul.

"What do you mean at last, I have been sat here listening."

"Remember the dragon," said Arin.

"Oh boy do I, you came on the dragon," said Paul.

In reply Arin called Firedrake and Paul and Darren just stared in awe as she came closer.

"She will not harm you," said Arin "She will allow you to move close to her,"

That was enough for Darren who although he was amazed, he wasn't afraid. He saw all life forms as friends to study and so far had met nothing that challenged his belief. For him it was all his birthdays and Christmases for years to come all rolled up in one go. He sat beside Firedrake and when she moved he moved. It was as though he was glued to her tail. He was mesmerised. and quite upset when Arin sent the dragon back into the trees, remembering Sarah's words about her mother.

"Is he all right," asked Arin

"He's just stunned by Firedrake. Its love at first sight I think."

Darren turned his head proving his brain was still operating with them, despite his concentration.

"Oh no, You can only truly love one person like that," he said seriously," but I admit to being drawn to Firedrake. She is fantastic."

Chrissie laughed and patted his arm affectionately giving him a kiss on the cheek.

"I think I can take being upstaged by a dragon. Well what's the plan, people," she asked "You have got one Sarah."

"Not exactly," said Sarah.

"I thought you were going to sort it last night," commented Chrissie.

Enchanting Sarah by Morgan Fitzsimons

"I didn't have time and anyway we need to get Sorrel's input first," replied Sarah.

Somehow her ride on Firedrake had become an experience she didn't want to share but they didn't have long to wait before Sorrel came back. He stepped around the ash tree and called to Sarah.

"I see you have a new friend."

"This is Arin and before we talk about what we have to do, he needs to ask you something." She explained how he came to here at this time.

"I have been trying to find a way back to my father. I believed Hemlock had the key to it all, but now I see that isn't so," said Arin.

"It would seem the Dragon Master cult has survived" said Sorrel."Everything you knew Arin has disappeared into the earth, but they seem to have remained here hiding their real function and purpose from mankind."

"Can you tell me if my father died in this massacre of the Enchanters or is he with Blackthorn?"

"Who was your father," asked Sorrel.

"Alder, who served Asoril as I did in the wars against the Dragon Masters."

"I knew him," said Sorrel. "Asoril died to allow the White Queen to escape. Your father went on to serve Asphodel. As long as I knew him he searched for his son who was taken from him by the sorcery of Aorcha, the Dragon Master. As I remember he was connected with The Great Wyrm of Groa the Sorceress. Your father never gave up searching."

Arin was still and silent.

"It was meant to be Alder and you rode at Aorcha to protect your father and so you suffered his fate."

"How do you know this," said Arin.

Enchanting Sarah by Morgan Fitzsimons

"Alder told me! He was immensely proud of his brave son," said Sorrel. "And he *was* at Dark Mullein that day to honour Lilia his queen and Asphodel, his High Lord Enchanter and he died with them as they all did."

Arin walked away from them to stand alone by the ash tree. He was gone then, he would never see him again and his home would have merged with the land while he was in a sleep like death. It would have been better if he had been dead altogether.

There wasn't anything anyone could really say to make it easier. His world was shattered, his goal snatched away from him. It was cruel but he had to know the truth.

He swung round suddenly, "How did he die, did you see it."

""I arrived after it was done, or I assure you I would not be standing here now," replied Sorrel

"Give me something that I can focus on, something to give me purpose."

"I will not be responsible for turning you to revenge and hatred. It would be so easy for the darker nature to possess you, but you can help prevent more deaths and more suffering from the beast who actually performed the deed."

"It was this Tal-git, wasn't it."

"That is so and now a dragon master seeks to bring him back, but there is no place for all that here."

"It is enough for now," said Arin. "The Dragon Masters do exist here even though they are not always obviously visible. I thought I caught a glimpse of one who looked like Aorcha. I could be mistaken as his was the last face I saw, but if he is here I will find him. This Hemlock is also a Dragon Master, though he isn't known to either us."

"Aorcha," said Sorrel, "I was right about him being involved with the Wyrm of Croa. You do mean the one who served Monkshood?"

Enchanting Sarah by Morgan Fitzsimons

"He usually has her symbol somewhere on his person," said Arin.

"That is equally worrying if he does still live, It was rumoured he was the son of Monkshood, but one was as evil as the other, whatever their relationship." said Sorrel. "If you need something to focus on Arin, Sarah has the blood of Elf Kings and Enchanter War-lords together and she has need of us."

"That is true, I will help you if you will allow it," he said to her. His voice was stern and resolute but with her new found awareness she sensed his pain and knew he cried inside for his loss, not just for his father but a whole way of life that was gone forever. He could never find his way back to it, but he wasn't going to demonstrate his grief.

"We need to find this Jefferson Hemlock. He could really be anywhere. One of these plans show a island called New Helleborine," said Sarah.

Enchanting Sarah by Morgan Fitzsimons

Sorrel began to laugh. "The nerve of the creature. He has given his island the name of the lands we lived in all those years ago."

"It fits the ego of Dragon Masters," said Arin. "He would like to believe he conquered it.

"Is this where he will go with the book and the bones of the dragon?" Sorrel asked.

"He said he was going to the castle so that may not mean this island," said Sarah. "If I remember right, there was a picture of a castle."

She had all the papers with her and she moved to the patio at the end of the large upper garden. She spread it all over the table and to the onlooker they were a group of young teenagers planning a trip.

"There were other documents among the papers on his desk referring to many other places so I suspect he has homes and business connections in many parts of the world."

Enchanting Sarah by Morgan Fitzsimons

Sarah's mum shouted down the garden. "I take it you are still going to Chrissie's. Is there anything you need me to do?"

"Just breakfast mum. My stuff is already in Darren's car."

Sarah's mum disappeared into the kitchen.

"There is another island map here that appears to have had some volcanic action in the past. The scribble over the corner says Darkenwald. Yet another sheet has a range of mountains and the name Curithir on it."

That got Sorrel's attention and he sat bolt upright on the grass at Sarah's feet.

"I can only hope the names do not reflect the nature of places I know."

"Why is that," asked Chrissie.

"Darkenwald is a place where the Dragon Masters created their monstrous life forms for evil purpose. It is a place with fire in the depths of the earth. Curithir is the dwelling of sorcery and occult magic and the creatures they controlled. That too was a place of fire in the depths underneath." said Sorrel.

"Maybe he is just marking where they used to be," said Paul.

"When I first saw you, I had thought maybe you were something he had created," said Sarah apologetically to Arin.

His eyes flashed as he removed the glasses to stare at her. "You *what?* Do I look like a monster to you?"

"Not now that I know you, "she said quickly.

"That still implies I look like one."

"Don't be daft Sarah, without the ears most girls would think he was gorgeous. Well maybe even with the ears. They are interesting I suppose, and he has a very masculine presence."

"Hey just a minute what's all this?" put in Darren. "I thought I was your guy. You aren't supposed to notice other guys."

Enchanting Sarah by Morgan Fitzsimons

"Now *you* are mental Darren, I notice all the boys. It's great fun. I just don't get involved with any of them, no one is as interesting as you Darren," she laughed and gave his arm a squeeze.

"I should think not," he said, as he turned one of the pictures the right way up.

"But it's not what I meant," said Sarah.

"I think we should move on," said Sorrel, "you are behaving like children."

"I am a child," said Paul," at least my dad always says 'that child of yours has messed up again, and she says 'half of him is yours, and he says which half and she says the trouble half."

"Enough!" Sorrel smiled at him. "Let's get on with it.

"Perhaps we should list stuff. What is our goal for a start," said Darren.

"We have to stop the raising of Tal-git. The goal should be to put a stop to Jefferson Hemlock too, but that won't be easy. He seems to have a network of power that is frightening in its scale," said Sarah.

"And you think dealing with Tal-git will be easier," said Sorrel with a grin.

"I think it may come down to destruction of humans involved in the process. My conscience will not quibble at destroying evil creatures but a man is a little different," said Sarah.

"This Hemlock is nothing more than an evil creature, all dragon masters are and whoever is tainted by them will also be formidable. I will have no difficulty squaring it with my conscience," said Sorrel.

"Neither will I Sorrel, my sword is at your disposal." He drew it and Sorrel looked in astonishment.

"It is the Eagle sword of Ainarr Asvaldur himself. I thought it was your father's."

"He gave it to me when I became a warrior," said Arin, and Sorrel cursed himself for bringing back the sadness to the young elf's face.

Enchanting Sarah by Morgan Fitzsimons

"Before we do anything, you both need to realise swords and bows are not today's weapons. We don't make a habit of sword fighting in the street or firing arrows at people." said Sarah. "It's the best way of drawing the attention of people we don't want to notice us."

"I didn't exactly arrive here yesterday," said Arin. "I have learned some things about survival here, It didn't take me long to catch on to Elves being a myth these days and anyone talking about wizards and witches is a candidate for what do you call it , a fun farm."

Paul laughed, "You mean the funny farm, that is itself a joke term. But yes you are right they would lock us all up and throw away the key."

"The swords are useful with certain elements of the enemy, but in dealing with the whole, you need to take into the equation an Elf Warrior's skill lie in much more than weapons, and an Enchanter's skill is much more than you can know," said Sorrel.

"That I will definitely agree with," said Sarah.

Enchanting Sarah by Morgan Fitzsimons

"Hemlock has the book, but has yet to recover the bones of Tal-git." Sarah went on to point out. "But I think this Castle he mentions could be here somewhere." she pointed to a picture of a range of mountains in the highlands of Scotland way up in the mountains in the North.

"So before we do anything else we need to get to the bones before he does," said Chrissie.

"But he could already know where they are and we don't," said Paul. "How can we possibly find out?"

"Maybe we could reason it out, "said Sorrel. "He died at Dark Mullein so isn't it likely that's where his bones will be."

"I don't think that would help as we don't know where Dark Mullein was, but Hemlock seemed to know where the bones were so it's likely he has them now or he is about to get them. We need to go over these papers and see if there is anything helpful. Darren you are good at research so while we are looking, get on your lap top and see if any activities are recorded in any news articles about Jefferson Hemlock or an associated group."

"Right," he said and brought his lap top from the car.

"Chrissie and Paul you need to check all these papers. I am going to my computer to see what I can find. Sorrel you stay with Darren and Arin can come with me. By the way, much as I dislike doing it, I am still not telling mum the entire truth here, so say nothing at all. It would take too long to convince her and dad what's going on. I will tell them afterwards." She really couldn't get her head round how she was going to do it so like most teenagers she shelved it until there was a better moment, but usually in life there never is.

Chapter 8

Close Encounter

Arin left his sword and coat on the seat and followed her inside. His leather jerkin, boots and trousers didn't look out of place and as they passed Sarah's mum she gave them a brief look. She was so used to Sarah's ears she didn't see anything amiss with Arin. She just got a brief glimpse of what she surmised was a friend of Darren's age. His height didn't worry her, She was used to youth's of all shapes and sizes passing through, friends of her sons, from short lads of eighteen or so to fifteen and sixteen year old giants.

"This is Arin Mum. We need some info from my computer," Her mum nodded as she continued piling up the toast.

Enchanting Sarah by Morgan Fitzsimons

She went into the computer room where her brothers and dad's computers were laid out. She sat in front of her dad's and watched Arin's reaction. There wasn't one.

"This holds no surprises for you does it," she said.

"I do have access to them in my sanctuary. I will tell you when there is time, but it is rather complicated. I have learned things related to my search and to Hemlock, but many practical things I still do not know."

She accepted that and typed in Jefferson Hemlock.

"My computer's up in my bedroom. I am not sure of my way around dad's."

All sorts of things came up and they waded through them. He chaired several trusts and was connected all over the place and had homes and bases in different countries as she expected. It was like tracing a spider's web so enmeshed was he in the financial and the philanthropic world. Hemlock Associates, Hemlock Industries and various other names came to light and there were hundreds of names linked to those. It seemed never ending.

"Dragon Masters are never philanthropic as you call it. They are purely motivated by self," Arin commented.

"So it's safe to assume he has some other purpose or something he wants to hide wherever we see his name connected with some good works."

"Definitely.!" Arin replied.

"Here's something," she said excitedly. "He is chairman of an archaeological society and funds various digs including one group specialising in ancient bones. There are mentions of past finds but not what they are doing now."

"This is a link," said Arin. "It's called the Drake Archeological group"

She grasped his arm "But what tells you that?"

"Drake is an ancient name for Dragon.Remember Firedrake?"

Enchanting Sarah by Morgan Fitzsimons

She swiftly printed out what info she thought would be useful.

"Maybe Darren can find what they are doing now. He seems to know where to look for obscure research info."

Sarah's mum called to her "I'm off to work now Sarah, behave at Chrissies. Don't let Paul do anything stupidly embarrassing."

"Ok mum," she called back.

They returned to the garden to find everyone munching toast and drinking juice.

"I see mum's been here," said Sarah.

"I kept out of sight, I thought it best," said Sorrel.

"She is great," said Darren. "I wish my mum was like her. Well she's ok, but it would be good if she did things like your mum."

"We are all different," said Sarah "and there's nothing wrong with that. My mother would love to play the harp and the piano and the violin etc like your mum, but she can't."

Enchanting Sarah by Morgan Fitzsimons

"I suppose so," said Darren cheerfully.

"Hurry up. I need you to find where this group is currently digging." She gave him the print out and he munched as he pulled out his Blackberry and surfed the web.

"I quite like the way you toast bread," said Sorrel. "Food is different but it tastes good."

"It's good but not always healthy," said Arin.

"You have noticed then," said Paul.

"The people I stay with have very healthy diets with lots of fruit around," said Arin.

"People?" said Sarah.

"I am not alone in my sanctuary," he said. Sarah briefly wondered what that meant.

"Got it!" shouted Darren.

"I still have your data stick in my pocket," said Sarah."Download the info!"

Darren did as he was bid and Sarah went into the house to print it.

Enchanting Sarah by Morgan Fitzsimons

"This is a very useful tool," said Sorrel.

"You get rather used to it," said Darren.

"Ok where's the dig," said Paul.

"It's in Wales," said Darren. "It's on some inaccessible mountain side, where there are sometimes still snowcaps in the summer"

Sarah emerged from the house with the details and they got out the map.

"By the way," said Chrissie, "Darren said we were camping so his dad gave him the seven seater car for the week."

"Just like that," said Paul. "Darren, don't ever complain about your parents to me."

"I suppose they are generous," he answered as he finished his toast.

They worked out the journey and started putting some stuff in the car. They had enough money at their disposal thanks to Darren, to pay for hotels and cafe's so they just needed a change of clothes and even those they could buy. Sarah brought the papers and Darren checked he had his plastic.

"It could be risky flying the dragon in daylight." Sorrel pointed out.

Firedrake emerged from her cover again and Arin went to her.

"I will fly alone," she conveyed, "I always find you. I can hide much better alone. You must guard the Elf Lady."

"True," he said "Very logical." Turning to the others he told them her decision.

The weapons were put in the rear compartment and Sorrel and Paul climbed in the back seats leaving Arin and Sarah in the middle with Chrissie with Darren in front.

"Even you can't get lost Darren. There are signs all the way, but I will have to change places with Chrissie when we get to the area of the dig," said Paul.

"That's fine by me," she said.

Enchanting Sarah by Morgan Fitzsimons

Mum had already left for work and dad had gone long since. Charlie was home so Sarah didn't need to lock the doors.

"I'm off with Chrissie and Darren now," she shouted.

"See you," replied her brother engrossed in his game.

Sarah had left her a big note in the kitchen. "Thanks for breakfast mum. I will phone soon. Love you. She blessed the invention of mobiles as they would assume she was calling from Chrissie's, which in a way was true as Chrissie's place was now Darren's dad's car. They had no idea what they might find, but Darren at least was quite excited at the prospect of even more intriguing creatures. Just as Darren was about to drive off, Sarah's phone rang.

"Where the hell are you Sarah. We can't win this without you!"

"Just a minute, "she said and placed the phone so it didn't pick up what she was saying.

Enchanting Sarah by Morgan Fitzsimons

"It's Nigel," she hissed.

"Sugar," said Chrissie, "you forgot the Maths and Science thing didn't you."

"The head will send me out to a firing squad. They'll kill me if they lose."

"Not while I am here," said Sorrel and Arin together.

"It's just a figure of speech, they won't actually kill me but they will be real mad. It is so important to the school and the city I suppose."

"Well its only two hours," said Darren "We can give you two hours. I'll drop you off in the car and we can introduce the guys to Starbucks or MacDonald's or something and pick you up at the end of it."

Sarah ran back indoors to grab her blazer. They would have to make do with the t shirt and jeans. Darren drove her round to the Regional College and she dashed inside. Arin felt suddenly extremely uneasy. Something triggered off that Elf intuition.

Enchanting Sarah by Morgan Fitzsimons

"I think I'm going to stick around a bit," he said. He tossed his coat into the car. I will keep out of sight. There are lots of trees over there.

"What is it," asked Darren.

"Just put it down to that uncanny sixth sense, elves supposedly have. I just don't feel right."

"Your just being over sensitive," said Sorrel from the back, thinking maybe Arin was just a little smitten with the pretty Sarah.

They drove off and Arin found a place to wait. Sarah found the team waiting and she joined them rather hastily. Everything was as normal. There were the usual head hunters from the colleges and universities in the lecture theatre, as they always were for these events. The students taking part were all in the top 1% bracket in the country. This was the first time Sarah's group had the opportunity of taking home the Sixth Form trophy because Sarah now was the required age to take part and was such an exceptional student.

Enchanting Sarah by Morgan Fitzsimons

Meanwhile the others invaded MacDonald's and had an amusing time with Sorrel wanting to try stuff. He was fascinated by the kid's birthday party going on in the corner, particularly with the MacDonald's clown, which it took some time to explain. He just loved the balloons but could see no real use for them. Why blow them up if you were going to pop them? He acquired several which he ducked all efforts by Paul to burst them, much to the amusement of the children.

The event was progressing well and Sarah stood out like a beacon, not only her ability but as Sorrel had said, she was acquiring that iridescent quality and positive presence of Elf, she sort of radiated a brightness. One of the guest visitors presumably from a college, or maybe a well known organisation, seemed quite taken. He leaned forward in his seat his eyes fixed on her. Her fringe covered the mark but her hair moved when she did, revealing glimpses of the slightly pointed ears.

When it was over they were expected to talk with the guests and Sarah tried to duck it, but was collared by Nigel who pulled her over to meet some of them. The keen guy reached to shake her hand and the elf instinct kicked in sending a shudder up her spine. He wore the usual suit and looked quite expensive, and sported an ID badge listing him as Director of the Hodges Science Research Laboratories. It seemed credible, so she thought. He couldn't be here if it wasn't. He was pushy and after the trophy went to Sarah's group, he was persistent. She slipped away as soon as she could only to find he had followed her and was now flanked with several colleagues. They followed her outside and one of them caught up with her and grabbed her shoulder, rendering her unconscious. They carried her out to the car but Arin had seen them, and picked up on both Sarah's plight, and the men with her. He recognised them, not as humans, but Salwed, which literally meant darkened, painted black with pitch. Arin recalled humans had called them Pitch Elves. They tossed their hats into the car after her and drove off flanked by two motor cycle riders. Arin raced after them as they took off down country lanes. He had no trouble keeping up with them, and they passed no other cars which were fortunate as Arin would have been noticeable. They arrived at a house in its own grounds and Sarah was bundled out of the car. Another Pitch Elf came out to them.

"What is she here for?" he demanded.

"I believe she is Golden Elf," was the reply.

"Where did you find her?"

"She is from the local college where we were looking for recruits to use in the company."

"You took a local girl actually from a college? We are supposed to recruit them not kidnap them. What the hell were you thinking?"

"We were told to look out for Elf," he said

"You could have watched her and taken her at a more appropriate time when she wouldn't be missed. This way will result in public outcry, snatching her from a college building." He turned and went inside. "Fetch her in!" he called back. "I'll decide what to do with her."

Arin had heard enough. He had surprise in his favour and walked out to grab both Pitch Elves at once smacking their heads against the car. The leader twisted his fingers but Arin was faster and he was held in the air and with a jerk, he was dropped to crack his head on the paving stones. Sarah was coming round but was in no shape to run. Arin grabbed the nearest parked motor bike and jumped on it. The Ryder appeared overhead to attack the motor bike rider as he came round the corner. Sara swayed on her feet.

"Quick, jump on," he said and she did, clasping him round the waist.

"Have you done this before," she gasped. He roared off with Ryder racing him overhead. He followed the country lanes back to the area of the college, stopping when he was in the vicinity and he was sure there was no pursuit.

"That was exhilarating; He laughed as Sarah phoned Darren giving them the name of the lane they were parked in.

"Maybe, but had you ridden one before?"

"Not exactly," he grinned "but I have studied the principal involved. Add a little Elf intuition etc no problem."

Sarah shook her head and got off sitting on the grass until Darren came. Things were likely to get a little hair raising with this young elf around if he took such risks, but she supposed he had been prompt in his actions and he had saved her from these creatures, whatever they were.

Chapter 9

The Lady Vanishes

Sarah threw her blazer with the phone in it on the seat and climbed in after it. Arin looked anxiously out of the window as they moved off again in the car.

"Don't worry Firedrake will be fine. She isn't going to take any risks," said Sarah.

"I'm not worried about her. The hawk has gone back to her," he said. "He says he intends to watch over Firedrake on the journey if I continue to be vigilant over you until you are together again. It seems I have his approval."

"How can you know so easily what they communicate? Is it something all elves can do with any creature? Anyway I can watch over myself. "

He ignored that remark. He took the charge seriously if she did not and childish comments were pointless.

"All elves have these skills in some small measure, call it enchantment if you will but the Dulcamara have more gifts and abilities than most. It's a question of using them and growing in them."

"I wouldn't know where to begin," said Sarah.

"From what Sorrel has said your ancestor is this Blackthorn I never met, and his abilities were greater than any I have known and some of that must be a part of you."

"Maybe so, but it is all new to me."

"You know of mind walking, and indeed few are able to do it. I am one of those who can and it has proved useful." He was still looking out of the window, even while speaking.

"Something troubles you Arin, "said Sorrel from behind him."

Enchanting Sarah by Morgan Fitzsimons

"I dislike this way of travel. It is so confining. I doubt I can stay with it for most of the day."

"I feel just the same. We could get out and run for a bit I suppose," said Sorrel.

"And where will you run to," said Paul. "You need us to find the place and we can't all run. In any case how would it look to have two people outrunning a car?"

"They would have to catch you to give you a ticket," said Chrissie.

"A ticket?" Sorrel questioned.

"There are speed limits on roads and if you go too fast, you get a ticket and pay a fine. Faster than the car means faster than the speed limit."

"The best thing is to have a nap until we get into Wales. You will like it much better. The landscape is much more what you are used to," said Paul.

Enchanting Sarah by Morgan Fitzsimons

"I'm sorry it will take so long," said Darren," but I am not old enough to drive on the motor way which is much quicker."

"Quicker maybe, but I think the surroundings would make it even harder on them," said Paul.

Sorrel put his head back on the seat and closed his eyes.

Arin was still restless.

"Maybe you could tell me some things that would be helpful," suggested Sarah.

"It is not for me to do that," Arin said and Sorrel grinned, his eyes still closed.

"You are a female elf and should learn from your parents," said Arin.

"It may have escaped your notice they are both human. I don't see any other Dulcamara elf around, female or otherwise."

"That's true," said Sorrel, "She has the right of it." his eyes still closed.

Enchanting Sarah by Morgan Fitzsimons

"You are at least some sort of relative, you should explain to her," Arin said to him sticking the shades back on.

"There are some things I can help with but she is quite right, I am not Dulcamara Enchanter and only know what I have observed. I have no experience myself and you have."

For some reason he couldn't even explain to himself, Arin was a little disturbed by the idea of teaching Sarah

"There are many things you should know I suppose, but not all at once," Arin said at last. "I didn't have time to experience all aspects of being Enchanter. Some things are still to come for me also."

"Perhaps you should begin with the small things and let everything take its proper place in due course of time," Sorrel said from the back seat.

"You see you would be a far better teacher than I would," said Arin.

"Isn't time something we may run short of in this conflict with Hemlock?" Paul said.

"Maybe so," said Sarah.

"My mum says cross that bridge when you come to it, and maybe that's how you should move forward," said Chrissie.

"Very well, I will try," said Arin."I know you can mind walk, but do you know you can focus your thoughts on something or someone, and you can travel to where that is, even though you have never been there. You just need to be familiar with that which you seek."

"Just a moment," said Sorrel," that's not a small thing." He sat up in the seat.

Arin ignored him. "If for instance you fixed your thoughts on Ryder or Firedrake and want with all your being to be where they are, you can go there."

"Now, I can do that now," she was excited at the idea.

Enchanting Sarah by Morgan Fitzsimons

"Do you want to try it," he said, "It's better than being trapped in this car."

"You can't let her wander alone. Anything could be where they are. She would be in danger from any dragon master with the ability to sense her in the vicinity." Sorrel was clearly perturbed.

"She wouldn't be alone. I would be with her."

Sorrel gasped." But there must be complete trust for that. Have you ever done this before?"

"I haven't but my parents have and I have witnessed it. My father talked of it after my mother's death. I think it helped him get through it. My skill and experience is stronger than yours so I have trust you Sarah to allow me to lead. That means obeying without question if there is danger. You will have to trust me to watch over you and keep you from harm." He held out his hand, "Will you do that?"

"I trust you, I will do as you say," she said, "Let's go."

Enchanting Sarah by Morgan Fitzsimons

"I could take you but the whole idea is for you to do it. You must take me. Fix your thoughts on Ryder. Touch the mark above your eyes."

She did as she was bid and he took her hands touched the mark on his forehead with her finger tips then put his arms about her and they were no longer present. She was floating up into the clouds and it was typically raining a little and she actually felt the spray of the rain as they rushed to where Ryder was. She was at that moment sitting with Firedrake deep in a dark belt of trees keeping out of sight. The two of them knew at all times knew where their charges were, and would be able to join them when they were ready. Ryder felt her presence. Firedrake communicated with Arin.

"You are being followed," she said.

"I felt it was possible. How many are there?" he asked.

"Two," she said. "They know you,"

"Keep watching," said Arin.

Enchanting Sarah by Morgan Fitzsimons

Even as he spoke a dark swirling presence entered their consciousness making straight for Sarah. It wasn't something mind walking, it was something directed at them. She couldn't breathe and tried to shake it off but Arin was there imposing his will upon whatever it was. It writhed and choked and Sarah could hear a screaming sound and knew whatever it was it no longer existed.

"You must go back," said Ryder. "Someone following knows you are here."

Arin drew her away "fix your thoughts on the car," he whispered and the moment she did they were drawn back to the confines of the vehicle.

"Next time I will prepare you for such encounters so you can deal with it yourself."

"I was afraid," said Sarah "I will need time to be that confident."

"What happened," demanded Sorrel.

"You were right in that something sensed her and tried to choke her," admitted Arin.

Enchanting Sarah by Morgan Fitzsimons

"What something."

"I understand we are being followed by at least two creatures. It's my fault. My presence makes you fair game for any of Hemlock's creatures who spot us and we don't really know where they might be."

"I think that's a good point from Firedrake, they know you. You need different clothes so you look less conspicuous." said Sarah.

"Right now we must rest but I presume we will stop at some point to eat so we can find me some clothes then. I have other clothes back in my sanctuary but I wore these to reassure Sorrel I was who I said I was."

He closed his eyes and this time he did sleep.

He awoke to Sorrel shaking his arm.

"We were going to get you some modern clothes," he said.

Enchanting Sarah by Morgan Fitzsimons

"You realise it probably will make little difference. They can sense what I am," he whispered to Sorrel.

"I do, but it will reassure the others."

He followed them into the clothes store where Sarah found a black long sleeve top and a wine coloured one. She thrust them at him along with a black leather jacket, a pair of jeans and fedora style hat. He disappeared into the changing room and emerged looking totally different with the leather coat and wine coloured top, the jeans and carrying the hat in his hand. He still wore his arm braces with the leather jacket. Sarah impatiently took the hat and reached up on her toes to stick it on at a rakish angle, covering the tops of his ears. Chrissie clapped her hands.

"I'm keeping the boots," he said firmly.

"Shades of Johnny Depp," commented Paul.

"Who or what is Johnny Depp?" said Arin.

"A famous actor in the movies, everyone had heard of him," said Paul.

Enchanting Sarah by Morgan Fitzsimons

"Movies?" asked Sorrel.

"It will take too long to explain," said Paul.

"I have seen some of these movies, films, whatever. You are not missing much," said Arin.

"Ah but I bet you haven't watched Lord of the Rings," said Paul.

"Never heard of it," said Arin.

"What is it," said Sorrel curious as always.

"It's a story about elves and you see it as moving images." said Paul "I will show you one on my cameras when we are back in the car."

Darren held up his card but Arin shook his head and produced one of his own from his dark green coat.

Sarah immediately felt a rush of disappointment. Had she been wrong to trust him? Where had he got the plastic from and was it Hemlock?

"I haven't actually used it so I am unsure of the procedure."

"Simple," said Darren."Do you know your pin number?"

"I have an excellent memory," said Arin.

"Follow me then," he said and led the way to the cashier. She cut the tags from the items and he bought the black top too. His own jacket and pants were put in a bag and Sorrel took his coat and Darren showed him how the card was used. The cashier read the name on the card and raised her eyebrows. Arin hastily took it from her. Sarah had spotted a pretty hat in 20's style and promptly bought it with her own money pulling it down over the ears.

"You know it might be cold where we need to go, shouldn't we get some warm anoraks or something" said Paul.

"Good idea," said Darren

They put the purchases in the car and went to eat.

This time Darren went to a Chinese eat in place. There was some laughter over the food as Sorrel tasted different things and mastered the use of the fork. He loved the fries and the burger which Darren had ordered with everything on it but it was different from the one he had eaten at the Macdonalds. He also loved the rice dishes.

"It was worth being here for the food experience," said Sorrel, as he watched in fascination as Paul squeezed a bottle to put tomato sauce and then mustard on his fries.

Arin ate very little, but Sarah noticed he did know how to use a fork and he actually sampled some of the rice dishes using chopsticks quite deftly. He seemed preoccupied and barely spoke as they continued the journey.

They saw the sign Welcome to Wales and all the sign posts changed to Welsh with English underneath. The landscape began to change as they travelled country lanes and they found themselves at last in the hillsides of Wales. When they reached the mountains and the steep passes, Arin just had to get out of the car as did Sorrel.

"This is more like the world I knew," said Sorrel.

"Which way must we go," he asked and Paul checked the map and pointed. "You see the road way ahead as it curves beneath the mountain. That is as far as I can see."

Arin reached into the back of the car for his sword and strapped it over his back while Sorrel slung his quiver in place and his bow on his shoulder. Like two children they raced off running so fast the watchers gasped,

"Me too," said Sarah and legged it after them.

She was incredibly fast but they were faster and to be fair they had no idea she was behind them, they were so exhilarated to run free. Darren started the car and followed the road. They reached the two Elves who were sitting on a rock looking down on the road. They strolled down but on reaching the car they saw Sarah wasn't in it.

Arin swiftly swung round to look back. "Ryder will not be impressed that I lost her so easily."

"Where is she, "asked Sorrel grimly.

"She followed you," said Paul.

"Follow this road to the end and wait for us," Sorrel ordered.

Arin was already racing back the way he had come and Sorrel lost no time in following. A silent Darren drove the car to the end of the road as it curved around the steep inclines. The steep rock faces became woodland and the road went on to end up on one side of a bridge that crossed a river deep in a valley below. They didn't cross but sat in the car and prepared for a long wait.

"I can't just sit doing nothing," said Paul.

"Well why not sort out all that info Sarah printed out. It will be useful to organise it into stuff on this guy's business and all the different projects and the stuff about the island,"

"Ok," said Chrissie and she got the folders from the back of the car and Darren demonstrated a few useful features. The front seats turned round and faced the back and the middle seats formed a flat area.

Enchanting Sarah by Morgan Fitzsimons

"Wow," said Paul, "Your dad doesn't stint himself does he,"

Darren just grinned "He can afford it," and laid out the papers to be organised. It was bit boring but useful and he didn't want to have to think about what could have happened to Sarah.

Chapter 10

Finding Sarah

Sorrel caught up with Arin who was crouched on the ground examining the terrain.

"She slipped here and fell," said Arin.

Sorrel had great tracking skills in the old days. He was a little rusty now but he didn't seem to have lost the ability.

"I count three other than Sarah," he said.

"Make that four," called Arin who had moved on. "Someone stood here and watched."

Enchanting Sarah by Morgan Fitzsimons

"Can't you sense her anywhere," asked Sorrel.

Arin closed his eyes and was very still. He filled his mind with her image and sought its match but could not feel her presence.

"She must be unconscious. I am picking up precisely nothing"

"Then we will have to find her the hard way," said Sorrel.

They followed the tracks which led them into the cold places where the tracks could be seen leading down into what appeared to be a small valley. They were high above it crouched on the skyline so they could not be observed from below.

Arin closed his eyes and found Firedrake. "I may need you, but do not come yet until I call."

"Ryder is coming," Firedrake conveyed and Arin felt Ryder's anger..

"Do you see anything Sorrel?"

"There is someone down there but how many I can't tell."

Enchanting Sarah by Morgan Fitzsimons

Without warning a dark shadow of wings passed over them.

"Eagles?" questioned Sorrel.

"It looks the right place for them," said Arin.

Even as he spoke there was a rushing of air, a mighty displacement caused by a huge wing span. The most beautiful of golden eagles cane to land beside Arin. It was at least a meter across each wing if not more.

"Yulir," said Arin. "You have come back to me."

He put out his arm and the bird rested briefly on the leather arm brace he wore over the sleeve. He perched on a rocky outcrop as Arin stroked his feathers, meeting the eyes of the huge creature "The Dulcamara female elf with the golden hair, have you seen her?"

The eagle picked up the distress within his friend and Arin saw what the bird had seen, Sarah being carried over the rocks and down into the valley below. He had known they were being followed but then he wasn't prepared for Sarah's impetuous behaviour. That didn't stop him from blaming himself and now a bunch of Darg's had her.

Down in the valley, Sarah opened her eyes to find herself bound. She looked around and took in her surroundings. It seemed she was in what looked like an old shed, with gaps in the walls where the wooden planks had rotted and fallen.   There was a view of a small stone farm house through one of the gaps. That too seemed derelict. She turned her head and looked straight at a hen sitting on old straw. This must be in an old hen house where some of the hens were still in occupation. Turned her head the other way and stared straight into the face of the most horrific apparition from her worst nightmares. She screamed the shock was so great and went on screaming. The screams penetrated Arin's mind and he was rigid for a moment. "Sarah, Sarah, show me where you are. "

Sorrel had spent too much time with Blackthorn not to know Arin had made a connection. Arin raced off down to the bottom of the valley with Sorrel alongside. Sarah had stopped screaming and Arin picked up the images as she saw them.

"We are looking for a stone house with outbuildings of some kind, an abandoned farm I think," he told Sorrel.

"Did you see who took her?"

"Some kind of Darg, I have seen them with Hemlock."

Sorrel spotted the two left on guard before Arin did.

"This is like being home," said Arin, "This I can deal with."

Yulir took a rapid dive and brushed over their heads startling them and Arin and Sorrel took them from the back. Sorrel's target was killed instantly with an arrow, but Arin held his creature flat on the ground with the sword drawing blood at its throat. The tail was threshing a little and even though these creatures were a bit smaller than they were used to, they were still larger than the elves. The tail was the most lethal weapon and Sorrel noted with approval the young elf warrior knew his business keeping the creature down. He locked his eyes with the Darg for a moment.

"They are under a permanent order to take anything that looks like an Elf to Hemlock. That's for me I suppose, but it netted them Sarah, just as it did in the college grounds. This lot are going to frighten her a lot more than those who took her at college. They looked almost human, but she will not have encountered anything like these before. They are taking her to the dig site so she can be sent on from there."

"Then we are close to that too," said Sorrel.

Arin's attention left the creature for a moment, but it was enough to have him rise, his jaws snarling and the great claws to rip out and go for Arin's throat. Arin calmly side stepped and slashed the creature a death blow.

They moved on the building where Sarah was. "I think she is alone now. The rest of the creatures are eating in the farmhouse," said Arin.

"We should be grateful they are not eating Sarah," said Sorrel.

"True but probably their fear of the master is greater than their appetite for elf."

He spoke the last words as he went through the doorway and Sarah heard him.

"What do you mean their appetite for elf?"

"They like to roast and eat them," he said.

"Cut me loose" she said. "I would like to be somewhere else."

"You could have been free of your bonds anytime," he said. "Just focus on free hands and twist them."

She tried it and held them up as the bonds loosened. "Why didn't you tell me that sooner?"

"We didn't need you running out and alerting them before we got here," he said.

She burst into tears. She really was scared, never in her life had she faced anything so terrible before. It was like something on a movie screen that hadn't seemed real until the creatures touched her and bound her and the reality of it came home to roost. Sorrel comforted her and she wept all over his jacket. Arin moved to the open doorway her tears disturbed him but underlined the fact her experience was no more than a new born elfling. It wasn't any comfort to know he had been right about her being scared. Sorrel was a bit shaken himself, not that he was scared but he hadn't fought Darg's for a long time and it was more tiring than it used to be, unlike Arin to whom it seemed only yesterday.

"You know I am beginning to feel my age," he said over Sarah's head.

Arin laughed, "Only just beginning to?" he said.

"You can smile but has it occurred to you, if you hadn't been fixed in time by Aorcha you would now be either dead, or much older in human terms than I am. Technically you are in years if we are to count time as humans do, but I suppose physically you were in limbo so can still be considered a mere elfling."

"Have you got your breath back O ancient one?" said Arin grinning.

"We need to deal with the others. I don't think it would be a good idea to let them communicate their find to their superiors," said Sorrel.

"Point taken," agreed Arin. "Do you know how many are in there?"

"At least four more," said Sarah, then she saw the eagle as it came down to Arin once more.

"Yulir will attack with us," he said.

"You found him again," she said."He is as magnificent as Ryder."

The eagles head pivoted towards her and she met the unblinking gaze. She could have sworn he heard her and understood who Ryder was. The four creatures chose that moment to come outside and move toward the hen house. Several more eagles appeared and hurtled after Yulir as his great claws reached the nearest of them. There was a terrifying screech as a furious Ryder appeared and flew straight at a Darg and ripped at his eyes with his claws.

"Stay here Sarah, while I show Grandfather Elf here a thing or two," said Sorrel.

"In your dreams laughed Arin and was already charging forward, leaving Sorrel to run after him. His sword flashed so fast he met his target while Sorrel had his bow in his hand equally speedily and he shot in rapid succession. Sarah had her first experience of the kind of violent dangers they had once faced, and were still facing now in her time. Talking about it wasn't the same as living it. It was impressed upon her this terrible evil could not be allowed to touch upon the people of her time. They had enough problems without Jefferson Hemlock and the Dragon Masters. She didn't think she would ever have the courage to laugh in the face of these creatures. It was gratifying to see them erased into the landscape.

"The dig must be nearby. We could find it now with Firedrake," said Arin.

"First we must let the others see Sarah is safe, we can't leave them waiting at the roadside. Then we can find what is happening at this dig."

"They could have already found what they are searching for," said Arin.

"I realise that, but a short period of time won't make a lot of difference."

The hawk came down to face to face level with Arin.

"I know," Arin said, "but losing her wasn't intentional."

The hawk did sympathise a little, he knew the contrariness of humans, but never the less he had trusted Arin, but then again, he was still young and had much to learn about human females.

It was a lot faster going back to the car than it had been searching earlier. Chrissie hugged her and the weapons were returned to their resting place under a blanket.

"Your phone rang while you were gone," said Chrissie. "It was your mum but I said you couldn't come to the phone. She assumed you were in the bathroom and said she would call tomorrow."

"Well done, "said Sarah.

Yulir had not followed, but Arin wasn't worried he knew now where he was and Yulir would find him again when he was needed. Ryder deemed Firedrake to be in fairly safe territory now and they flew over the car as they passed over the bridge finally swooping down to find refuge in the gorge below. Darren drove over the bridge and into the little village which was really a few rows of tourist shops and hotels. They booked into one, the girls having a small suite with a sitting room area and a balcony patio overlooking the rushing water of a river running over many layers of rock creating small waterfalls. The sound had a familiarity for the Elves. There was an old

Enchanting Sarah by Morgan Fitzsimons

fashioned street lamp built into the rail which came on when it went dark. The girls and Darren sat at the table with glasses of clear spring water. Sarah had discovered it was all Arin would drink. He didn't like the taste of most things he tried and was accustomed to a drink made with honey, Paul leaned over the rail to look up the valley, the twilight mist creating a haze over the water, while Sorrel sat cross legged on the wooden floor his eyes closed as he related to the natural elements around him. The hawk sat on the balcony rail, his amber eyes surveying Arin, who hastily took the hint and dropped down at Sarah's feet. It was such a lovely place with no sign of the evil lurking out on the hillside and Arin was experiencing a brief moment of peace sitting there in the twilight, the breeze ruffling his hair, but even as he experienced it he knew it wouldn't last.

The mood was broken by Chrissie.

"You lot can sit out here all night but I'm going to sleep in a bed while I can. Good night Darren," she said pointedly. "This is the girl's room and our balcony, so go and find your own."

Enchanting Sarah by Morgan Fitzsimons

When they had gone, Sarah saw Arin had left his jacket. She picked it up to put it to one side and his bank card fell out of the pocket. She picked it up wondering once more how he actually got it. It was responsible to gather what information she could, so it wasn't snooping. The name on the card leapt out at her, Arin Inazo O'Neill. The name sounded familiar but she just couldn't place it. How did he get a name like that if he was just Dulcamara? Again her doubts surfaced and she shook Chrissie who was already drifting.

"Which room is Darren's," she said, but she just got a murmured reply.

She would just have to search the web herself and she scrabbled in her pocket for her phone. She keyed in the name and it picked up on the Inazo O'Neill giving her The O'Neill Foundation. There was a lot of info about Gregory Inazo O'Neill and his interests which could quite easily be a part of Hemlock's set up. O'Neill was involved in as many companies as Hemlock seemed to be. Why had he been reluctant to tell them more about his sanctuary? Was Gregory O Neill part of his sanctuary, or was Arin using a false identity?" There was really only one way to find out and being Sarah she acted before thinking and she marched to the door. She knew he wouldn't be inside the hotel but somewhere out among the trees. She wanted direct answers before they went any further.

Chapter 11

Ardreth Eryri

When the others had retired to their rooms to prepare for the next day, Arin had reappeared only to swiftly leave the hotel making for the trees down by the water just as Sarah thought he would. He was engrossed in his thoughts and raised his head, his eyes glowing fiercely from beneath the hat brim as Sarah stepped out in front of him.

"Where are you going," she said, "Maybe I shouldn't have trusted you."

"Don't be childish," he said.

"I am not a child," she said crossly, "but it is possible you are not all you seem. I want to trust you!"

"Then trust me," he said simply.

"Not until you explain this." She held out the card.

"So you are not so trustworthy either, to steal my bank card from my pocket."

"I did not," she said hotly, "I found it on the carpet. How could you think I would do that!"

"I didn't think you did, but now you know what it feels like not to be trusted."

"How did you actually get here though, what actually happened? Surely if I must trust you, I can be trusted with what happened and where you found sanctuary."

Her words conjured up images he wanted to shut out. The panic rose in him and he felt his mouth, his throat and nostrils, full of dust and rubble and his breathing became laboured. The sensation of choking, suffocating, filled his existence. He tried to explain but gave up and instead he took her hand and put her fingers against her mark then his own.

"Let me share it with you then you will understand and believe it," he said.

She was immediately in a state similar to mind walking. She was either walking in his mind, or he was talking mind to mind, she didn't really know. She was conscious of the experience he wished to share and scrabbled at the claustrophobic rock encased about them.

He felt the dragon move beneath him; she gave a mighty heave and the rock disintegrated into millions of fragments, freeing the eagle at her head. For the diggers, it seemed like the rock came alive and took the form of a dragon. Searching for the bones of a dragon was one thing but facing something living was another and they downed tools and ran screaming from the cavern. The lights shining on the rock face were knocked over and discarded in the rush but they had served their purpose, the light acting as some sort of trigger to melt down. The dragon continued the thrust and emerged blinking into the light of day, her eyesight impaired by her long sleep. The eagle that followed close after in no way resembled any bird of today, but seemed more a prehistoric creature of stone with a huge wing span. Arin however was totally disorientated. He had been encased within the very substance of the mountain for so long; he was unable to adjust and could see only shapes moving against the light. His sword was still in his hand as it had been when he was transported and he just slashed with it blindly at what he perceived to be a threat. He couldn't understand what they were shouting either, the human dialect having changed over the centuries. There was a surge from Firedrake to Arin enabling him to know what was being said. The man he had later come to know as Mason was yelling at the fleeing men.

"Get back here, you bastards," he fired off a weapon held waist high and a stream of bullets blew up dust clouds from the crushed rock. They stopped in their tracks.

"Remember who pays you. Mr. Hemlock will pay millions for a real live specimen."

It made little difference to the situation. Some of the men began to fire weapons and Mason screamed at them to stop. He wanted the dragon alive. Firedrake had every intention of staying that way too and opened her mouth to breathe. The dust and debris had dimmed her fires somewhat but her feeble attempt at flame still had the effect of a flame thrower as it seared over them. Arin was barely conscious but as Firedrake took to the air, he caught a glimpse of a tall man staring at him from the doorway of one of the tents. The face turned up to him was just like Aorcha, the dragon master who had sent him to oblivion, but Arin only caught a glimpse and a distorted one at that, and couldn't really be sure. The dragon flew on, but she too suffered the effects of the long incarceration, as did the eagle tagging along wearily behind. She searched below and lighted upon the garden of Mitsouko.

Enchanting Sarah by Morgan Fitzsimons

Mitsouko was the Japanese wife of Gregory Inazo O'Neill. His great grandfather was an Irish immigrant to Texas and had ended up an oil billionaire. Although his company had extensive holdings in Texas, his main home was in California, in a beautiful Hacienda combining the old Spanish style with colonial elegance. His son had married a Japanese wife. Greg's father had maintained his wife Magumi's garden in her family home in Japan. It now belonged to Greg's wife Mitsouko. It was her place of peace while she waited for her son. It was as though Firedrake knew the occupant. She was drawn down among the trees and allowed her burden to slip down to the grass where Mitsouko found him.

Sarah caught her breath at the image.

She looked like something from a Japanese painting in her rose coloured kimono, belted with the deep sash and the graceful wide sleeves flowing down. She wore her hair looped up with combs and looked every bit from another age. She fitted in perfectly with this traditional Oriental garden with trailing blossoms and a pretty bridge over a stream. She knelt and brushed back his hair.

"I knew if I waited Inazo, you would come."

Arin was still covered in the dust from the rock in which he had been encased and he was torn and bleeding. He was as exhausted as if he had clawed his way through the rubble of an earthquake to reach his mother, which she was convinced he had.

"Gregory, come and see," she cried out.

Her husband had come running when she cried for him.

"It's Inazo, "she said. "Our son is alive, he has come home,"

Whoever he was he needed help and in no way would Greg put his wife's frail hold on life at risk by denying her words. She took command of the situation which in itself was a miracle and Greg's manservant helped carry him to where he was bathed and his clothes taken to be cleaned. He was barely conscious and wrapped in a robe when she was allowed to see him again. His long black elf hair had reached his waist but it was so matted with rock that it could not be loosened so they had begun to cut it. Arin became extremely distresses and raised a hand to the length still there and feebly ran his fingers down it to reveal a last long gleaming lock of hair. It was some time later Greg made the acquaintance of Firedrake and Yulir. The two were quite content to allow Mitsouko to care for Arin and she had not been afraid of them at all. When Firedrake withdrew into the trees, she had accepted her reticence to be seen. When Arin recovered he explained to Gregory all that happened and the only thing that convinced Greg of the youth's sanity was meeting Firedrake. He was real so the rest of it had to be. He was fascinated but as soon as he could he drew Arin to one side.

"My wife believes you to be our son Inazo and to be fair, you do look a great deal like him. "

"Your son?" said Arin. He struggled to focus on Greg for his eyes were still weak from the long darkness.

Enchanting Sarah by Morgan Fitzsimons

"Our son was a victim of an earthquake on a visit to a member of the family here in Japan. He was just 17 then. There was no body found, just some of his things. That was a year ago and Mitsouko is still here in her family home, still waiting for him to return. I come as often as I can, but my business interests are vast and wide. She won't come back to California without him."

He sighed and went on "She is very fragile with a heart condition and the death put her on a knife edge mentally and physically. If she believes you are Inazo, I cannot tell her the truth."

"I understand," Arin said quietly, "but I am not her son and need to find my father."

"I accept that and perhaps we can be of service to each other," said Greg.

Nothing would persuade Mitsouko this was not her son and Arin was finally persuaded to accept it for her sake, for wasn't his loss as great as hers had been. He understood her pain and the more he learned of Greg and how he used the power of money, the more he respected him. Greg's grandmother had been Japanese and her father had followed the way of Bushido. He had been Samurai, so Greg respected Arin's integrity born from his High Elf Warrior class.

In Arin's time, foster parents were a natural thing so their acceptance of each other was born out of need which soon became respect and affection. He had to live somewhere unobtrusively and this was the perfect solution.

He looked so like Inazo but for Greg there were subtle differences, His son had slightly almond shape eyes and this youth's eyes were European in shape. He could pass as Greg's son though for Inazo had only the black hair of his mother and in all else his appearance was like his Irish grandfather.

"I have not been here very long but while searching for answers I became part of the work of the Foundation, and as Gregory's son I crossed the path of Hemlock Industries and some of his other organisations."

Enchanting Sarah by Morgan Fitzsimons

"But you didn't stop looking for your own father," Sarah said

"I think I knew in my heart he was lost to me but I had to try, and now, knowing what Hemlock is about and that Aorcha may be alive, I have a purpose for being here at least."

"You want revenge for your father," somehow she had not thought it would be Arin's way, and she wasn't wrong.

"Not revenge, justice perhaps and certainly both he and Hemlock must be stopped. They have pulled too many strings behind the scenes for far too long and it's time to fight back."

"I see," she said.

"I will take you to meet my foster family as soon as I can, I must admit the work Greg's people do is beginning to grip me, but we have to sort this first."

"What do you intend."

Enchanting Sarah by Morgan Fitzsimons

"He intends to go up there without the others," said Sorrel as he stepped round a tree.

"You as well," said Arin.

"I think you are right to leave them to sleep in peace but you will need us," said Sorrel.

"Come then, "he said."Firedrake can carry three up the mountain as easily as one.

He climbed up quickly and easily and placed Sarah in front and Sorrel got behind him and they took off.

They found the dig site which was fenced off with high wire fences.

"Drop us on this side," said Arin "Any night guard is less likely to notice us without you."

Firedrake duly landed and allowed them to slide down. They vaulted high and over the fence with ease and landed on their feet on the other side. They covered the ground quickly taking in the surroundings. There were several wooden structures and one stone built building which was the base office. They spread out first of all looking for the actual areas where digging was taking place. There were several trenches opened but nothing revealed any artefacts still there.

"I have a feeling about this," Arin whispered. "These trenches suggest they are looking for buildings of some sort as well as artefacts or bones."

"But what?" said Sarah.

They checked the shed like buildings finding one containing crates which were labelled with possible dates of contents but nothing related to what they were looking for. A door opened and they hid behind trees when several guards emerged to do a patrol check. They shinned up to the tree tops and waited while they passed below. Someone opened the door of the stone building and a shaft of light illuminated the area in front. A man stuck his head through and called to one of the guards.

"Has everyone else gone home for the night?"

Enchanting Sarah by Morgan Fitzsimons

"Have you lost track of time again professor? I suppose you missed your evening meal again. I 'll see if we can rustle up some sandwiches and a mug of tea in about an hour."

"Bless you Evans," he said, and went back inside. When the guards moved out of sight checking the perimeter, they moved to the door and followed Arin inside.

The Professor looked up from the things he was poring over.

""Don't be alarmed Professor," said Arin in a quiet voice, the tones taking on a deep rich quality that held the man rigid. "I just want to talk with you for a while."

"Who are you?" he asked.

They were standing in the shadows but Arin moved into the light. "What is it you are looking for here? Do you seek the bones of Tal-git?"

"Not now," the man answered."We realised they had been removed before we came. They were stored in some facility or other. I can't remember which."

"Then why are you still working here."

"Mr Mason wants me to find some ancient dwelling that was here from a time when myths and legends were born. He says the discovery will change our whole view of our history."

"And what is this place you look for?"

"The Ardreth Eryri of Ainarr Asveldur," was the reply.

There was a sharp intake of breath from Arin.

"But you are beginning to suspect you are looking for it in the wrong place are you not?"

"How can you know that?"

Arin removed his hat and the professor's jaw dropped. "You exist then? It is true what Mason says?"

"I don't know what he says," said Arin, "But I do know this is not Ardreth. I lived in a place very near it millennia after the passing of Ainarr, it was called Drake's Ridge. May I look at your research?"

"But of course," said the professor. Arin studied it all carefully and showed nothing of his excitement as he worked out the possibilities.

"Why does Mason want you to find Ardreth?"

"The president of Hemlock Industries, who pays the bills incidentally, wants us to find an artefact that he believes is still there."

"What artefact?"

"They haven't told me that yet," he said, "I have to find the home of The Ardreth first."

"We must leave you now professor," said Arin, taking a short stick from his belt. He clicked it open. It formed a staff decorated at one end with silver and gold. He tapped the professor very quickly three times.

"You will forget our conversation or that we were ever here."

Enchanting Sarah by Morgan Fitzsimons

The professor dropped his gaze back to his work as they silently left. They didn't speak again until they were over the fence and back with Firedrake.

"That was interesting. Does that mean somewhere near here is the Ardreth Eryri?"

"It does," Arin was brief.

"I will meet you back in the wood where Firedrake was. I have a sudden urge to run back," said Sorrel.

Arin and Sarah climbed on Firedrake and took to the air at which point Yulir returned to Arin. He was accompanied by another eagle, a little smaller but still impressive.

"They want us to follow," said Arin."Of course! I am totally stupid. The eagles will know where it is. The words mean the eagle nest of the Ardreth. It is what Yulir has been seeking"

"What is the Ardreth actually?" asked Sarah.

Enchanting Sarah by Morgan Fitzsimons

"The personal War Band of Ainarr Asvaldur. The Ardreth Eryri was their fortress named after them, invincible and very inaccessible."

Firedrake followed the eagles and they rose over the higher peaks to where several more eagles had gathered and were wheeling around in the magical moonlight. The dragon floated down to land on a flat up thrust of rock, where their excitement mounted as they saw steps cut out of the stone leading down. Neither of them noticed both Firedrake and Yulir taking off again to fly in the direction of a high ridge on the mountain side. Sarah clutched Arin's hand as he led her down them, to where carved stone arches could be seen leading into the mountain. The rooms they could access were empty and silent and they couldn't move into lower areas which were blocked with falls of rock and the rubble and sediment of ages gone by. Arin rubbed at some of the stone walls revealing carvings of extreme beauty as all Elven craft work was.

"For the moment I think it virtually impossible for anyone else to find this place. It needs a Yulir and a dragon to track it down, or even access it for that matter. Whatever he wants from here he isn't going to find it before I have the time to explore the place."

He stood at one of the window openings and pointed to a long high ridge further over among the hills.

"That was Drakeridge. I played here as an elfling and my home is somewhere down there. At least I know now where it is."

He sat on the ground and closed his eyes briefly and she could feel his pain as his memories engulfed him. She sat down beside him and grasped his hand and they sat there together. He gripped her hand tightly and pulled her to her feet.

"We need to get on with the more pressing task," he said, "Thank you for caring,"

She could feel the sorrow at losing all he held dear, his people and his way of life.

"You are not alone here Arin," she said once more impulsive. "We are of the same origins you and I.

Enchanting Sarah by Morgan Fitzsimons

I am beginning to understand what my heritage means and the responsibility of it and the place I am being led to. I am finding it a lonely place."

"You have made a difference by just being here Sarah. If you were not, then there would be no one to share memories with who actually knows what Elf is."

He walked out onto what appeared to be a stone balcony still holding her hand and leaned over to look at the fabulous scene before them. There was a little moonlight, enough to make the landscape mysterious and magical and Drakeridge curved in the form of living dragons. All around was empty and silent and magnificently stark and beautiful, nature at its most magnificent. Sarah shivered a little in the cold air and Arin instantly removed his leather jacket and wrapped it around her, the anoraks being back in the hotel. He held her close against his body warmth and it was quite natural to be there.

Enchanting Sarah by Morgan Fitzsimons

"It feels so safe I wish we could stay here forever, it so beautiful and unreal, like living in a dream," said Sarah.

"I would like that, but sadly we have to live in the real world, but maybe we could escape here sometimes when it gets too tough down there."

"You won't forget you said that will you?" Sarah said.

"I will not forget," he promised, "But we need to go back now," He was reluctant to move because he had realised in those few moments, keeping her safe was the most compelling thing in his life. She had become the most precious creature in his world now, she had the elfin beauty that fascinated, and was extremely intelligent, witty and fun, but she also held dear all the things he lived by and she was one of his own people. Sarah didn't want to go either. She was entranced by the surroundings and as most girls of her age would be, she was fascinated by this lonely youth who was of necessity an adult and yet a youth, together, presenting her with a mystery, an enigma she wanted to unravel, but he was right and they must go back to the others before dawn came. High over head Firedrake returned to wait for them as they climbed up the steps to where she was. Arin wondered fleetingly where she had been but forget it as he helped Sarah back onto Firedrake's back and they soared high above looking down on the magnificent site that had once housed The Ardreth of Ainarr and the curving ridge where once Arin's home had been and would never be again, but seeing it had perhaps given him some closure and he could begin to make a new beginning.

Enchanting Sarah by Morgan Fitzsimons

Chapter 12

Questions and Answers

Sarah couldn't sleep in the few hours left and made her way back down to the trees opposite the hotel. Sorrel was there before her.

"You knew humans of my age in the past. How different would they be to those of today?"

"I hadn't thought about it, but any male was judged an adult when he could wield a sword. This was true of elves as well."

"But what about females," she asked, "Were they warriors/"

"Some were, but many elf females were small and delicate and used a bow or a staff.

She contemplated her feet swinging below the tree branch she was sitting on.

"At what age did they marry then?"

Sorrel smiled realising where this was going. The young were ever curious.

"Life was short for man and they married young but for elves age and time matter little, we live so long. Time is almost a constant for us; it doesn't register as linear and unfolding time. The past is always so much the present too. You child, were born out of time. The way you look now is probably how you will look a hundred years from now, yet everyone around you will move on in so short a life span."

"I hadn't thought of it," she said slowly. "It is hard to envisage being here when everyone has gone. How can you know that will happen to me?"

Enchanting Sarah by Morgan Fitzsimons

"Nothing is certain, but I do know when Elf partners with human, their offspring have always been either definitely human, with all their characteristics, or definitely Elf, with all that entails. These elves have also inherited the long life which ends early only in battle."

"But we can't really know for sure," said Sarah.

"My intuition tells me I see an ageless elf, with the fragile beauty that draws everyone to her like moths to the flame, and it will still be so even when you are very old. You can use that quality to lead, be a shining example as Lilia was, or you can use it to gain power over others, to enthral people to do your bidding, and for selfish pleasure. That path will however destroy the very thing which gives you that beauty. It will gradually fade and you will lose the enchantment."

"I had not realised it was so crucial, so strongly drawn a line, "said Sarah.

"It is so! That's what happened to the Dragon Masters, and other Elves before them. They began as elves gradually corrupted by their own desires and became black as pitch in the heart and soul. They became masters rather than guardians, reflecting their own darkness. They turned more and more to the sorcery of the dark witches and wizards, powerful drugs and other ways to enhance and bolster up their dominance."

"What are you saying exactly?"

"I am saying the enchantment; the magic is all the same, it's what you choose to do with it. The way it's used changes the individual for good or bad according to their own choices."

"I think I understand you, but how will I know what is the right way?"

"It is very difficult because the expectation of your present way of life is so different. You can't go wrong if you follow Lilia's example. She was always gentle, considerate of others, kind. She had a strong will but a purity and honesty and a joyous spirit, that made others want to be worthy of it. She was courted by many and was always gracious."

Enchanting Sarah by Morgan Fitzsimons

"I am flattered you think I could be like her."

"Don't underestimate that," said Sorrel. "Maybe goals are different now and things once prized are no longer, but I can't believe truth and honesty and purity of spirit are of little value anymore, if that were so it would be as though we never lived."

"I think many have those values still, but we tend to notice the bad more than the good. But I have to say it is getting harder to discern truth from lies and greed and self advancement called philanthropy. People have grown so good at deceiving, particularly in government and politics."

"Make no mistake," said Sorrel, "Greed, deceit and selfishness abounded in my time, being a warrior was a necessity, more so when the Dragon Masters evolved."

"One more thing The Dulcamara are Elves of Shadow, they have a darker side," said Sorrel.

"In what way? asked Sarah.

Enchanting Sarah by Morgan Fitzsimons

"The Elves of light- the Golden Tribe have all the attributes and qualities their name conveys. I must admit we do have that one annoying trait of arrogance because of it."

Sarah laughed as she knew sometimes it was a trait she demonstrated on occasion herself. It wasn't a trait she had just from the Golden Tribe though Sometimes teenagers spoke with the arrogance of youth on occasion, believing they had to be right and the adults didn't understand them When really we were all young once and went through growing up. It often wasn't a lack of understanding perhaps, as much as a desire to protect their loved ones from what they understood only too well.

Sorrel continued his explanation.

"The Dulcamara on the other hand, come to life in the enchantment and mystery of the twilight, they have a fire and passion of the heart and soul that drives them. They are chivalrous, loyal, steadfast, virtuous, and honourable and all the things you would expect, but it does not come naturally. It is down to the individual will and choices and how they use the enchantment. It is too easy to indulge self, to look for power over others."

"But we can all be guilty of being a bit selfish sometimes," said Sarah.

"For any of the Dulcamara, it was the tip of the slippery slope. Once they begin to enjoy self indulgence it led to a need for more and more and the transfer from shadow to the depths of darkness is complete, particularly if they succumbed to drug inducement to enhance their power of enchantment"

"What kind of drugs could they have had access to so long ago? Today they have all sorts of drugs that damage. "

"Probably quite a few of them were developed by this Hemlock and his Industries. The drugs they used would kill humans, monkshood, digitals, deadly nightshade, all from nature but deadly when mixed by the Dragon Master Lord Monkshood."

Enchanting Sarah by Morgan Fitzsimons

"Today its cocaine, heroin, ecstasy and many others, including opium from the poppy that people use. But as far as magic goes, isn't the source of the magic important? Doesn't that affect whether the enchantment is good or bad."

"Not exactly! The power of enchantment you and Arin have recourse to, originates with the dragons through the Enchanter Lords. Ainarr Asvaldur like Blackthorn was a child of both light and shadow. His grandmother Merle was a Shadow Elf Queen, his grandfather father an Elf of the light, the High King of the Twilight Star.

"But what exactly is the enchantment?"

"It would take days to explain it, and even then I am not sure I could. It's all relates to the forces of nature, an extension of the harmony and understanding together with the blood bond of the dragon, the enchanters can transcend the boundaries beyond all the senses and move in the supernatural, their understanding allowing them to move beyond the natural laws. It is much more complicated and interwoven than that, but it's the best I can do to briefly convey a little."

"But I haven't bonded with a dragon."

"To deal with the situations of his day Ainarr was given Domgeorn the sword eager for Doom Justice created by the Dwarves of Eridia for the White Dragon Queen and the Black Dragon King. He bonded with both dragons by the Blood Oath and their blood increased his powers of enchantment and it passed to all the Enchanters of his line."

"So why aren't you an Enchanter."

"The line separated again in his children. The girl was golden and became Queen and the boy dark elf and Enchanter War Lord. She ruled all and he held the Dulcamara in her service. All born of this bloodline bearing the mark were Enchanter Lords. Arin's father Alder was a cousin to Asoril the father of Asphodel. He too had the mark. Both Golden and Shadow lines came together again in Blackthorn"

Enchanting Sarah by Morgan Fitzsimons

"It is a fascinating story, and hard to believe I am a throwback to this line."

"It is very simple really. There is a difference between the natural abilities of Elf and the Enchantment. The Golden Elf has a pure life force, a positive presence, an iridescent quality. And in common with the Shadow Elf Enchanters they have a little supernatural wisdom, more than learning. They have an uncanny knowledge beyond the five senses. You must have noticed how your sense of hearing has increased. In the Enchanter this knowledge and these extra senses are greatly enhanced, and is the foundation for the Enchantment to function. As has been said before, it isn't the enchantment itself that is important but how you use it. It is all in the choice you make. I can't stress that enough. What you believe or say is not the most important, it is the doing that counts."

"I can agree with that Sorrel. The abilities I seem to be developing need to be used, and stopping the Dragon Masters is an absolute necessity and we are all there is. The authorities won't believe it and would probably treat Arin and myself as the enemy."

"From what Arin says I think that is so. People are afraid of what they can't understand."

"Could I compel people to do things they didn't want to do?" Sarah asked.

"There you have the truth of the danger. You could, and it would be wrong. Everyone has to choose their own way. You are curious aren't you, and it's that curiosity that leads to the act of trying it, just to see if you could and so it grows."

"I think I understand what you are saying, but it is a human trait to be curious especially when you are my age. You want to know it all and experience it all, so why not so long as you don't hurt anyone else in the process?"

"Because there are consequences to every choice you make good or bad. Now you can't now get away with the excuse 'I am hurting no one but myself,' because in hurting yourself you will be turning to the darker side of your nature, damaging the Dulcamara soul. You will be creating an ultimate evil. You have to be very sure of what you are doing and why before you actually do it."

"Being a teenager in today's environment is hard enough without all this."

"Tough," replied Sorrel. "But one thing I have learned, life in the world of men is never easy."

"I suppose that's true. We make most of our problems ourselves."

"Arin encounters the same difficulties you do, but he has at least grown up with the knowledge of the consequences which enables him to deal with it better," said Sorrel."And it has been my experience that men as well as elves, can rise to great things in adversity."

"I seems I still have a lot of catching up to do," she said. "I suppose some people are attracted to those who are very different and others to those who are similar in their tastes and background."

Enchanting Sarah by Morgan Fitzsimons

"You offer both together." Sorrel smiled at some inner thought. "You are an enigma, someone quite different from another time another place, and yet you have the most obvious attraction."

What might that be?" she laughed.

"You are one of his own! You are timeless just as he is. You will need each other."

"How did you know?"

"That you like Arin," he smiled. "I have been around a long time, remember, all this talk is leading somewhere and you are female so your interest is obvious."

"There speaks the arrogant male again and it's not just the prerogative of Elf."

He stood up to go, but turned back to her. "You like Arin and he seems like any other youth of Charlie's age, but he has the maturity and reliability of the warrior background he comes from. It makes you feel dangerous and safe at the same time and you can't quite understand that."

Enchanting Sarah by Morgan Fitzsimons

He had put her confusion exactly as she experienced it.

"There is a bond, because like you he is a product of the past, a strange phenomena, a throwback that probably has an existence way into the future and the loneliness of that will throw you together anyway. The hard part is dealing with this new way of life which neither of you chose nor had time to come to terms with before you were actually in it. It would make sense to help each other but that depends on if you can become close or not."

"That sums it up fairly well I suppose,"

"You want to take refuge in the safety your parents provide yet you are drawn to explore the things that draw you into the world of adults. I never had that problem, because we don't count time or age, it has no relevance, but you are between both worlds."

"I find myself hovering and questioning too much and I am still a creature of impulse, "said Sarah.

Enchanting Sarah by Morgan Fitzsimons

"I would say just take it as it comes day by day. Be yourself and trust your instincts. It is one thing that is very reliable in the Elf. Finding common ground may not be as easy as it might look. Just because you have to come together to survive doesn't mean you will find it easy to be friends and it could prove impossible if one loves and the other doesn't. It is hard to tell if he is here because he likes you or because he is obliged by heritage, to protect you." He muttered the last words to himself but she heard him.

"Thank you for putting that into words," she said and ran back towards the hotel.

Sorrel looked after her in dismay. "All those words and all I achieved was her running away," Sorrel said to the hawk sitting above them, who wisely said nothing at all.

It was dawn when they gathered on the balcony. Arin told them he had the details of the possible whereabouts of Tal-gits bones.

"There was reference to it in the Professors papers."

Enchanting Sarah by Morgan Fitzsimons

He pulled a crumpled sheet of paper from his jacket pocket and passed it to Darren who flattened it and read it.

"They are not in a museum as such," he said. "This says the bones were not identifiable as any known species and were transported to a prohibited government research facility, along with some other bones with human similarities."

"How far away?" said Paul.

"Just a few hours drive," said Darren but it's likely a restricted no access facility."

Sorrel grinned at him. "I don't think that's a problem do you?"

"Point taken," said Darren. "Let's get moving then."

They paid the hotel; bill and piled in the car again, leaving Firedrake and Yulir to follow them though Ryder was quite visible from the car.

"What was it you did to the professor," asked Sarah of Arin.

"It was a little Siedr magic using the rune staff. It saves my personal energy to use it."

"But isn't that evil, Sorcerer's magic?"

"The enchantment belongs to neither Elves, sorcerers, witches, nor anything else, but they make it theirs when they use it and either preserve its purity or taint it with their purpose."

The car swerved to one side of the road as Sorrel spoke Darren was listening so intently.

"Keep your eyes on the road," said Paul from the back. "You aren't the greatest driver in the world."

"At least I am getting you there," said Darren.

"So long as your purpose is we arrive in one piece," said Paul.

""But what is the difference between light Elf and Dark Elf apart from their physical appearance? Chrissie asked."

"In simple terms, Light Elves rarely can be corrupted whereas Dark Elves have to struggle with it," said Arin.

"So you are nigh on perfect then Sorrel?" said Chrissie laughing.

"I suppose you could say that," said Sorrel.

"I forgot to add arrogant to the description," said Arin with a smile.

"We have already agreed on the arrogance," Sarah said.

"True," said Sorrel," while I might say most of the Dulcamara Lords of my acquaintance, were true warriors of integrity, their sense of chivalry and honour un matched, but they were not born to it, they have to choose it."

"Thiers is a constant struggle to resist the darker side of their nature. They have so much power at their finger tips you see, and can so easily be corrupted by it. You may find it easier Sarah so much of the golden elf is retained within you," said Arin.

"Humans have a similar struggle," said Sarah. "There are so many temptations within easy reach in today's society. It is easy to succumb to all kinds of abuse."

"Well I'm tempted every day to beat up dear Bradley," said Paul.

"He's a sixth former and twice your size little brother," scoffed Sarah.

"Remind me to teach you a few tricks," said Arin.

"Cool," said Paul.

"Don't encourage him," said Sarah.

"How far have we come," said Chrissie who was now bored with the discussion "Are you checking the map Paul?"

"We are almost there so we need to know what you intend to do, "said Paul

"A short mind walk will be helpful," said Arin. "It will be fairly dangerous if it's an official place. There are most likely military guards with modern weapons."

"You know the capability of such things then," said Sarah.

"I have not wasted my time with Gregory," answered Arin. "His research facilities and business interests are vast."

"Have we missed something?" asked Paul.

"Nothing of concern,'" he replied.

"Now who is arrogant," grinned Paul.

Sarah ignored him.

"Does he know where you are now," asked Sarah.

"Of course," he held up his state of the art mobile. "I can use this fairly well now and I can tap into a phenomenal amount of information back at Greg's HQ."

"Should I be surprised," muttered Sarah.

"I prefer not to use it very often. I understand it can be used to track your whereabouts. Greg tells me this one is very special and just about as trace proof as it can be, but we can't be certain it isn't tapped into by Hemlock 's lot."

Sorrel interrupted, "You want us to wait somewhere out of sight while you mind walk."

"That is the sensible way to start."

"It would be faster if we each took a half of the buildings," said Sarah.

"It would be but it would be dangerous for you."She ignored his statement, fully prepared to use her own initiative.

The facility was way outside any occupied area and surrounded by overgrown fields and dense clusters of trees and wild undergrowth. It had the inevitable wire fence with coils of wire on the top There were warning signs plastered everywhere denoting the coils were electrified and the ground were patrolled with dogs. They drove past the huge gates where sentries were on duty and continued along the lane finding some cover far enough away not to invite suspicion among the trees where they parked. To any interested observer they looked just a group of teenagers out exploring the countryside for the day. Ryder flew over the whole place and came down on a tree branch. Sarah looked into his eyes and saw what he had just seen. There were quite a lot of troops around, either on guard in doorways or in groups exercising or training. It was quite a sprawling collection of buildings with some hangars and huge outbuildings. Arin sat quite still and Sarah knew he had already left them and promptly followed. Inside the main buildings were offices and meeting rooms with a variety of technology. Some areas were guarded. The outbuildings were strongly guarded and inside two there were huge boxes and crates all labelled and sealed. There were too many of them to check individually. One outbuilding had cells in which there were people confined. If one of the boxes contained the bones they were seeking, it was going to be a daunting task to find which one. They really needed to access records which they could only do in the flesh. They went back through the complex office buildings pinpointing the records office which was lined with filing cabinets and several booths with computers in them. Back at the car they explained what they had seen.

"I am afraid you guys will have to wait again but the best way to do that is to act like tourists having a picnic," said Sarah.

"We'll keep it simple so we can take off fast," said Chrissie.

"If we do find the bones are there, we will have to use Enchantment to move them and that could cause us some problems," said Arin. "We may have to come back to the car make another plan."

In the event they didn't have to go to search to find the container with the bones. The container came to them.

Chapter 13

Taking the bait

The three Elves went over the electric fence with
care. Arin watched anxiously as Sarah went over,
but she had no difficult with the somersault, she
was so light and agile. As they slipped through the
trees to enter the buildings they saw a huge lorry
in the open area being loaded with a large crate.
The roof had been slid back to leave a large cavity
allowing the crate to be lifted and lowered with a
crane and they waited patiently for it to go so they
could enter the buildings. Once it was fixed in the
lorry the roof slid back into place and was
secured. The back doors were shut by the armed
guards inside with the crate. The man in charge of

the operation spoke to the driver as he scribbled on his hand held screen and got a signature from thehim. There were two armed guards next to the driver.

"Remember the contents of the crate are precious to the Hemlock Corporation and must be handled with care."

The watchers registered that and looked at each other. Could it be what they sought?

The driver started the engine. "It's just a load of old bones, why all the fuss!" he muttered under his breath.

That settled it and Arin led the race up over the roof to the end of the building where the lorry had to pass. They moved very fast and were not spotted from below. Arin jumped with Sorrel landing on the roof of the huge lorry. Sarah was not so fortunate. A group of armed men turned the corner, policing the roof perimeter. She was last to jump and was seen. A weapon slammed with extreme force into her delicate ribs which had little protection against the force of the blow. She fell unconscious from the roof to the ground.

"Stay with the bones Sorrel," Arin ordered, and with the long ease of obeying Blackthorn, Sorrel nodded as Arin leapt down from the moving lorry which was already through the gates. He landed on the ground. He pulled out the mobile and called Darren. "There is a lorry coming down past you in about a minute. Follow it and see where it goes. Sorrel is on top. Just follow it!"

He heard rapid fire as he went over the wall again but the place was teeming with armed men. It wasn't exactly the place to mind walk and she was unconscious anyway. The source of the shots led him to where Ryder had screamed down to her side and viciously attacked all comers and they had fired at him and he had taken to the air again.

Sarah had been swiftly loaded into an ambulance on the instructions of Mr Mason no less who was there to supervise the transportation of the bones but seeing the golden elf realised the prize he had. He wanted her alive as much as Arin did and he wasted no time. The ambulance with an escort screamed out of the place like a bat out of hell with Arin going back over the wall and sprinting after it. Above him he was joined by an anxious Yulir and the Ryder was actually flying high over the ambulance. He ran faster and longer than he had before and was exhausted by the time the ambulance turned into the hospital grounds. At least he was where she was and he could find her now. He needed to mind walk again. Yulir had now come to rest beside him with Ryder and they sat patiently in the shelter of the trees waiting for Firedrake.

Sorrel meanwhile was still on the lorry which kept going until it reached a dockside and ships. He was aware of Darren following and caught glimpses of the car now and again. He parked it discreetly and told Chrissie and Paul to stay put. Sorrel joined him, explaining the bones were still on the lorry.

"They seem to be shipping them somewhere so I will just ask where the ship is bound." He walked along the dock to where an old man was sitting watching the proceedings.

"Do you like the sea and ships then," he asked the old man.

"It's in me blood boy. Used to serve in merchant ships. I'm out to pasture now but I come down here to watch them coming and going most days."

"Do you actually know where they are all going?" asked Darren

"What's it to you,"

"I wondered where that one was going," he asked and pointed to the ship where the bones were loaded as they spoke.

"Why that's one belonging to some trust or other. It's off up to the North of Scotland, calling at Liverpool first then way up to the Highlands somewhere. I think it's something like Highland Heritage Trust or some such thing."

Darren passed him five crisp ten pound notes.

Enchanting Sarah by Morgan Fitzsimons

"Have a drink on me sir, it's not often I meet an old sailor."

The bemused old sailor in question wasn't objecting and looked up from the cash to thank him, but he had gone back to the car.

"We can't do anything more," said Sorrel.

"I'm hungry, "said the practical Paul. "I vote we eat and wait for a communication from Arin re Sarah."

"We don't know where they are right now so that would make sense, and they can get to us faster on Firedrake than we can get to them," said Chrissie.

Accordingly they found the nearest fast food drive through, then parked up the car to wait once more. At least it kept Paul from voicing his worries, though Chrissie contented herself with coffee to clam her nerves.

Back at the hospital Arin mind walked leaving Yulir to watch over him. He persuaded the Ryder the best way to help Sarah was to fetch Firedrake so they had a means of escape. He moved swiftly, seeking Sarah. She filled his mind, his heart, his soul; he had no problem finding her within the hospital. Outside the place was now surrounded by military vehicles and armed soldiers discreetly positioned. As he moved down passages inside he came to a point where things changed a bit. There were armed guards on every floor and at the nurse's stations and although it seemed quiet where Sarah lay, he spotted Mr Mason and his minions. She lay still and silent on the hospital bed and a doctor was writing a report. The doctor was speaking to Mason.

"She had quite a severe blow covering the stomach area and lungs which has broken her ribs, but the whole injury is causing her inner organs to fail. There is nothing I can do to stop it. She will die fairly quickly."

"He will know and he will come. He could fix it you see," said Mason "Mr Hemlock wants to take him alive. If the girl lives it will be a bonus."

"If you say so, Mr. Mason, but I don't see this being fixed."

"Hemlock says so and he is usually right. I have my people stationed everywhere on this floor and the moment he heals her, we can take him"

"Why wait?"

"I am advised by Mr Hemlock, his species is quite formidable and he would likely escape us, but in the weak state he will be in after bringing her back from near death, he will present no problem."

It was a neat trap but he was going to walk into it. There was no way he put his life before Sarah's. He checked the room swiftly. There was a large window. That would have to do. They definitely wanted the dragon alive so he doubted they would shoot at her. He looked down and below was a small courtyard building on all four sides. He rushed back to Yulir. Firedrake had arrived and he and told her to hover outside the window.

"Whatever, happens you must fly off with Sarah immediately."

Enchanting Sarah by Morgan Fitzsimons

"What about you?" Firedrake communicated the question.

"They will probably capture me but I will escape them. Trust me and do as I ask. I know what I'm doing."

He knew the risks were far greater than he was conveying but it didn't stop him. There wasn't much time so he just walked in through the front entrance and made for the room where she was. Some of Hemlock's people did try to stop him and he left them dead or dying as he passed. Once in the room he waved his hand in the direction of the window knowing it was now open and ready. She lay where he had last seen her, looking so fragile and helpless, still in t shirt and jeans. He felt Sarah's pulse and panicked, he was going to lose her. It was almost too late. Wasting no time he turned up the t shirt and located the damage placing two hands to cover the whole. The light from them spread under his fingers across the damaged area and into the ribs. It took much of his strength to maintain the level of healing, because she was so near death. She coughed and opened her eyes. While she was still confused, he rammed his hat on her head and he lifted her slight form, his breathing already laboured. The window opened as he came to it.

"Quickly now, on to Firedrake."

She obeyed and wriggled across, but there was no way he had strength enough to follow her.

"Go," he said and before she realised he wasn't coming, Firedrake swooped up in the air, careful of her burden.

"Go back! Go back," cried Sarah, but Firedrake obeyed her beloved Arin trusting to his skills.

Arin hadn't wanted to lose the hat because she chose it, and his last sight of her was the large hat crammed over her ears as he passed into oblivion. Mason rushed in with guards and seized him. They knew they couldn't hold an Enchanter without the right restrictions and rushed off with him on a stretcher trolley. Mason ran straight into a snag as he was accosted by the Federal agents working with military officials. They all thought they were obeying superiors which they were in a sense; only the top of this particular structure was the hidden Jefferson Hemlock. There was great excitement to have actually captured an alien being, a different life form.

"We need to put him in the special room we created for him," said Mason."It has to be done before he wakes up. We can't contain him outside of it." It's in everyone's best interests we move fast.

He was rushed out to an ambulance with a military escort, accompanied by the Federal agents and taken to the prepared place. Mason had hoped to avoid the presence of the other officials. But he knew Hemlock wanted to keep relationships with them as sweet as possible. Sarah knew he was in the ambulance below. It wasn't by Enchantment or mind walking, but the affinity of the heart that told her where he was. She told Firedrake to follow as best she could. Firedrake was bonded to Arin and had no difficulty knowing his whereabouts. It was daylight but they just had to risk being spotted.

Enchanting Sarah by Morgan Fitzsimons

Firedrake flew as high as she could go without having Sarah freeze. To Sarah's dismay, they ended up in an airport.

"Now what!" she said. "I think I need to mind walk and listen to Mr Mason again."

She fixed her thoughts and went to stand behind Mason. She could see Arin still unconscious on the stretcher.

"You need to keep him unconscious until we reach The Eco Biological Research Base in Florida, It's mostly manned by our people but protected by the government."

The man with him was puzzled."Why there," he asked.

"Because its best suited to dealing with the species our prize represents."

The man nodded.

"Why all the military interest?"

"All our research is made available to the government. They are protecting that," said Mason.

The man tapped his nose significantly.

"We pay for it and in today's economy that helps too." Mason added.

They had placed the stretcher on the jet.

"Our eta is 8 hours from now," Mason said, and made himself comfortable.

Sarah bent over Arin but in this form she could not touch him or reach him. "I will find you again," she said into his ear. "I promise." She could not achieve anything by staying with him so she must go back to Firedrake.

She transferred the information to Firedrake who advised her to go back to Sorrel.

"But we have to follow the plane," she said in distress.

"Not so" said Firedrake. In the allotted time you will get on my back and desire to be where he is.

Enchanting Sarah by Morgan Fitzsimons

We fly up into the air and come down in the right place. I have done this before many times with Arin."

She reluctantly turned her attention to Sorrel and came down where they were waiting. They had moved to where there was tree cover anticipating Firedrake's need. She explained events and how she could follow him. She accepted it would make sense for Sorrel to come with her.

"What about Yulir where is he?" Sarah said.

"He will either be flying after the plane or he may even have taken up residence inside it somewhere. He will not leave Arin but will watch for his awakening." said Sorrel.

"I am a bit puzzled as to why the government is interest in such as Arin? Do they think he is a spy or a terrorist or something," said Chrissie."

"Think about it, what do those ears say to most kids today?" Darren said.

"Spock of course!" said Sarah. "That's it isn't it. Mason has them convinced he is an alien life form."

"Exactly," said Darren."That makes it a lot more dangerous. What Mason is claiming, indicates to the official bodies, Arin could pose a threat to human society."

"I think you three should go back to Chrissie's for the moment," said Sorrel. "I will go with Sarah."

"Take your phone with you and call us," said Chrissie.

Sarah pushed it into her jeans pocket. She took a clean top from the things in the back of the car and disappeared behind a tree to change and then grabbed her jacket. She picked up his hat which was a bit large for her, but she would keep it until she could give it back to him. She had to keep confident there would be an opportunity, or she might just lose it, which wouldn't help him at all. The others departed with a tearful Chrissie and when about eight hours had passed, Sarah and Sorrel set off on Firedrake with The Ryder flying in her wake. Up they soared and came down again in Florida where they had taken Arin.

"Are we actually in Florida," she whispered and she had to believe it as they flew over Disneyworld and sandy beaches with the strangest looking palm trees their trunks patterned like dragon skin, but Firedrake pressed on to fly over a huge complex of buildings bristling with military presence. The main building had many floors with smoky glass in abundance. One side of the building had a mass of the interesting palm trees and other foliage ending at a river edge. Along the bank she could see logs lying in the sun and it registered they must be alligators. Firedrake came down into the palms.

"Well at least you blend with the background," she said to Firedrake. "Time to take a look" She sat cross legged on the ground with Ryder beside her and Sorrel notched his bow with an arrow, taking no chances.

Chapter 14

The magic of technology

Sarah floated up into the air and made for the buildings that were heavily guarded, yet she just didn't know where to begin. It looked so large and daunting, but she had to start somewhere. Help was at hand in the shape of Yulir, who swooped down and up into the air again sitting on the rail of a small balcony in front of a heavily barred window. It belonged to the tallest building which had quite a few floors to it. In fact all the windows on that side of this particular building were very heavily barred, but this particular one was at the very top. She moved up to the balcony and considered the bars. She willed herself into the room beyond them and it was empty. She moved on into the next one and discovered within it, was a cage. It wasn't like any cage she had seen however; the bars were beams of light. The spaces between them were fairly wide but not wide enough to allow someone of Arin's build to pass through them. They still had him unconscious and she remembered the discussion Mason had. It was likely they had drugged him, and she hoped it wouldn't affect him too much.

She wasn't too sure about the bars as they had said it was a special prison made to contain Arin. She couldn't take any chances with it. She had no idea if she could mind walk through something built specially to contain an Enchanter. Still she was very slim and small and if she went through sideways, she should be able to pass through safely. She had no idea if her mind would take her through solid barriers so she moved through the gap. She breathed a sigh of relief as she bent over Arin. He was still breathing. She needed him to wake up, but again she couldn't reach him while in this state. There was nothing else for it but to return and pass through these beams while in the flesh. She would have to do it in the dark as well because Firedrake would be immediately spotted depositing her on the balcony in broad daylight. She went swiftly back to Firedrake, explained to Sorrel and they waited as darkness fell. They passed like silent shadows over the palm trees and Sarah and Sorrel were deposited on the balcony. They moved inside and Sarah looked through the bars shock holding her rigid when she found he wasn't there. She moved back and signed to Sorrel he wasn't where she had left him. They peeped out through the door into the corridor. It was empty so they moved down the passage uncertain of what to do next. Sorrel had taken the lead, when she was grabbed from behind and a hand pressed against her mouth. She knew who it was the moment he touched her. He let her go as soon as he knew she wouldn't cry out, but not before he had snatched back his hat. Sorrel was as silent as Arin expected him to be.

A group of Hemlock's private army was turning the corner and Arin whispered, "Duck into that room or you might be caught in the crossfire." He and Sorrel advanced to the threat.

She obeyed instantly, but unfortunately the room was already occupied. The woman facing the window had beautiful blonde hair and a perfect figure in the all in one military suit. She turned and faced her and Sarah was now totally in shock. The face could have been beautiful, the mouth sensuous with perfect rose lip stick and the right eye was fringed with black eyelashes but the left side of her face was what the nauseous experiments had made it. The eyeball was completely exposed and parts of the brain visible and reinforced with glittering implanted pieces. Although she looked human in form, she could have been born of man or Elf originally but had ended up what the Masters had made of her. She had a belt around the waist with various items clipped to it. They had been busy while Arin was sleeping and the development of new technology over the intervening millennia had been used to their benefit. Sarah's attention was caught by the rapid movement in the female's left eye. It would not be noticeable to the human eye, but Sarah's eye sight was now as sharp as Sorrel's was. This wasn't anything to do with enchantment, but was a skill given to all elves. The female's eye was picking up images and transmitting them. Sarah looked around, but there were no computers visible. Wherever the information was going there wasn't a computer or anything else similar, visible in the room.

"You are the golden elf female. I have a report concerning sightings of you," said the woman. "Remain where you are and you will be collected in a moment."

Sarah made for the door and something shot past her arm as she reached for the door handle. She looked back and saw the female was using her own finger as a weapon. She was using the 'magic 'of the implanted technology. Sarah increased speed to pass through the door and for a brief moment was almost invisible to the female, she moved so fast. She was into the corridor where she had left Arin and Sorrel. They were surrounded by several bodies or what was left of them. They were just smouldering heaps, some of the implants having melted from whatever had been done to subdue them. Arin just grabbed her pulling her with him down the corridor. His senses more experienced than Sarah's, were operating at a much higher level and he whisked her into the first empty room he came to. Sorrel had his back. Arin crossed to the window running his fingers around the frame, and it came away into his hand. They went through it and came out up on to the roof. The roof was fairly flat with up thrusts of structure in which doors led back into the top floor of the building. They sat for a few moments so they wouldn't be seen from below. Sorrel was watching the door they came through.

"You didn't trust me to escape on my own I see," Arin whispered.

"And how would you do that without Firedrake?" she hissed.

He ignored that! "I mind walked the whole place while I was restrained. They were unaware I was conscious. This top floor is the province of this private army. The rest is all military"

"But what kind of creature were those part flesh, part technology things? I know they can do a lot of things we never thought of, but I wasn't aware it was still anything but unachievable conjecture and fiction," said Sarah.

"With Dragon Master Sorcery, the impossible is possible. They have experimented with all sorts of creations from altered dargs to TAB's," said Arin.

"TAB's?"asked Sarah.

"Technically Altered Beings, it's the name they are tagged with in the advanced research section of The O'Neill Foundation. They are altered from people, elves, dargs, ferrishin whatever."

"Hemlock is very plausible," said Sarah "Everything we saw in our web searches showed how he has penetrated into establishments, with what seem like impeccable credentials and is well into the US government. He is highly esteemed and the same in the UK, and in many other places, using his money and his magic to control.

"It would seem so," replied Arin.

"Is he here now?" said Sarah

"Apparently not!

Sorrel's ears were twitching a little as he listened to their whispering voices.

"This place is run by a military general who is also a Master. The thing , this top floor needs to go. We need to put it out of action before we leave. They are performing a whole lot of monstrous experiments here that I am sure the government is unaware of. Whatever we do though will deplete our chances of escape. We will need to use Enchantment."

She thought about that."How about you show me what to do? It would be less difficult if I was weakened, you or Sorrel would be able to carry me out of here while the other is free to fight. I can't support you."

"True, you need more practise. Much as it goes against my ethics, it has merit as an idea."

"We are here now because last time I couldn't help you. Why didn't you just carry me out first?"

"You would have died while I was doing it," he said briefly.

She hadn't realised how close to dying she had been. "But how can we shut them down?"

"There is a central source controlling the technology even that implanted in their bodies. We need to destroy that! I need you to follow me and do exactly as I say. It means relying on my ability to make the right choice at the time."

"Ok "she said briefly.

"There are two males and three females in the room operating the systems. Sorrel and I will deal with them." He was so close she could feel his breathing and she turned her head to look at him. She wondered what it would be like if Arin kissed her and her startled eyes met his. She turned away again in confusion.

Enchanting Sarah by Morgan Fitzsimons

"You will need to concentrate on the central controls and simply will its destruction. Direct your vision and your hands at it and send your whole energy force to destroy."

She nodded.

"Keep low for a start." He moved across to the far side stopping when he was above the central computers. He cautiously opened the door and moved into a short stairwell leading to the top floor corridors. They encountered two of the security patrol. Arin gave them no opportunity to register him, but hit them at the neck with his hands as he walked between them. He caught them one on each arm and lowered them down. Bending over one he made a sharp movement with his fingers and an eyeball popped into his hand. Sarah gave a shudder of revulsion but saw the sense of it when Arin walked to the door he sought and pressed the eyeball to the security panel. The door slid back and he had entry. The occupants were also altered creatures, just like the woman she had encountered. There were no windows in this room which meant escaping elsewhere. Sorrel and Arin had silenced the occupants without much difficulty. It was so unexpected, they had the advantage.

"Concentrate yourr mind on the destruction of this place. It is an abomination that they alter minds and play with genetics to further their own ends. Keep that in your head, touch the web and raise your hands towards the controls in the central panel"

She did as he said and he turned to deal with a couple more of the TAB's. Sorrel was out in the corridor with his bow in his hand. He could still shoot it faster than the opposition could register his presence. She saw the computers through a haze, and heard Arin's voice saying words she was beginning to understand how to use. She picked up the inflection and the chant came from her lips. Around her she saw a menacing mist rising, but it didn't threaten her. It ebbed and flowed around her. It was positive yet negative at the same time, negative in that it was destructive, yet positive in talking action against the evil practises surrounding them. She could only liken it to the breath of a dragon, as it swirled and billowed around the room enveloping the control panel which began exploding in bursts of brilliant light. It spread to other systems and in some cases shut down the beings as well. Some of them were simply separated from the central information system and were intact, but left to their own initiative. Sarah swayed on her feet and Arin picked her up and put her over his shoulder and went back the way they came. The attack on the system had created a lockdown to his consternation, and they would have to find an accessible stairway to the roof through all the smoke. The windows now were covered in a thick heavy metal which he may be able to cut through but he couldn't risk ending up dropping Sarah. He would have to get Sorrel to take her in the event that was necessary. He turned a corner and checked the first door he came to, but the room was in darkness as the lights had failed and the window was now like those in the corridors. Someone was seated at the desk calmly waiting for the clamour to cease. A female got to her feet and sat against the front of the desk.

"So we have the Enchanter Lord and the Golden Prince," she said.

"How can you know me," asked Sorrel.

"You were a formidable warrior in your day, so I am told, though it isn't your calling. But now the battle is with a much younger generation."

She was in shadow but they caught glimpses of a tantalising figure and rich dark hair wearing a uniform of sorts. The glimpses of the face showed her to have alluring beauty and the ears swept up high. Arin had already placed Sarah against the wall.

"I am Melusine," she said. "Does that mean nothing to you?"

Sorrel looked blank but Arin gave an involuntary start.

"Ah I see the young Lord remembers me."

Enchanting Sarah by Morgan Fitzsimons

He did and he wasn't messing about with the menace she represented. He simple raised his hand and twisted it with words in his language. They were harsh and strong but Melusine was so arrogant, she didn't see it coming. She twisted with them clawing at her throat and gasping she fell unconscious. He remembered Melusine as she was, in the past, not a wife but the companion of Aorcha, and as deadly and cunning as the golden serpents she had wound around her breasts. Sorrel asked no questions but raced out and Arin tossed Sarah up again. Locating a stairwell they went up it and Arin passed Sarah to Sorrel. She actually wasn't unconscious now, just weak. He burned a hole through the metal shutter in seconds and they passed through it. Underneath them there was pandemonium now, and fire and smoke pouring out of all the upper rooms. Sorrel allowed Sarah to stand and she looked down below to the courtyards. There were masses of soldiers all carrying very up to date weapons. They were swarming all over the place. They were wearing

Enchanting Sarah by Morgan Fitzsimons

USA military uniforms and were definitely not Hemlock's private army.

"We have a problem Arin?" Sarah called.

He looked across at her, his eyebrow raised.

"Those men trying to capture us, we can't kill them."

"They will kill us," he said, "Therefore we must kill them first."

"But they are not Dargs, altered beings or what have you, they are soldiers of Greg's country and an ally of mine. They are hunting us because they were lied to. They are deceived by Hemlock's staff. If we kill them, we will definitely be the enemy and we won't be able to put it right."

 "What do you suggest I do then, hold up my hands and say kill me? I doubt Sorrel would agree with that either.""

"Isn't there some kind of enchantment something that will immobilise them, for a bit?"

Enchanting Sarah by Morgan Fitzsimons

"I have an idea," he started to laugh. "I am not a wizard but I do know the seidr magic. There is a battle magic that uses shape shifting. Normally it's the seidr warrior himself who shape changes, but with a little innovation..." He began to chant, not in his own language but that of the ancient ones. He spoke the rune chants of the galdr repeating the chant and suddenly all the soldiers in the area changed into animals, wolves, wild boar and even bears, but some were just harmless ducks, pigs, sheep etc.

"I had meant them to all be the same," he said doubtfully.

"Well it's better than killing them."

"It isn't going to last long," he warned. Yulir had already spotted them and got Firedrake who now had free passage to the roof and they were soon on her back and soaring away from the scene. Even as they went the bewildered soldiers found themselves in strange positions on the ground but as Arin said, they were still alive

Enchanting Sarah by Morgan Fitzsimons

He ordered Firedrake to come down at the Ranch to check in with the O Neill Foundation.

Chapter 15

Back at the ranch

Firedrake landed them in the woods which were part of the grounds around the Old Spanish Hacienda style property. As they walked up to the main house Sarah was struck by its sheer beauty, the curved arches and beautiful polished wood were in perfect harmony with the natural setting and the flowers and trailing foliage made a gorgeous splash of colour in the sunshine.

"Who is Melusine," she asked? "I caught a glimpse of her and she seemed absolutely stunning."

"Stunning is the word. I will tell you more later. Don't let the beauty fool you. She has a mind like a steel trap. She was the partner of Aorcha, a Salwed, a Pitch Witch, sorceress, whatever description fits. She was responsible for the death of my mother."

She sensed how much he still felt the hurt after all this time. Before he could say anything more, the doors were thrown open and a manservant appeared.

"This is Toshiro," said Arin. "He runs this place and we are all have to toe the line, well I do anyway."

Toshiro smiled a she bowed and Arin bowed back.

"And you must be the Lady Sarah," he said as he made the Japanese bow of welcome.

"Konichiwa, Lady Sarah," he said. "Master Greg is in the long gallery," he said to Arin. "Don't run Master Inazo!" he called after him shaking his head as if Arin were a little boy.

Arin bounded up the graceful stairs, the rail beautifully carved, and they followed him with interest. The Lady Mitsouko, Sarah recognised form Arin's memory. Arin kissed her fingers,

Enchanting Sarah by Morgan Fitzsimons

"Mama Mitsouko you are looking very well," and then he hugged her twirling her about to stop beside Sarah. He had no difficulty usually with calling her mother, for his own had been killed when he was very young, but the recent encounter had brought it all back and he was attempting to put it from his mind..

"And you are the fascinating Sarah," she said.

"Am I," said a startled Sarah.

"If my son is to be believed, but I see you are as he described. Welcome Sorrel, you see I know your name also. My son has talked to us about his friends."

"Problems my boy," said Greg.

"Nothing we couldn't sort out," he grinned. "We do need to gather some information though, and there are things I must tell you that I could not say on the phone."

"Fine," he said. "Get the tough bits out of the way then we can eat and sort out what you need."

Enchanting Sarah by Morgan Fitzsimons

"Sounds good to me," said Arin.

"Mitsouko will you tell cook there will be three more guests for dinner"

"There are others here," Arin was a bit alarmed.

"Just some of my long time buddies, Colonel Moorhead and Major Herrick, Colin from the FBI. I think Josh the CEO of the Foundation was going to pop round but he may get caught up in something else. They are all concerned about the activities of Hemlock Industries and the like. We were going to have a chat. Your input could be useful."

"But I can't sit down to dinner in jeans with guests like that," said Sarah.

"You could my dear and outshine us all, but Mitsouko will take care of that. It's one of my old fashioned peccadilloes that we dress for dinner. I too am a creature of constancy," His eyes twinkled at her. He was not that large a man but somehow conveyed stature and presence. His voice was rich and deep and she suspected he probably had a good baritone.

At that point another man came into the room, one of Mexican origin this time.

"Ah, Ricardo, take Sorrel will you and loan him something to wear to dinner. This is Ricardo, my secretary when I am here. He speaks several languages and is most useful."

The Ricardo in question was of Sorrel's build and incredibly slender, but with broad shoulders and looked more like a Spanish toreador than a secretary. Sorrel loved new experiences and when he learned Ricardo also was keen on horses he was very interested and asked if he could see them.

"But of course," said Ricardo." We can look now before dinner. There is time." He showed no curiosity as to who Sorrel was but just accepted his attire and the bow. He perhaps shared his boss's knowledge of things, or maybe was just beyond surprise.

Enchanting Sarah by Morgan Fitzsimons

"You might like to meet Chief Iron-fist as well. He still loves to shoot his bow though I assure you, it's mostly at static targets these days, but he does do a bit of hunting now and again. He is in charge of the stables."

Greg ushered Sarah and Arin to his study and they sank into the comfortable chairs.

"Now what is it you have to tell me?"

Arin still found it hard to adjust to his father's death. He looked at Sarah and she responded by explaining what she had from Blackthorn and Sorrel.

"So you are telling me you have lost your father, and the life you knew, and there is no way to reverse it?" he said.

 Arin nodded.

"But you are my foster son and I have arranged to make you legally my heir, so you have a future and a home here. I know I can never equal the warrior your father was but I honour what he made of you and I believe he would approve."

Enchanting Sarah by Morgan Fitzsimons

"I must be honest with you Greg. Right now I still yearn for my old life and I don't know if this is where I can be, but if I do choose to stay it will be as your son. I doubt I can ever get used to the lifestyle and you will find my needs for myself simple though I will shamelessly exploit the situation in my drive to rid the world of the Dragon Masters."

"That will do me Arin," he said "I have to say though, this Dulcamara elf is a great deal prettier than you are, She is like a fairy tale princess with a little enchanted mystery thrown in."

"That may be because she is descended from a queen," Arin said. "Come! I will deliver you to Mama Mitsouko."

A little while later they gathered for dinner and Mitzouko came in one of her kimono's with a wide sash and long flowing sleeves and behind her came Sarah in a Spanish gypsy top with a full embroidered set of Spanish skirts complete with fan and the pale blonde hair sported a beautiful large rose and a pineta comb, Her eyes were demure over the fan but that elven mouth smiled provocatively as the fan quivered. The youthful image was replaced by a provocative young female who could not fail to tweak hearts. The other guests were certainly impressed which seemed to amuse Sarah more than anything. Arin wore the typically Spanish style evening suit with a wide sash that fitted with his surroundings and his thick black hair with the long plait over his left shoulder. Sorrel was just as resplendent in a frilled white shirt and waistcoat borrowed from Ricardo who wore what could have been a complete matador kit. Arin and Sorrel each held out an arm to walk her into the dining hall so she linked arms with both of them. This was great fun and she was enjoying being the centre of attention. It was a moment of time she intended to make the most of an forget all the horrid things that had suddenly become the norm. Ricardo had been much impressed with Sorrel as he whispered to the horses, calming down the big stallion that had given so much trouble and knowing exactly what herbs to use to heal a sick foal who had laid down and given up, but was now standing and eating.

"You will need to bring him back Arin if he will come, or maybe he will stay now for a while. The stable hands can't get enough knowledge from him" said Ricardo enthusiastically.

"Arin knows as much as I," said Sorrel. "It comes from an affinity with nature and its creatures."

"How come you kept that quiet," said Ricardo.

"My attention has had to be on other things," answered Arin, "but maybe there will be time."

During dinner they talked mostly with Sorrel about things Elf. Greg's friends knew about Mitsouko and her belief in her son, but it seemed they were acquainted with Arin's origins in some way, whether the truth or as a genetic throwback, Sarah couldn't be sure, but they didn't refer to it in Mitsouko's hearing. They all knew Jefferson Hemlock and others connected with him and had concerns regarding Hemlock's network but so far had not been able to prove their suspicions enough to take official action. All they could do was be watchful and alert in their dealings. General Moorhead already had heard of the destruction of the top floor laboratories, but not the truth. His suspicions of the true state of what had actually been going on there, were confirmed though Arin and Sarah. They were strengthened in their resolve of vigilance and determination to expose Hemlock but accepted they needed far more than they had to bring him down. Arin explained they were going to pursue the whereabouts of the bones and information would be relayed to them through Gregory. Sorrel wanted to check on the stallion and the foal before they left. While they waited Sarah walked in the garden where Arin found her sat on a bench.

"I love the scent of the flowers here," she said as he dropped down beside her.

"I wanted to talk to you," he said.

"I wanted you to talk to me. There are some things I need to understand. I was trying to understand the difference between the Dark Elves and Dragon Masters. Do you truly believe in evil as a presence or is it just a label. Is their good and bad?"

"I hadn't really thought about it in that sense." He replied. I am, as an elf, more inclined to put it in terms of light and dark and it isn't always clear cut. Enchantment for example can be positive or negative; it can be either or both and still be used for good purpose. A negative move can have a positive effect as the outcome."

"I see where you are coming from," she said. "I am familiar with such moves in playing chess."

"If you consider light Elf and Dark elf it is easier to see because you see the golden elf who has a perfection of race that encompasses his actions, his appearance everything about him." Arin went on. "He has an innate goodness, but he can still lose his temper, attack you if you step over his boundaries and if you make him your enemy, you will regret it, but I have never known one lie or twist the truth to his advantage."

Enchanting Sarah by Morgan Fitzsimons

"But you are most of those things, "she said "and you are Dulcamara."

He laughed at that. "The Lord Enchanters are actually descended from Ainarr Asveldur. They kept the dark side of him, but the other qualities were hidden within. We are creatures of fire and temper but choose to be straightforward, honest, fair and intensely loyal. We love with passion and can hate with the same passion too. We have no fear of dying either. It isn't so much when as how. I suppose we are closer to man than he might think for we too must choose how to live. "

"That is true I suppose," said Sarah

"Even when enmeshed in the pits of depravity, we can choose to do something outside the box we are trapped in, but we can't regain the skills of enchantment," Arin went on.

"How do you see courage then?" asked Sarah. "How can you face an enemy when he is a reality in front of you when it's just your skill against his, sword or magic?"

Enchanting Sarah by Morgan Fitzsimons

"It comes from your perception of what is right which becomes the courage of doing what is right. It's not an impetuous rush into the worst of the fight to kill and be killed, any animal can do that. Courage is only meaningful and true if you live when it is right to live and die when it is right to die."

"I think I see," said Sarah, "but I don't know if I will be capable of that kind of courage, though I suppose no one does until they are faced with the choice."

"It is a great misapprehension that valour is something that throws itself blindly into the jaws of death. For me, its facing death for something worth dying for," said Arin

"Like your father's life," she said.

"I did that because I loved and honoured him."

"So what is your definition of Enchanter?"

"I can tell you what my father taught me," said Arin "A Lord Enchanter worthy of the name should have tranquillity, a calmness of spirit that isn't surprised by anything, but isn't afraid to deal with it either. He respects life, laughs at the storms. He is magnanimous and can love. He takes action even though it weakens him, but it is not action misspent. Asphodel was all these things as was my father. Asphodel had a noble spirit that showed benevolence yet forbearance. He was fearless and prized fortitude. He was just and chivalry itself, "

"There are men who are capable of these things, particularly in the wars fought today." Sarah was thoughtful. "Whatever is wrong with the reasons for war there is no denying your kind of courage and heroic spirit still lives in man. You know as you spoke I could also see the similarity to the values of Bushido which were also those of a specific group of people that has gone as a way of life.

"Gregory talked to me of this, "said Arin "but he too has this same noble spirit and would be considered a true knight by my father, he just uses different weapons. But Asphodel would not see value in the Samurai act of suicide; he would see more value in living to try to rectify what had brought you to it, though he would understand the acceptance of responsibility for your actions."

"Maybe we are not meant to be here, maybe it's all just a mistake." said Sarah

"I don't think that is true," he protested. "Everything has a purpose and everything has a time, but the Dragon Masters have continued pouring their pitch so we too are here out of time to do something about it. Everything they do is set against the natural order. If we put it into today's terms maybe we are natures virus sent to eliminate them."

She thought that very funny. "So I am a viral infection am I? Have they got an antidote?"

The thought went through his mind that he certainly hadn't, but did he really want one? That brought him back to what he had wanted to talk to her about.

"I am not sure how I should say the things I need to say, but I have to explain them."

Enchanting Sarah by Morgan Fitzsimons

He caught her hand and held it

"I am aware there is an attraction between us, and you are curious, and it isn't that I don't want to respond either, but you have to understand I am not like your brothers or Darren or any other youth you know. They have this fun loving light hearted approach to life, such a curiosity, much more like Sorrel than me."

He was searching for the right words to use. "I was born during a siege. I grew up wielding a sword in one hand and the power of enchantment with the other. I was leading warriors when Mike's age and fighting fearsome battles. Death was a daily companion. It isn't the sort of background for playing kissing games."

"You didn't have time for a girlfriend?"

"I don't think your understanding of it is the same as mine, in any case   in this time and place you represent Lilia and it is my place to protect and serve you. I can't go against what I am."

Enchanting Sarah by Morgan Fitzsimons

"What exactly are you? Do you have a heart that beats and feels emotions like everybody else?"

"Oh I definitely have a heart," he pulled her hand to feel it beating quite fast. "but my role model was Asoril's son Asphodel. He was I remember, a warrior of fire and passion and temper, but his devotion to Lilia gave him another dimension. He would follow his father into her hall and wait behind him until he had greeted her. He would then go on his knees and kiss her hands as his queen and rise to his feet taking her with him to greet her as her chosen one, the very essence of romantic chivalry, yet a few hours before he had been slashing off the heads of dargs. He ruled his warriors with an iron fist yet the same hand was capable of holding Lilia as though he held a fragile butterfly. She was the other half of him. I think we all envied him that. "

"Are you seriously telling me you are keeping your kisses for your one true love? That is usually a female prerogative."

Enchanting Sarah by Morgan Fitzsimons

"No, I am trying to explain why I can't be light hearted about it, but I am obviously doing it badly."

"It isn't immoral to choose to kiss someone in your world, is it?" Sarah asked. "In mine it isn't a binding contract."

"Nor was it in mine, but the way I lived shaped what I am and such things must have meaning for me."

"So what you are saying is it wouldn't mean anything if you kissed me, Well I don't recall ever asking you to," she was angry now.

"On the contrary it could mean more than you would like, and you did ask, you ask me with your eyes."

Her answer was to leap up and as he came up with her she made to kick his shins really hard, but the next thing she knew was she was being fiercely kissed, so she just ran and he thumped the wall angry with himself for his sole intention had been not to kiss her and frighten her away and now he had done just that.

They prepared to leave, each being extremely polite and distant with the other. Greg was highly amused by the silliness of the young. It certainly didn't make it any easier when he leapt up behind her on Firedrake and took her back to the garden.

Chapter 16

Pitch dwarves and Paintballs.

The others had reached home and as his parents would be at work Paul thought it would be a good time to pick up his laptop. He didn't want to face any awkward questions. Darren and Chrissie obliged and decided to have a quick snack while they were there. Chrissie made sandwiches while Paul got his laptop. He scribbled a message for his parents to say he had taken it, love you both Paul and Sarah. They went down to the old garden to eat the snack. Minutes later they had a shock when a small face peered round the tree and two small males trotted out to face them. They were as short as Paul and wore black leather biker jackets and jeans.

"Would you be the one called Paul?"

"That is my name," said Paul cautiously.

"I am Bogbean, and this is my friend Frogbit. We still pop out into the world of men occasionally just to lark about," said Bogbean.

"We like a bit of a laugh though of late we have sighted too many Pitch people for my liking," said Frogbit.

"Definitely more than I would like," added Bogbean. "Which leads me to why we are here."

He fell silent for a minute thinking deeply.

"Well," said Chrissie, "Why are you here?"

Darren was gobsmacked again and was lost for words.

"You see we ran across this bunch of Pitch Dwarves and they were arguing as they usually do and we picked up the mention of Paul and the

Enchanting Sarah by Morgan Fitzsimons

Lady Sarah. It seems they had found Sarah by accident and they kept it quiet so they could surprise their masters with their brilliance at catching an Elf when no one else could."

"That is to our advantage," said Frogbit cheerfully, "as we can outsmart them any day."

"True ! " said Bogbean,

"Now if they had told Ferrishin or Masters, it might be a different story." Frogbit went on.

"Speak for yourself you old fool," said Bogbean indignantly," I can handle any of them anytime."

"Maybe in your younger days, "but you are a little older now," said Frogbit.

"Older, what's a millennia or two, look at Sorrel if you doubt me."

"Well yes but you have to allow he is Golden Tribe and was always the better warrior anyway,"

"Maybe he could run rings round Uncle Bartsia, but he never stood face to face with me," said Bogbean.

Enchanting Sarah by Morgan Fitzsimons

"That would be a bit difficult anyway," said Paul. "He is twice your size."

"Don't you start! You're no bigger than I am. I heard all about you and Sarah from Sorrel.   I didn't know where Sorrel was or where to find you so we went back to tell Blackthorn what I heard."

"It wasn't too pleasant as we had to own up to our sneaky visits to Bogbean's uncle Bartsia who was mad as fire," said Frogbit.

"But Lord Blackthorn just thought it was funny." said Bogbean cheerfully. "Anyway we were sent to warn you."

"Warn me of what," said Paul.

"It seems their plan is to capture you and use you to control Sarah. They really do want to impress the Dragon Masters ."

"I see," said Paul "and did they say *how* they planned to do it?"

Enchanting Sarah by Morgan Fitzsimons

"They seem to have gathered a lot of information about you and some of them are following you everywhere watching for an opportunity," said Bogbean

"Well now you know you can watch out for them" said Frogbit "Shall we move on now Bogbean?"

"Hold hard little frog," he replied. "This promises to be much more fun than anything else we planned, pitting my wits against that lot."

"Who are you calling little frog? You aren't much bigger, "said Frogbit indignantly.

"Well it is your name isn't it, Frog-bit, little frog, don't stretch your brain too much,"

 Paul was obviously amused and Darren fascinated again.

"Anyway, it looks like Sorrel isn't here and I don't think he would be too pleased with us if we abandoned them to the Pitch Dwarves."

"Oh please do stick around," said Darren, "but we are leaving for my house now."

Enchanting Sarah by Morgan Fitzsimons

"In that car I saw at the front of the house? asked Frogbit.

"I would rather it was a motor bike but I suppose it will be fun," said Bogbean. "Can we go now?"

Darren led the way to the car and they climbed in the back and knelt on the seat staring out at the traffic behind.

As they turned into the drive the man next door waved at Darren.

"I rather like your garden gnomes," he called. "What a great idea, biker garden gnomes, where can I get one?"

Chrissie stuck her head out of the window. "They were custom made for Darren," she said sweetly, "and they aren't gnomes, they are dwarves. Surely you can tell the difference, they are much moré handsome than common old gnomes"

Darren continued up the drive to the rear of the house.

Enchanting Sarah by Morgan Fitzsimons

""Gnomes, GNOMES," squeaked Bogbean. I was never so insulted. Turn back while I put a spell on him."

"Its ok, said Frogbit, "she put it right, well said Miss Chrissie."

"I suppose she did, it was well said," but he was still a bit miffed.

"Tell you what," said Paul, we may have to wait ages for Sarah, why don't we liven things up with a bit of Paint balling, rather than sit here depressed."

"Good idea," said Darren brightening up a bit. It was the one energetic thing he loved to do.

"Paint balls, "said Bogbean, "what are they?"

"Oh I think you will like it but if you come with us you will have to stick a cap over those ears til we get you kitted up."

Bogbean loved a fun experience and agreed with enthusiasm. Darren gave them each a Liverpool football cap which they cheerfully donned making their way back to the car again. By this time it was early evening and they had already forgotten why Bogbean and Frogbit were there at all. The Pitch Dwarves they mentioned however hadn't forgotten their plan and were unobtrusively following. When they reached the Paintballing club Darren showed his Membership card so the costs would all go on his account. They got the kit and had fun just putting it on. They had overalls to keep the paint from their clothes and flack jackets to protect the chest, leg pads and arm pads and helmets, plus never ending questions from Bogbean and Frogbit. They collected the paint guns and Darren showed them how to load the balls. There were guns that fired single shots at a time and guns that fired multiple shots like a machine gun with rapid fire. Darren and Paul were experts and even Chrissie was a good shot. First they had some practise shots to get the little guys used to it. When Bogbean saw the bright coloured splats of paint he hopped up and down with glee.

Enchanting Sarah by Morgan Fitzsimons

They didn't notice the group of Pitch Dwarves who followed them in. The attendant simply thought they were all with Darren and carried on with his conversation with the pretty girl on the refreshment counter. Darren and co were now out in the big barn like building, and dodging round haystacks firing at the targets when the Pitch Dwarves appeared. They had acquired guns too but were totally outside any rules. It stood to reason as they didn't know them anyway. They started to fire at them and hit Paul squarely on his face which fortunately was protected by goggles, but he now couldn't see where he was going and fell over a bucket of balls which rolled all over the place. Frogbit promptly slipped on them and sat down with a great thud which burst the balls he landed on covering him with bright yellow all over his rear He scrambled to his feet with yellow hands and proceeded to leave yellow hand prints on anything he touched. He raised the paint gun and fired back and missed the Pitch dwarf, hitting Chrissie smack on her chest, splatting her bright purple.

Enchanting Sarah by Morgan Fitzsimons

"Whose side are you on," she yelled, "the enemy is that way,"

She pointed frantically at the Pitch Dwarves trying to back Paul into a corner by hammering him with shots and he was dripping with paint of various bright colours. Darren got mad then and started to shoot back and he never missed, so in no time the Pitch Dwarves were barely recognisable. By this time Bogbean had realised who they were.

"Get back to the car Paul," he shouted, but Paul had recovered and determinedly re-loaded his gun.

By now it was a bit difficult to tell one dwarf from another as they were all splatted with so many colours. Frogbit started splatting a Pitch Dwarf and whacked him up in the air to come down with a huge splat as he landed in a net full of paint balls. He tried to scramble out, but only succeeded in rolling the net out into the woods, finally catching it on some brambles. The head peered over the top and the voice that cried for help was that of Bogbean who alternately was yelling and spitting out paint. The battle then raged out into the woods after him, which were part of the Paintballing experience anyway.

"What are you doing out here Bogbean? While you were playing with yourself, I caught one of them."

"You caught me you fool'"" said the now raging Bogbean.

Darren cut him free and he spent some of the rage on chasing the Pitch Dwarves.

"They aren't giving up," are they," said Paul.

"We really do need to get back to the car," said Chrissie. "We need to lose them."

They plotted a way back, but the enemy was always in the way. One of them swung a gun butt at Frogbit and sent him down with a bloody nose, then hammered him with paint balls. Bogbean rushed out and pulled him up. "Come on Frog old fellow," he said. But the old fellow was really incensed now and he shook free of Bogbean and roared straight at the one who smacked him down, landing on him with such force he knocked him out, exchanging a bit more paint in the process.

"Tenacious little sods, aren't they," said Darren.

"Which ones, the bad guys or the good guys," laughed Paul.

"Take your pick," replied Darren

They couldn't get back through the building and the only option was to move through the trees on to the car park path, where the pristine, seven seater stood. Before you could say splat, they started firing at them again, but this time Bogbean and Frogbit had had enough and they marched through the hail to down each one by using the paintguns as clubs. They were surprisingly strong and came back triumphant with the dwarves scattered on their backs. Darren turned to get in the car and was horrified to find it covered in glorious splats of a myriad of colours.

"Dad's going to kill me," he groaned.

Enchanting Sarah by Morgan Fitzsimons

They all quickly climbed in and Darren roared away. They looked at each other in triumph and howls of laughter at the sight they presented until it dawned on Darren the inside of the car was going to be as bad as the outside. They called at Darren's house wondering what to do next.

"We can't put this all over the garden," said Paul.

"We could stand on the paved courtyard at the back," said Darren. "There's a hose and a tap and the yard is well drained. If we hose the paint off, it will disappear down the drains, then we can take this stuff off and wash the overalls. Let the lot dry, and I can take it back."

"Sounds like a plan," said Paul. They walked round to the courtyard and Darren connected the hose to the tap and they had another merry five minutes as he chased them all with the hose, but Paul got his own back when he grabbed the hose to turn it on Darren. Once they were all hosed down they removed the soaking wet gear and piled it on the paving stones. Their clothes underneath were all wet. A roar from the side of the house got their attention.

"Darren!"

"It's your father," said Chrissie.

"What on earth is he doing back. He shouldn't be here for another week at least."

"Get out here Darren I want an explanation"

"Stay here you lot," and he raced round to face his dad.

He spent the next five minutes explaining and he fiddled about with the car as he was talking. He accidently popped the boot and to his horror there was the face of a Pitch Dwarf staring up at him. He slammed it shut and leaned on it.

"I know it looks bad, but a day in the garage should have it back looking like new."

Darren's dad tossed him back the keys which Darren had left in the ignition.

Enchanting Sarah by Morgan Fitzsimons

"All I can say is I hope you aren't so careless in future. I was going to surprise you when I came back but you can have the keys now. I bought it for your birthday and I'm sure as hell not having it standing in the front drive. Park it at the back where you parked your old car. It's your responsibility now, Enjoy," and he strode back to his own car.

"Where are you going," called Darren.

"Back to the conference, I only came for some extra papers we needed."

Darren went back to the others. "Did you get all that!

Chrissie laughed.

"You won't laugh when I tell you there's a Pitch Dwarf in the boot."

"Let's get back to the garden. Arin and the others may be back."

"Leave the dwarf in there while we figure out what to do with him." Darren took out the keys and pressed the security lock control.

"He can't get out of there in a hurry."

"Arin will know what to do with him," said Paul.

They all piled in the car and went to Sarah's hoping they had arrived."

They moved into the garden and Bogbean stood there still rather wet, with his nose in the sir.

"Do you smell something strange," he said to Frogbit.

Frogbit sniffed, "Pitch," he said.

"Well there is a Pitch Dwarf in the car boot," said Paul reasonably.

"This is outside, coming from down there," and Bogbean pointed toward the little wood.

"Stay here Chrissie," ordered Darren. Cautiously he and the Dwarves went down to the bottom garden.

Enchanting Sarah by Morgan Fitzsimons

From the little wood came some of the Pitch Dwarves. The paint had dried on their boots and bodies but they had discarded their shirts and jackets revealing the heavy black swirls on the skin and although they presented a very funny sight, no one was laughing. In their hands they carried quite formidable axes, with the cutting edge polished and gleaming, but still marked with the dark stains of blood that was grained into them. Chrissie had followed and was frozen with fright. Bogbean and Frogbit could probably have taken them on, but they had no weapons with them. Bogbean grabbed a fallen thick tree branch but it wouldn't last a moment. Nevertheless, he valiantly stood between the others and the dwarves. At that exact moment there was a rustling sound from way behind the Pitch Dwarves and three of them fell with Arrows in their chests. At the same the same time one appeared behind Darren and the others, whirling two axes and running past Chrissie, who he knocked down as he passed. Darren went down beside her and the creature went for Arin with the axe instead of Darren and was struck down in the blink of an eye with Arin's sword. The last one was knocked out with a blow from Arin's fist.

Darren grabbed Chrissie carrying her to the garden seat. There was a bruise forming on her temple and blood trickled down from the broken skin. What had seemed such fun had suddenly taking on new meaning and they saw the enemy and the dangers clearly for the first time, just as Sarah had days before. While Sarah tended to Chrissie, Arin and Sorrel carried the dwarves into the little wood placing them on the ground. Arin spread his hands over them, and they faded down into the earth beneath."Why didn't you do that where they fell," asked Darren, ever curious.

"I didn't think Sarah would like to have the image of Pitch Dwarves in her garden every time she came down there," he replied.

Chrissie was sitting up now with no sign she had ever been hit but she was shaken.

"You need to come out to the car," said Darren. He started to explain what had happened as they followed. Sarah, Arin and Sorrel stared at the now Technicolor splat vehicle.

"What on earth did you do to it," said Sarah.

Darren continued explaining amid chuckles from Sarah.

"It was funny at the time but now it's not so amusing," said Paul, "Darren's dad was hopping when he saw it. Fortunately he didn't find the Pitch Dwarf locked in the boot."

"It does get worse," said Darren.

"Can it," asked Sara still grinning.

"Oh yes, Dad said he'd bought it for my birthday so I could deal with it."

Sarah did laugh at that.

"Everyone will see me coming," cried Darren.

"You say one of these dwarves is still in the boot?" Sorrel asked. "He must have been the beacon to find you all again."

Enchanting Sarah by Morgan Fitzsimons

Darren opened the boot at a gesture from Arin and the paint covered dwarf got out. He took one look at the Enchanter facing him and fell over his own feet trying to dive back in again.

He was hauled out by Sorrel and marched down the garden.   As they went he addressed Bogbean.

"I take it this all started with you Bogbean?

Bogbean beamed at him. "I suppose you could say that."

When they reached the bottom of the garden he saw only one Pitch Dwarf left rubbing his head and trying to stand.

"We can do a deal," he said "I have information to trade."

"What information could you have that could possibly interest me," said Arin coldly.

"Shut up you fool. The Salwed will kill you," said the one on the ground

"I think I'm more scared of the Enchanter Lord than the Salwed," said the one standing.

"This Salwed has a daddy and a granddaddy who is Dragon Master. That scares me," said the one who had been on the floor, and had now managed to stand.

"But they are not here and I am," said Arin, "and you are beginning to seriously annoy me,"

"Egg, Egg" he cried in a panic. "You will want to know about the Egg. Promise to let us go and I will tell you."

"Why would an egg interest me," said Arin.

"It is a Dragon's Egg," he replied.

"We promise to let you go," said Sorrel.

"There have been tales about the Egg for years but my cousin claims to have found where it is," said the dwarf. "He is working for one called Jason Carr. He has been looking for a long time."

"You are talking of a real Dragon Egg?"Arin said.

"It has been here from the time of Asoril. The Dragon Master wants it. Something to do with putting the flesh on the bones."

"Where is this Egg?"

"I can only tell you Jason Carr knows and my cousin has almost found it."

"I know Jason Carr," said Darren. "I doubt there could be two like him. He is a fellow student at university. His parents are very wealthy. He has more money than sense."

"That is so, he is what you said, a student," agreed the dwarf.

Arin promptly tapped them with the rune stick and they passed out in a heap on the floor.

"Stick them under a tree somewhere and they will have forgotten us when they wake up," he said.

"Now Bogbean," said Sorrel sternly," you will go back and tell Blackthorn everything. Tell him we are still on the trail of Tal-git and the Dragon

Masters. Tell him there are more than we thought and it may take longer than I expected."

After promising to come back to see Paul if they were allowed, they trooped off through the portal. Darren and Sorrel loaded the two dwarves in the car and drove them way out into the countryside and left them under a tree as directed. .

Chapter 17

The Sword Gift

"I don't like the sound of the putting the flesh on the bones bit," said Sorrel, when they got back.

"It sounds to me as though it's linked to the transformation of the bones," said Paul.

"At least we know where to find Jason Carr, at least I do," said Darren. "He has a particular circle of friends who are always with him. They party a lot and it's supposed to be the in thing to be invited to Carr's bashes. He always throws them at a club in London. It's a private club which seems to be made available to him when he wants for his private parties."

"Have you ever been to them," asked Arin.

"We haven't," said Chrissie, "though I have always wanted to see why they are so popular, but it's not really Darren's scene."

"This particular half term is Kevin Seddon's twenty first birthday, so Carr and his cronies will have been in London for that last night as it was to be at the Rothschild. Seddon invited me but I 'm having a much more interesting time with you lot, however that means Jason Carr will be somewhere there because he has one of his parties tomorrow night, or rather his twin sister has, at the Black Drake Club."

"Black Dragon," said Sorrel.

"Good grief ," said Darren "So it is!"

At that moment, Bogbean stuck his head round the tree. "Sorry to interrupt but Blackthorn wants Sorrel and Yulir to come to him. He says it's important."

"You will need to go then," said Sarah. "I wish I could see him."

Enchanting Sarah by Morgan Fitzsimons

"If you did you would not be able to take the key with you. Your journey could only be one way."

Sorrel made his way to the portal. "I will not be too long."

Bogbean joined Paul and was followed by Frogbit.

"I see I'm stuck with trouble again," said Paul drawing Arin's attention to the dwarves.

"You had better behave and try taking proper care of Paul. If they give any trouble whatsoever, pack them off home. Darren, try phoning the hotel and asking if Jason Carr is there, if you have any problem getting an answer say you are me. The Inazo O'neill name usually opens doors."

"You can't be serious!" said Chrissie.

"My sanctuary is Gregory O'Neill and he is my foster father, did I forget to say."

"Is that true Sarah," she said

"I just found out, I met Gregory and his wife Mitsouko," she replied, and wished she hadn't as she remembered the incident in the garden.

"Is it possible Darren to find out what Jason has been researching? That may tell us more about the egg," asked Arin.

"I can't but my friend Dennis probably could,"

"You mean by accessing his college computer," asked Paul

"That's exactly what I mean. He is a hacker, the best I know."

"A Hacker?" said Arin.

"He can hack into the most sophisticated computers."

Darren made a call to the Hilton as suggested.

"He is apparently still at the Hilton until tomorrow. Now I will call Dennis."

He talked earnestly into his mobile before coming back to them.

Enchanting Sarah by Morgan Fitzsimons

"Dennis says Jason logs in on the library computers quite often. He always uses the same one. Dennis is actually in there at the minute fixing a programme for Margaret who runs the library. He will send the results to my lap top in the car. Come on Chrissie we can sit in the car until Sorrel is back."

"We need to be gone before Mum gets back from work if we want to avoid awkward questions." said Paul, just as Sorrel reappeared with Yulir.

"I am sorry guys but for the moment you will have to make do without me," said Sorrel.

"But we need you," said Sarah

"I know, but I am afraid my lady Aeshna needs me more at this time."

"Lady Aeshna?" said Sarah.

"My partner," he said. "We got a little angry with each other," said Sorrel, "Which is most unusual for me, so she left me to my own devices for a while, but it seems I am to become a father after all this time."

"How exciting for you," she said "You will make the most marvellous father,"

"Will I," he sounded a little doubtful.

"Of course you will and you must go back," she urged.

Arin looked a little stunned "Your son will need you Sorrel, friendship is a marvellous thing, but can't compare with a son or a partner who needs you."

"That is true, so Blackthorn sent you something to make up for the loss of my sword. He has sent you Domgeorn The Sword Eager for Doom Justice. It is the meaning of the runes carved upon it. It can only be raised for right causes and to deal justice on behalf of the line of High Elf Kingship."

"He trusts this to me, but I am the youngest warrior ever to serve Asoril."

"You may be, but Blackthorn says you will need it to settle accounts with the Dragon Masters. HE has asked about you and was very impressed with what he heard. The mere fact you have it will make them afraid. He has appointed Yulir to care for it and all you need do is hold up your hand and ask for it."

Arin immediately held up his hand, "the sword Yulir," he said and Yulir flew over his head with the sword in his claws and it dropped into the hand of Arin as though a magnet drew it there.

It was the most beautifully crafted sword he had ever seen with runes entwined on the blade and the black and white dragons on the handle.

"I can't believe he would trust such a thing to me."

"He trusts you will serve the descendant of a queen with it, Blackthorn always referred to it as the sword of Asphodel. So it is only fitting it should serve a Princess like Sarah."

"But I am not anything so grand," she laughed.

"I have to differ," said Sorrel, "blackthorn called you Princess and he should know."

Sarah hugged Sorrel. "We will miss you," she said.

"I was just beginning to know you," said Paul.

"But I will come back," he protested. "Aeshna would not expect me to neglect a right cause if I could make a difference. I do think the sword will be a far greater advantage than my presence would be though. Take care of her," he shot at Arin. "Whatever she says she is still as royal as I am. "

"Definitely the arrogant Golden Prince," laughed Arin. "I will take care of her," he affirmed, suddenly quite serious.

Sorrel disappeared as he had come.

Arin held up the sword for Yulir to take it.

In fact he was genuinely shocked that Blackthorn thought him worthy enough to wield it and determined he would not let him down, but he also accepted Sarah's was someone he must give his loyalty to.

Enchanting Sarah by Morgan Fitzsimons

Darren came back from the car with news from Dennis. "It seems Jason has been searching through archives and ancient writings following a trail of sightings through the ages. His notes on his computer say an egg was last reported in 17th century having been found by a pitch elf. He took it to a Dragon Master who through occult magic and a pitch witch sorceress, decided its origin had been the Area of the ancient Ardreth and if they returned it there, it may possibly hatch in familiar surroundings. The sorceress apparently then poisoned the Dragon Master so she alone could possess the secret of the egg. Before it began to affect him he slashed off her head for the same reason just before the poison hit him. The egg was last seen disappearing over the mountain skyline of North Wales. It's all considered to be a fantasy in the archives but Jason knows it's not."

"So now we know why Hemlock wanted to find the Ardreth site. The Egg is the object he wants to find there," said Arin.

"Does that mean there is a connection between Jason Carr and Hemlock?" Sarah asked.

"I believe it does," said Arin. "So we need to go to London and encounter this Jason."

"Paul you are too young to get into any where Jason is. Take these two," he nodded at Bogbean and Frogbit, "over to my place and see if you can keep them out of mischief. Try them in the games room or watching films. I should think they could play some of my games quite well,"

"Fab," said Paul. "What about your dad though. "

"He's definitely gone back to the conference. He only popped back for papers he was missing."

"Just make sure they don't wreck the house," said Chrissie.

"I rather think they will take to computer games," said Paul."We can send out for pizza."

"Good idea said Darren. "Better still I will drop you off and park the car up. We can take a taxi to the station."

"Pizza, "said Bogbean. "I don't think I know that one,"

Enchanting Sarah by Morgan Fitzsimons

"You eat it," said Paul.

"Will I like it?" asked Frogbit.

"Judging by what you ate last time, I would say you will love it," said Paul.

"Did you bring your weapons this time," said Arin, knowing they would be very skilled with them even though they were fun.

In reply they each held up a large axe which disappeared from view when they lowered them.

"I am trusting you to watch over the boy," he said.

"Very funny," said Paul.

"Let's go then," said the dwarves and they marched out to the car.

Sarah rang her mom to tell her she was invited to a university thing with Chrissie and Darren. Sarah's mum hoped she would choose to go to the same university Darren went to. Sarah had already been invited as a guest by several of them, Darren's included. She approved as Sarah knew she would.

Enchanting Sarah by Morgan Fitzsimons

They took a train to London. It was the quickest way to get them all there in just over an hour. The trip was uneventful. Darren and Chrissie spent the time looking at castles in the highlands on Darren's laptop. Arin had taken a seat opposite Sarah and had his head back with his fedora tipped forward over his eyes. They couldn't go on in this uneasy silence, but Sarah didn't know how to get back to their previous friendship. As she thought about it she knew they couldn't go back, if she did anything it would have to move forward. She looked up to catch his fierce eyes staring at her from under the brim of the hat.

"What do you plan to do when we get to where this Jason is?"Sarah asked him.

"I have no idea," he said. "First we must find him."

"Book a table for lunch at the hotel where he is," Darren called across. "We should be there before lunch."

A taxi deposited them at the hotel and Arin asked for a table outside in the hotel garden. It had the advantage of overlooking the inner dining room and the hotel desk.

"Please put the table in Mr. Darren Cresswell's name. I prefer to remain out of sight of the press."

"But of course sir," effused the man on the desk.

They were shown to the table which was beside a long swimming pool. They sat back relaxing under the umbrella's in the late morning sun. Arin stayed by the desk to call Greg. Darren noticed there seemed to be quite a few young people from his university there and several people greeted him. He wasn't part of their crowd as a rule but his father was sufficiently wealthy for him to count, and his mother was world famous. At the far end of the pool was their quarry Jason Carr. He looked quite bored.

"Would you believe it, but he is sitting right there," said Darren. "We don't have to look for him at all.

"It *is* the man himself, Jason Carr," said Chrissie.

Enchanting Sarah by Morgan Fitzsimons

His gaze was idly wandering but his attention was caught by the small fair haired figure sitting with Darren of all people. There was something unusual about her. He got to his feet and strolled up to where they sat.

"What are you doing in the big city Darren? I always thought you gave our party's a miss. Can I buy you a drink old man?"

Jason dropped into the spare seat at their table. His eyes never left Sarah as she sat with Darren and Chrissie.

"Who is your friend Darren," asked Jason.

"Aren't you lowering your credibility a bit sitting where I am," said Darren. He did not like Jason or anything about him and despite their mission; he found it hard to be pleasant.

"It would be impossible," said Jason with extreme arrogance. "Your daddy may be well off. It's a drop in the ocean in my circles, but he does have all the right contacts, so that makes you one of the in crowd whether you choose to be or not."

Enchanting Sarah by Morgan Fitzsimons

"Then what are you doing here."

"Oh I am just in town for the break, what brings you Darren? You don't usually seek the flesh pots."

"And I'm not now," he replied. "The girls are shopping. I'm just along to carry it."

"I'm a little intrigued by your lady friend and it had crossed my mind to encourage that brain of yours to join our circle. Now is as good a time as any to show you a bit of high life while you are here. For starters join us this evening at the Black Drake Club. Kayla's throwing a disco style party for something or other. Bring your friends of course." He didn't wait for an answer but strolled back to his table. They all left laughing and joking, just as Arin arrived at the table.

"Who was that," he asked sharply.

"That was no other than Jason Carr," said Darren.

"I just had a feeling of something familiar and menacing at the same time, but I didn't really get enough time to analyse it, it was so fleeting," said Arin

"You right about menacing. He is a menace who seems to think money and privilege get you anything."

"He certainly was intrigued by Sarah. He couldn't take his eyes off her," said Chrissie. "Though I wouldn't have thought she was his type."

"What is his type," asked Sarah.

Chrissie looked around and pointed to a stunningly gorgeous tall girl with long dark hair. She had a low cut dress revealing quite a figure, the very short skirt giving full view of shapely legs in very high heel shoes. Her makeup was perfect and her lips scarlet and inviting.

"If that's the case there is little about me that would appeal to him at all," said Sarah.

"You have no real conception of what we call aelfscyne, or elf sheen beauty in your terms, have you?"

Enchanting Sarah by Morgan Fitzsimons

"What beauty?" she turned startled eyes to him.

"It is a perceived value in human terms. It is common to male and female elves, a quality that enchants, that draws people to it. I think Sorrel already mentioned an iridescent quality, a radiant brightness."

"I read about that in my Anglo Saxon research," said Darren. "I seem to recall it mentioned in relation to Helen of Troy among others. It has fatal quality about it likened to weaving a spell to enslave."

"But she wasn't an elf," said Chrissie.

"But who knows her ancestry?" said Arin.

"I hadn't thought of that," said Darren. "I suppose genetically it is possible to have one or two elf attributes if back in your past a human male or female got together with an elf of the opposite gender."

"You are definitely elf and can't escape drawing people to you even though you are unaware of it," Arin said quietly,

She just laughed and shook her head in disbelief.

"You're daft if you think I'm anything like a Helen of Troy."

"I should hope the only thing you have in common with her is her attraction, by all accounts she had too many lovers and ended up causing the destruction of a lot of good brave men," said Chrissie.

"If I remember the story rightly, I wouldn't say they were all good," said Darren.

"I must admit I think there is more to his interest than attraction," said Arin. "I just get this disturbing feeling, there is something in you he recognises, which makes me wonder how much more he is than he seems. My intuition is telling me Pitch Elf or maybe more."

"That sounds a bit more credible," said Sarah.

"This party is the best place to find out what we want to know, people let their guard down at parties." said Chrissie "I must admit I always wanted to know what went on at the Black Drake

Club. The word is his parents own it, but no one really knows. It's very exclusive. He is always having private parties for his in crowd and all Darren's friends talk about them being fantastic."

"It sounds very dangerous as well, remember Drake is dragon. It seems a bit more than co-incidence that we run into him with so little effort," said Darren.

"Well I can't party dressed like this," said Chrissie, looking down at her clothes in dismay.

"I said we were shopping, so let's forget it all for an hour and actually go shopping," said Darren.

"I'm up for that," said Chrissie, I just love shopping."

Arin shook his head in dismay. "It's definitely not my scene," he said. "Do you need me to go?"

Sarah promptly linked her arm through his and looked up at him fluttering her eyelashes her lips curving in that intriguing smile. She was determined to break through the barrier between them.

Enchanting Sarah by Morgan Fitzsimons

He laughed, "It won't work on me Sarah I am well used to the magic of Elf females," but he allowed himself to be led after Darren and Chrissie all the same.

In the event, they spent much more than an hour having quite a crazy afternoon. They tried on all sorts of things and the girls and Darren clowned about and succeeded in making Arin lighten up a bit as Darren put it. He couldn't help but laugh with them.

"I don't think I will ever get used to all these things being so readily available," Arin said. "There are far too many things to choose from. Why would you need all this stuff?"

"People want things just because a friend has it," said Chrissie. "They have become used to having what they want when they want it, and all the advertising stuff tells you, you want it and need it, when you probably don't."

"Everyone wants to be in fashion and looking as good as the next or better. Myself I prefer to be different, unique perhaps," said Srah.

Enchanting Sarah by Morgan Fitzsimons

"You achieve that without clothes or adornment," said Arin. They all burst out laughing.

"Ok what did I say?"

"It's ok we knew what you really meant," said Chrissie.

"Now what," said Darren? "We need somewhere to change."

"That isn't a problem," said Arin. "My foster father has a London flat. That's what I was doing on the phone, asking if we could use it."

They were past surprise where Arin was concerned and followed him as he called a taxi wondering if tonight's events would have any kind of result.

Chapter 18

The Black Drake Club.

The taxi deposited them at the entrance to a very prestigious building. The doorkeeper came to open the cab door and carry their packages and as Arin went inside someone rushed from the security desk. "My apologies sir we had no idea anyone was expected."

"No problem Hammersmith, we are fine." He said cheerfully and made for the lift with the others following.

"You have been here before then?" said Sarah.

"Twice with Greg," he said.

Enchanting Sarah by Morgan Fitzsimons

The lift shot to the top and they alighted into a plush corridor leading to two large double doors. He rang a bell and the doors opened revealing a man standing in the hallway of a beautifully decorated and furnished apartment.

"Mr Arin, is Mr Gregory with you? I had no notification."

"No Harris, he isn't with me and I am not staying, my friends and I need somewhere to change."

"Certainly," he said. "I will leave the gentleman to you sir, if the young ladies would like to follow me."

He was what everyone would imagine a butler to be and just the sort of person Greg would want to look after the place. He led them to a light and airy guest room and showed them the adjoining shower room and bathroom and politely left them, assuring them they only had to ring the bell if they required anything more. He was so like something from the previous century, they collapsed giggling on the big bed.

"Did you know about all this," asked Chrissie as she went around the room looking at the accoutrements.

"That Arin had found a foster father, yes I did, but I didn't think as far as all this. I don't think all this means anything to him personally. I think he cares about the people who took him in, but he still would prefer his warrior life. He said as much to Greg. If you remember he hadn't used that card before we met him, and he seems to prefer sleeping under the oak tree in our garden."

"How can you know that for sure." said Chrissie.

"He said he still yearns too much for his previous way of life. I think he finds it all confining. He is always looking back for the time of riding into battle with his sword in his hand and Yulir overhead. Then he knew his enemy and could eliminate him with a blow from his sword or a wave of the hand. He finds this deviousness today, of a hidden enemy coming with the hand of friendship, one he can't easily stomach. I will tell you the story of Greg some other time. Right now I just want to get on with enjoying the day."

They made full use of the luxury in the bathroom and there was everything they needed to dry and fix their hair. There was still an hour or so before they would leave for this club and Chrissie was thirsty. They put on jeans and tops and went to find Harris. He was in the kitchen and looked scandalised when they started to help him. They soon had him laughing with them He took the tea tray into the lounge where Arin was talking on the phone obviously reassuring someone all was well.

"Thanks Harris, he said.

"As you indicated you were going somewhere special, I took the liberty of asking Lady Mitsouko's London hair dresser to come and fix the young ladies hair."

The bell rang as he spoke. "That will be him now," he made for the door.

"Does it look that bad," said Chrissie touching her hair in dismay.

Enchanting Sarah by Morgan Fitzsimons

"Not at all," said Arin. "He is being helpful which is what Greg expects of him. Greg always offers his guests the best he has, and he seems to have taken a liking to Sarah anyway."

There was a young man with two pretty girls with him and they fussed around the girls and whisked them away to Mitsouko's dressing room.

"No cutting," said Sarah.

In no time at all they were manicured and made over. The hairdresser had caught the elfin look and asked Sarah what she was wearing. She obligingly took out the dress and the hairdresser arranged her hair with a beautiful white flower over a black one perching it at one side over the top of her ear and swathing her hair over the other.

"I must admit to feeling fab and ready to take on anybody," said Chrissie.

When they had gone Sarah put on her dress and stared at herself in the mirror and this small fragile creature stared back, and she just couldn't see this elf sheen thing at all.

She joined the others feeling a little self conscious when Arin held out his arm and escorted her to the lift having thanked Harris. She eventually took a peep at the guys. Darren looked great in his dark blue jacket flecked with something glittery and a plain round necked shirt and a small trilby style hat pushed back on his wavy hair. Loosely draped around his neck was a luridly brilliant pink silk scarf with tassels which Chrissie had insisted on. He winked at Sarah and defiantly put on his large round glasses. She didn't really look at Arin until the door man held the taxi door open, and Arin waited for her to get in. She felt a totally unaccustomed shock to her system. No male she knew had managed to shake her composure to this extent. He wore a plain steel grey suit, beautifully cut with a matching waistcoat and a plain black shirt, and of course the fedora. The Elf charisma needed nothing more. Perhaps he should have applied the term aelfscyne to himself, though she chuckled at the thought of him being considered having a radiantly pale brightness.

When they arrived at the Black Drake Club, lots of others were also arriving. There were bodyguards on the door taking names, referring to the guest list and checking student ID cards. Darren gave his name and duly flashed his ID and they were ushered in. It was quite a resplendent place; its normal function that of a nightclub with a lot of shiny black and rich red and glittering chandeliers. This of course was one of Jason's private discos for his fellow students and the normal rules didn't apply. Although Sarah was curious she was immediately aware this was different from her brother Charlie's parties. On the surface it looked like any normal disco but there was this pervading sense of decadence in the accoutrements on the walls and the whole atmosphere. They followed the flow into the large room where the lighting was discreetly dimmed and guests were moving on the dance floor while glittering lights flashed over them. It was a typical disco style event but with much more opulence and style than most. The taped music was the latest stuff. They just observed for a while, watching the crowd reacting enthusiastically to the latest hit songs. The large screen on the far wall showed the DVD's of the stars performing the hits. They were ushered to a table and drinks placed on it that looked very enticing and innocuous. Chrissie took a sip before grabbing Darren's hand, hauling him onto the disco floor where he indulgently followed the rhythm of the music, surprisingly fitting in with everyone else and quite capable of the latest twists and turns for such a studious academic. There were groups of people all moving together. A lot of them were singing along with the songs. Arin looked on rather like an amused adult, though he looked no older than the participants.

"Have you been to a disco before Arin. "

"No, and I don't think I will again, the music is too loud and emotions too high."

"You sound like my mother," she said laughing.

Enchanting Sarah by Morgan Fitzsimons

"It is outside my experience, I have known nothing like it. I like the sounds and the excitement of some of your music, though I don't always grasp the meaning of the words in songs, I can feel the emotion of it. But this is too loud and too strident and there is something inside the rhythm that eludes me, but I will work it out."

He looked up at the sources of the colour flashes and the strobe lighting and frowned.

"What is bothering you?" asked Sarah.

"I don't exactly know," he answered. "You have been to such a party before. Does this feel the same to you?"

"I love disco's and dancing, "she said," but they are always lively and everyone is having great fun, and they clown about just as they do at Charlie's friends parties They have this kind of lighting and so on but all this cost a lot of money. It feels a little unreal, maybe more like a movie set. I don't know what it is but I do feel a kind of cold tingle. Sounds silly I suppose."

Enchanting Sarah by Morgan Fitzsimons

"Not so, it's your Elf instinct. It is telling you there is danger here."

He lifted one of the glasses on the table, holding it briefly to his nose. "These are laced with something. Don't drink them as they are." He stared at each glass very briefly and the contents changed colour.

"Its water now, "he said." It will not harm you. If you need to do it, just see water instead of what is in there and click your fingers, like so."

She sipped it through the straw and as she put it down someone grabbed her hand and twirled her into the throng. Arin looked about briefly and noted where there may be any threat lurking. It was easy to tell guests for most of them appeared to be this Jason's fellow students and friends, and were between 16 and twenty or so. He thought some of the girls looked quite young. His attention turned back to Sarah. A laughing, Sarah had entered into the mood of the music. She wore a deceptively simple black dress that floated over one shoulder leaving the other bare. He had already noted the trace patterns of delicate blue in the upper inner arm, but now her back was exposed as she danced and the dress revealed quite a bit of back. He grinned at the delicate blue patterns almost like butterflies that swirled up alongside her spine. He knew she would have some somewhere. So many youngsters had tattoos, temporary or permanent that it wouldn't stand out in a crowd as Elf. Her skirts floated and flared as she twirled revealing the delicate but shapely ankles above the deep pink very high heeled shoes. Her hair shone like elfin silver in the glitter of the strobe lights. Blue eyes looked up at her partner, eyes shaded with long lashes fringing the eyelid coated with blue and silver. She really was fascinating. But even as Arin looked a shadow came between them in the shape of a very sensual female who looked to be around twenty years old. Her hair was a very dark colour with hints of deep red and bright copper in it. Her makeup was faultless and the lips a luscious deep red. Her top of dark cobwebs revealed the long white neck and the curving shapes beneath.. The skin hugging matching tights ended before the ankles and her feet were encased in very high heel black strappy sandals. The long finger tipped with luscious red nails moved towards his face as if to touch it but he moved back.

"You are alone," she said.

"Briefly, the girl I came with has been pulled into the dance,"

"Then you must dance with me," she said. "I am Kayla, my brother is throwing this party for me. Are you a guest of my brother?"

"Darren Cresswell is," he replied. "My partner and I came with him.

His eyes narrowed a little as they took in the tattoos on her arms. She had one on her neck also. She pulled him with her and he allowed it and Sarah was astonished to see Arin moving to the music recognising the woman Darren said was Kayla Carr the sister of Jason. He hadn't seemed to like any of this, and yet here he was seemingly engrossed in someone totally opposite in appeal to herself. She felt somehow disappointed in him, but that was silly. The girl was very beautiful whereas her elfin looks were almost childlike. He was bound to react to such a girl as Kayla. It didn't stop her wondering what it would be like to dance with him. In fact Kayla puzzled Arin and the fact she twitched her finger in the direction of the disc jockey, did not escape him, and the music ceased its rhythmic beats and poured out a soft and dreamy sound and Kayla moved closer to her prey. Whatever her purpose he had caught on to what she really was. Arin twisted his fingers and everything froze. Nothing was moving but Sarah. He crossed to the young man dancing with her and lifted him to put him down in front of Kayla "You will not remember dancing with me," he said in Kayla's ear, and went to Sarah where he promptly resumed the dance with her. Everyone was moving again and it was like nothing happened. Realisation hit that Arin was holding her quite close as they drifted round the floor. It was one thing to wonder what it would be like to dance with him, but quite another to actually stay calm when it really happened and she fell over her own feet. Immediately he swept her to her seat and knelt to check her ankle. The pain left the moment he touched it

"Why did you change partners," she asked.

"I have no intention of being caught in a Pitch Witch trap and at the same time your partner was getting too familiar."

"There are definitely Pitch Witches here then? Anyway you're not my keeper."

Before he could answer that, they were interrupted, which was probably just as well or they might have got into another argument.

"At last we meet again. Is the lady hurt," Jason Carr asked.

"It's nothing a little rest won't put right," said Arin sitting beside her, pointedly putting his arm around her back.

Darren and Chrissie came back just then.

Enchanting Sarah by Morgan Fitzsimons

"Introduce me properly to your friends Darren," he said

Darren dutifully named Sarah, Arin and Chrissie who he vaguely already knew.

"It's a pleasure to welcome you to my party. Perhaps we can tempt you to become members of the club." He picked up Sarah's hand and kissed the tips of her fingers, quite ignoring Arin. She was hard pressed not to show her revulsion and to stop herself reacting to the cold frisson that racked her whole body. The danger bells were ringing over time. His eyes gleamed at the contact, but Arin picked it up and light began to dawn. He might not exhibit the ears but he definitely had them. Jason *was* the Salwed, the Pitch Elf the dwarf had referred to. Arin closed his eyes briefly and opened them again and the golden haired youth sat there in all his glory. His ears pointed high and his eyes were like dark coals. Under his jacket and shirt Arin could see the black patterns of the pitch elves, but these were more perhaps, some of them decidedly similar to the Dragon Master patterns. He seemingly had not yet become one. But he had the mark of an initiate to the order on one side of his throat. As far as he could tell this Pitch Elf picked up the aura of a golden elf that came from Sarah, but that was all. He hadn't enough skill yet to divine Enchanter unless it was blatantly presented to him. Jason turned his eyes to Sarah's and held out his hand She struggled to turn her eyes away but didn't really know how to stop herself rising. Arin's hand covered hers and his other arm round behind her, held her in her seat Jason raised his eyes from Sarah's and stared across at the eyes sparking fire under the brim of the Fedora.

"I think not, "said Arin. "perhaps later when her ankle is fully recovered."

One of Jason's friends appeared at his elbow and whispered in his ear.

"I regret I must leave you for the moment," Jason said and he reluctantly pushed back the seat. "Perhaps we can have a drink together later." He disappeared collecting his sister on the way, moving swiftly through the throng of people.

Enchanting Sarah by Morgan Fitzsimons

Chrissie took a long sip from her glass and pulled a face. "It tastes just like water," she said.

"That's because it is. The stuff they are filling up glasses with contains a substance you don't want to partake of," Arin said.

A waiter arrived with another tray of drinks and bottles. "Compliments of Mr. Carr sir," he said to Arin.

Once he had moved away Arin performed the same task, leaving simple water in the containers on the table.

"I would like to find out what his interest is in Sarah," he said.

"Well I wouldn't," she said. She was shivering and quite distraught. "I saw the real Jason just as you did and it terrified me. I could not resist when he held out his hand. Please do not leave me alone with him."

"That isn't going to happen."

Enchanting Sarah by Morgan Fitzsimons

"The music is getting quite elemental," said Darren, the beat behind the instruments is fascinating. "

 Chrissie stood up, her body swaying to the sound. There were lots of youngsters on the floor now twisting and gyrating to the sound and screaming above the music.

"I have been trying to work out what it is ever since I walked in here. The underlying beat and the so called back ground singing is a chant from the seidrkona magic."

What is Seidrkona," asked Chrissie.

"A female sorceress, elf witch, whatever angle you are coming from. The chant is harmless in itself. It is seidr magic like that of the rune stave I used. It's not exactly a subject I care to discuss, just accept   Jason's following are not here for light-hearted fun."

"You mean its music from some sort of ancient fertility rite," said Chrissie bluntly.

Enchanting Sarah by Morgan Fitzsimons

"Both him and his parties are very popular and well frequented, but they are all by invitation," said Darren. "Are you telling me it's just a cover for indulging in all sorts of depravity and taking advantage of female students?"

"That is what it looks like," said Sarah "and probably the other way round too."

Arin was a little thrown by the seeming forthrightness of his companions.

"This is too strident, too strong and combined with what they have all drunk. I suspect you will find it a little too hot in here anytime now and they will start removing clothes." No sooner had he said it than a girl leapt on the table and began stripping to the music, accompanied by a very young male.

"I think you need to take Chrissie out Darren. Grab a taxi and go back to the flat. She could become susceptible to it. I think it possible she drank something when we first got here."

Enchanting Sarah by Morgan Fitzsimons

"She sipped from the glass," said Sarah "before she danced with Darren."

Chrissie was indeed looking very odd. Arin reached out and touched her and she took on a trance like state.

"I can't heal her from it, but at least she can't hear the beat anymore. Walk her out and she will be better in the fresh air. We will follow you shortly She needs to sleep off the effect."

Darren held her hand and pulled her through the press, almost losing her to one or two guys who tried to grab at her.

"She feels sick, just needs a bit of air. "

The man on the door obligingly opened it and let them through and Darren waste no time getting her in a taxi. As Arin said, she began to recover but something still lingered as she spent the whole taxi ride kissing Darren who didn't at all object. She just appeared inebriated to Harris, who led the way into a guest room and turned back the covers so Darren could drop her onto the pillows. He discreetly removed himself while Chrissie tried to persuade Darren to stay.

"Why are you so awkward about, it after all I am nearly seventeen and can do as I please."

"That's the whole point it isn't as you please but it's that damn stuff talking."

"Don't you want to stay with me Darren? she said and knocked his glasses askew. He tried to straighten them but he got so mad in the end. He stood up and angrily yelled at her.

"You'd try the patience of a saint Chrissie and I am definitely not one. When you remember this in the morning you'll be mad at yourself, but if I stayed here you would be madder than a wet hen, and I'd just as soon not be on the receiving end of you in a temper."

She stared up in awe at this suddenly very tough Darren.

"That's the difference between me and the likes of Jason Carr. All his lot are looking for a night of self indulgence. I happen to love you, but you are still my greatest friend and I want it still to be that way in the morning, so ask me again when you are in your right mind."

He marched out and shut the door and joined Harris in the kitchen.

"Women," He said crossly. "Who invented them?"

Harris grinned into the cupboard and passed Darren a mug of tea, "Might I recommend a dash of whiskey in that sir?"

"You may Harris and I'm not a sir, I'm just Darren, a university undergraduate who at this rate is never going to make it." He settled his glasses on his nose and took a big gulp of the tea.

"I wouldn't say you were just Darren, I think you are quite exceptional and if I may say so, quite chivalrous."

"Don't be daft!" said Darren taking another gulp of the tea. "It's a dying art. It went out of fashion when Mrs. Pankhurst chained herself to the railings, or was it when Germaine Greer burned her bra. Do you think I could have a refill please?"

Obligingly Harris put another shot of whiskey in the tea cup.

Chapter 19

The terrible twins

Back at the club, Arin bundled Sarah through a door he had seen Jason pass through. The light was fierce after the dimness of the disco hall.

"We are not going to just leave them all under the influence are we? Some of those people in there probably don't what's going on."

"If I stop it now, I will alert those two and I want to find a bit more about them first. We still want to know what they need a dragon's egg for and where exactly this castle is."

Enchanting Sarah by Morgan Fitzsimons

They were in a corridor with various doors leading off. The opulent air of decadence still prevailed. One or two of the doors were open but the rooms empty. The sound of the music and laughter didn't get any less. Then Arin spotted Kayla going in to what was a very plush office. He moved quickly after her. She looked up from what she was doing and registered the guy she had been interested earlier, the one she thought was more than he seemed. Arin's eyes cut through the magic and saw her as she was this time. The black tattoos were actually a part of her skin and the ears swept up into her dark hair. One moment she was at the desk, the next right in front of him. She put a hand on his arm He blinked his eyes to be free of hers and instead flooded her with light so she was held rigid. "You will not remember Sarah," he said and she slid to the floor in sleep. He picked up the papers on her desk and saw the name of the castle on a letterhead. He turned to show Sarah. That was when he was first aware Sarah wasn't behind him. He frantically dashed into the passage but she was nowhere. He cursed himself for his stupidity in agreeing to bring the girls here. He should have known better than to bring what amounted to an elfling enchanter, to a place where they could find creatures such as these, that she would have no conception of, let alone know how to deal with.   The constraints of the evil in the place,   now surrounded him and was suffocating. The walls were closing in on him, crushing him. Even without that, he was feeling the weight of the buildings and the close streets and the high rises, all confining space and limiting his view of the sky. He just had to escape it. He raced up a flight of steps bringing him onto the roof. He actually shivered, what was this? Fear was a concept he understood, but had learned to channel into his sense of danger. What had Kayla managed to touch him with? He looked at his hands and they were shaking. Black shadows curled around his fingers, and he knew. He tossed his hat under the parapet moving away from the exit into open space and raised his arms wide as he cried out to the elements. The wind raced over the moonlit sky coming from nowhere whirling around him. It lifted his coat and his hair and as it moved around his body it came away carrying a twisting wraith of black smoke that became a female form which rose screaming on the wind. He staggered to the edge of the building and grasped the rail eventually raising his head to the creature as it rose higher and higher It was a Mara, a witch of nightmare.

"That bitch Kayla planted one of her creatures on me," he muttered angry with himself for allowing it.

He took a deep breath and raised his hand making a slashing movement and the wind stopped and the Mara hit the ground with a tremendous thud considering it had little substance, and what there was shattered into a shower of glass shards. He couldn't wait to replenish his strength he had to find Sarah. He groped his way to where he had thrown his hat and slammed it back on his head before going back inside. He sat on the top step to find her, risking his own vulnerability. His mind raced to where she was, finding her in a little room she had been locked in by her captor. He could feel her fear and see her shaking, but she pulled herself together and concentrated on the lock. Arin lost no time in physically getting to where she was. If she left the room he would have to mind search all over again. He actually ran into her making her way down the corridor.

"Did they hurt you?" he asked anxiously as he hugged her. The door to the adjacent office was open and he moved her inside for a brief moment.

"Just my pride and I really didn't mind that. I was whisked away and gift wrapped for dear Jason, but as it turned out he didn't find me at all attractive as a playmate, but apparently daddy would be delighted with him for finding a possible elf bride to boost the genetic line."

"So who is daddy and how ecstatic would he be to know you are Enchanter."

"Jason just didn't catch on to that, but ..."

Before she could say anymore Jason was in the doorway. He was shocked to see her there and his eyes narrowed at her companion. He opened his mouth and snarled and a host of black creatures came pouring from his mouth surrounding Arin. Jason reached out for Sarah but Arin gave him no time to do anything more. He said something in Dulcamara. He ignored the creatures and without fear, reached through them to grasp Jason's throat. He held Jason suspended by his throat and quite inanimate and the flow stopped. Arin's eyes flashed a pure white light that caught around Jason's head and took out the annoying creatures with it.

"You will forget Sarah exists," He said just as he had with Kayla, and dropped him.

"I know what he wants with the Egg," she gasped.

"Not now," he said grabbing Sarah's hand he dashed to where the music was still blaring out. He began chanting in the way of the galdr before he reached the room and even when he did the occupants could not hear it but the runes formed a clear sound, rhythmical, musical, but with a purity that was calming. His hands moved with it and the dragons breath curled around the dancing feet weaving its way round the room and they all collapsed in heaps fast asleep.

"You need to help me walk out of here," he said. Sarah curled her arm around his waist and gripped his hand with her free one.

They got to a taxi without further incident.

"What will happen to them," she asked once they were in the confines of the taxi.

"They will all wake up together in a few hours, when I click my fingers to be precise and they will all be embarrassed by their state of disarray. It's quite likely they don't know they are being manipulated so it may have some inhibiting effect."

She sighed "It's just as likely a lot of them do know what they are getting into but they do it just the same."

"We can't be responsible for them," said Arin.

Enchanting Sarah by Morgan Fitzsimons

"But why didn't you deal with Jason permanently. It surely would have been within your code of justice."

"Two reasons, one just because I am a warrior, doesn't mean I enjoy killing someone I have power over, and the other, I want him to lead me to his father."

"How will you achieve that?"

"By using myself as bait. He will know when he wakes up, an enchanter was here. It is possible his father is involved with the Dragon Masters or may even be one, and they are already well aware of my existence. He is going to contact someone and tell them all about what happened."

Sarah was alarmed but she knew he would do what he thought necessary whatever it cost him.

"Will they connect you with the O Neills?"

"I don't think so. In my encounters with them, I have managed to eliminate anything that may lead back to them. I intend to call Colin Holden and get him to tap into any calls made from The Black

Drake Club after I wake them up. I should think one of them will be only too eager to tell someone all about it."

They were out of the taxi now and into the building.

He quickly made the phone call outlining his need and then concentrated on Sarah.

"I have the name of the castle," said Arin "and you can tell me what they plan to do with the Dragon Egg."

They made their way into the lift, Sarah still offering support.

"You didn't tell me all he said, did you," said Arin.

She looked up at him with a frown.

"I might be lacking strength but I can feel your fear is still there."

"He *was* frightening and definitely strange," she said. "His hair is dyed you know, I suspect it's as dark as his sister's. He seems to be obsessed with golden. He said he would once again belong to the Cinn Radanta and be Lord of all things, his father had promised. "

"He has no chance," said Arin. "Ainarr was of the Cinn Radanta. It was the ruling family of High Elves. I maybe from his line but I'm an elf of Shadow. I can exhibit all the qualities I have from him yet never can I be a Golden Elf. A Pitch Elf has no hope of reversing what he is. He is that way because he or someone before him made a wrong choice."

"He can never change that?"

"He could stop behaving as he does, but he can't change the consequences of his bad choices. If he came from Dulcamara Enchanter stock, he could never regain the abilities he would have lost in the transfer."

"Why make the wrong choices if you know that," she said.

They had reached the doors which were opened by the faithful Harris. He threw his jacket on a chair followed by the hat and dropped onto the long sofa.

"Is everything Ok Harris," he said.

"The young lady is in the guest room and Mr. Darren is in yours. We can put Miss Sarah in the master bedroom but I 'm not sure what to do with you."

"No need to do anything Harris. I am staying right here and I think Sarah needs some company for the moment."

Harris placed a tray with glasses and a water carafe on the coffee table and departed.

"I asked why they did it?" Sarah said.

"Maybe once they start, they begin to believe they can survive, that they will be the one exception, or maybe they don't realise at first what they are doing, I don't really know. I only know how I feel myself, things fire up inside so fast to become a raging fire in no time and I could so easily act before I think and cause harm. I am fortunate in my father's training, but I must admit it isn't easy.

But you didn't finish what you were telling me about Jason."

She dithered about and he just caught her hand and pulled her onto the sofa beside him.

"I have the Dulcamara genes," she said, "and I am impulsive and I can get angry. Hasn't it occurred to you I could slip just as easily?

"You can talk about it now. He isn't here for you to vent your impulsive anger on."

"Maybe not but I don't want to talk about it." Impulsive yet again she put his fingers to his own forehead and then hers. "You can walk in my mind." she said.

"He is absolutely crazy, which is why he is so frightening. He is quite unpredictable."

Arin saw the memory of Jason standing in the room.

"Tell me about the bones of the dragon," she asked him.

Enchanting Sarah by Morgan Fitzsimons

"We have them and they will soon live as they did all those years ago. The runes in the book are so powerful they will transfer the life from the blood of the Dragon in the Egg into the bones.

"But you don't even have the Egg yet."

"It is only a matter of days," he laughed, "and I can deliver it to my father."

"But what can you hope to do with the dragon anyway. With today's technology you can destroy it without even having to come near it."

"Maybe, but the dragon can shut down today's technology faster and more effectively than any weapon."

"So why did you bring me here/"

"You are not exactly pleasing to me, but you will please my father. On the plus side you are golden elf, and it is my destiny to reclaim my place as Cinn Radanta."

"I don't see how I can have any effect on that," she said.

Enchanting Sarah by Morgan Fitzsimons

"In possessing a Golden bride I will possess all the radiant light and purity of a spirit you undoubtedly have. The more I look at you I see you are alfscyne."

"But that isn't really what you want is it?"

"But I can make you whatever I want you to be," he said.

She could feel the response in Arin as his rage began to bubble up. Hastily she let go his fingers and sat up straight on the sofa. His eyes were like fire but they calmed somewhat as he felt her nervousness.

"He has this dark spell from antiquity that he believed would make the transformation but he needed a particular auspicious occasion where enough power is generated to make it the right time for him to absorb me into himself. I didn't know what to make of that but it's either cannibalistic or obscene and either way I do not wish to breathe the same air as the creep. I think he's totally insane."

Enchanting Sarah by Morgan Fitzsimons

"You can forget it!" He said," I told you, when he wakes he will have totally forgotten your existence."

"His sources know the Egg is at the Ardreth but they haven't quite managed to find it though he claims his dwarves are in the right vicinity and they will scent it."

"Tomorrow we will consult with Firedrake and see if she can suggest where at the Ardreth a dragon would have left an Egg," said Arin. "We need to get a few hours sleep."

The use of Enchantment caught up with him and he gave in to the lack of energy and slept.

Reassured she curled her feet up on the sofa and she too gave in to sleep and woke up to find herself tucked in a blanket, her pink shoes askew on the carpet. Arin appeared from his room, showered and in casual clothes.

"Breakfast is ready! If you can shower and change fast enough I may leave you some."

"Breakfast, but it's still dark. What time is it."

Enchanting Sarah by Morgan Fitzsimons

"About 4am."

"You're crazy." She snuggled back into the blanket.

"We have to go in the dark as we are riding Firedrake. You can stay here if you want to."

She most certainly did not, so she dragged herself off the sofa and made her way to the room where Chrissie was still asleep. She showered and the water soon woke her up. She went to the kitchen where a pile of toast was waiting. She poured herself some coffee and sank on a chair. Arin held up his hand and clicked his fingers.

"There, they are all awake and somewhat embarrassed as I hoped and your new friends have forgotten all about the little blond elf as promised."

Darren appeared with his coffee mug in his hand.

"What is so urgent you woke me up at silly o clock," he demanded.

Enchanting Sarah by Morgan Fitzsimons

"I did bring you coffee," said Arin." we have to go before its light. What I need you and Chrissie to do is stay here at the flat on the computers in my room. Find all you can about this castle and of course the Carrs. I have this awful feeling daddy might be Jefferson Hemlock."

"You mean the terrible twins," grinned Darren. "I will try making the connection to Hemlock."

"Anything you find you can email or message to us both. And we may need to ask you for stuff so you will need to be alert."

"How long do you want us to stay."

"I will let you know. If you are ready Sarah, we can call Firedrake from the roof."

"If I can't find out about Jason's father my way, I will call Dennis again."

"Good idea," said Sarah.

"Take care guys," said Darren.

Arin strapped an empty scabbard to his back and they made their way to the roof, looking down on the quiet streets. There was hardly anyone to notice the shadow of dark wings over the buildings as Firedrake glided down accompanied by Yulir and the Ryder.

Chapter 20

Silvertrace

Arin communicated with Firedake. Sarah touched her so she could pick up what was said.

"Could there still be a dragon egg at the Ardreth surviving from the time of Asoril?"

"There *is* one there," she communicated.

"How are you so sure?" asked a startled Arin.

"Because it is mine! I had thought it destroyed, but when we found the Ardreth I was led to it. "

"I remember you were missing briefly. Why didn't you tell me?"

"It is well hidden and the time was not right for it to be. It has waited for me since the time of Asoril. There is life within the Egg."

Enchanting Sarah by Morgan Fitzsimons

"But now your child is in danger."

He pulled away and they climbed on her back.

"Take us to the Ardreth," he commanded. He put everything else aside in the need to keep Firedrake's child safe. She may never be able to have another. They shot up into the dark sky to come swooping down over the beautiful mountains. Over head they were joined by The Ryder and Yulir. Several eagles could be seen in the early light as the dragon came down and they alighted on the top.

Arin touched her again. "Can we go where you have hidden the egg, or is too far under the earth."

"It isn't here exactly." She rose again and carried them over Drakeridge, floating down below all the rubble and rock to a small crevasse into which she turned and almost touching the sides, she floated through into a cavernous space. They got down and followed her to the far end and through into another cave. She pushed aside some debris and there was the egg. It was an uneven shape and grey in colour, but as Firedrake came near it

375

became tinged with pearlescent green almost glowing in the dark. Sarah could see faint vein lines pulsing over it.

You left her at Drakeridge," he said in wonder.

"I put her here when we were last at Ardreth. It seemed fitting."

"You said she," said Sarah.

"I can feel her," he said. I am bonded to her mother. It isn't far off her time but you never can be sure," said Arin.

"I would not leave her if it was time." said Firedrake. They hastily covered the egg again, and moved back to the crevice. Ryder had flown in through the gap turning himself horizontal.

"He says if I permit he will stay with the baby," said Sarah. "He will guard her as he would his own."

"He trusts me with you then," said Arin.

"No he trusts me with Yulir," she replied sweetly. "He also has allies in the other eagles out there."

Enchanting Sarah by Morgan Fitzsimons

There was some agitation from Yulir hovering outside. They went through the crevasse and mounted Firedrake to rise up onto Ardreth again. They looked down over the scene below and saw movement. Arin closed his eyes and mind walked briefly down below. There were only a couple of scouts down in the lower valley but over the ridges was a lot of movement. The place was crawling with Dargs, Ferrishin commanders and just a few of the part technology monstrosities of Hemlock's creation. They were some way from Drakeridge but Arin wasn't disposed to take chances.

"We need to lead them away from Drakeridge," he said when he was back. "It looks like a Pitch Elf operation rather than a Dragon Master one. We can only be thankful for Jason's ego "

Why is that?" said Sarah.

"I believe he wants to show them all he can organise it without help."

"So let's demonstrate he can't!" she replied.

Enchanting Sarah by Morgan Fitzsimons

"If you drop us down where the few are I don't think you will be seen from the other side. I will dispose of them and we will make out way over to the rest. We can't destroy the vegetation as that will draw attention plus destroy the cover over Drakeridge."

Arin put up his hand and asked for the sword and it came into his hand as before, even as the dragon took flight depositing its burden below. Arin and Sarah rolled out literally at the feet of the scouts. The sword slashed and they fell on either side of him. They ran rapidly to the top of the next ridge and looked down. They could see a group of dwarves now as they emerged from an opening.

"This one is clear too," they called.

"This is getting monotonously boring," said the Ferrishin commander. At least he looked Ferrishin but when he turned his head, half of his face was artificial.

"Sarah, you will need to concentrate on the technology. There isn't too much of it, but if you can melt some of it down, it should destroy groups within the immediate area where you are. It will deplete you but I don't see any other solution. We must destroy as many as possible."

At that precise moment Darren chose to contact him. He swiftly replied to tell him the situation.

"Ready," he asked. She nodded and he raced down to take on dargs as he came to them, leaving Sarah to follow. She dropped down behind trees and concentrated on groups of the TAB's and once they had imploded she moved to the next. There were actually a couple of vehicles on the ground as well, but they went up with the rest. Arin was just amazing. She caught glimpses of him scything down all those who came against him. He was hampered somewhat by the need to preserve the vegetation but some destruction was inevitable as the technical stuff exploded. Arin dealt with the Pitch dwarves before they could scatter, then proceeded to lead those who were left in the opposite direction to Drakeridge. He grabbed Sarah by the hand as he passed and they ran side by side through the forest and undergrowth allowing themselves to be glimpsed occasionally. He had dealt with the biggest threat, namely the Pitch Dwarves who could have scented the Egg if they had continued searching underground. The prospect of capturing the Enchanter Elf drew the remaining troops like a magnet. He had used Enchanter skills as had she, the numbers justifying the need, and with all the running they were wearying a little, but that wouldn't have been a problem in itself, but for two unexpected happenings.

The first was entirely unfortunate and triggered off the inevitable result. They began to double back and retrace their steps, when a Darg came out of nowhere. Arin cut him down but he lost his balance and fell hitting his head on something very hard knocking him unconscious. If he hadn't been wearying, his reflexes would have kept him upright. Sarah ran to him and was promptly smacked on top of him with a crack to the back of her head. Yulir swooped down and tore a few of them as he came and he seized Domgeorn rising with it out of sight. A triumphant Darg began crowing and the second disaster occurred if you could call it that. A group of TAB's stopped their vehicle and a person of some authority stepped out. He strode across, his clothes showing him to be Dragon master.

"What is this fiasco," he demanded and looked down at his feet. Seeing the two unconscious bodies, his mouth began to curve in an awful travesty of a smile.

"You are forgiven, "he declared. "Put them in the vehicle."

Sarah was lifted and carried away and he stared down at Arin whose eyes briefly opened to see the shadowy face of nightmares. "Aorcha," he muttered.

"Alder's son!" Aorcha smashed him back into oblivion.

When they returned to consciousness Sarah woke first. Her hands and feet were bound and she was sitting in a corner against the wall. They were in a spacious room containing equipment that was obscure to her. They seem to be controlled by computers. Arin was connected to a device or machine, she couldn't be sure. It was a bit like a dentist chair with an intravenous drip attached to each arm. She could hear two of them talking. The Pitch Elves who had bound her seemed to have missed the mark under her fringe or they would have immobilised her more than they had, and she was thankful for that. As she listened it became clear this was Aorcha. The occupant of the hover chair beside him wasn't so clear at first but he was obviously very old and the most dark and twisted creature she had set eyes on. He was like a shrivelled raisin that was the only description that would fit.

"We are ready to proceed Lord Monkshood," said one of the Ferrishin, garbed in the white coat of a doctor. The scene looked like something out of a second rate B movie but it was actually happening.

"Get on with it then," he snapped.

"You are sure it will work on him. It didn't work on Blackthorn."

Enchanting Sarah by Morgan Fitzsimons

"This is no Blackthorn, he is all Dulcamara. There is no Lilia to help him in the struggle. When he comes round he will be on his own with nothing between him all the temptations this time has to offer. The pull of the drugs will be too strong to resist." Monkshood assured him.

"For a short time at least he will still have the full power of an Enchanter and we can use that to advantage. I am looking forward to it. How Alder would weep, revenge is definitely sweet," said Alder.

They all had forgotten the female in the corner. They had written her off as an immature golden elf, one with abilities yes, but no more than that. Her hair falling across her forehead almost covering her eyebrows, covered the pale mark of Enchanter, so they missed it too.

"I will leave you to get on with it. It's your revenge not mine. I just don't want an Enchanter running loose. I must join your father."

"If you are going to the castle, I will follow shortly to make sure Hemlock doesn't mess it up."

Enchanting Sarah by Morgan Fitzsimons

"Which is why I'm joining him."

One of the Pitch Witches pushed his chair through the door. He liked to have a permanent escort of at least half a dozen of them wherever he went. Sarah stayed still where she was thrown for the moment and simply concentrated her enchantment on the flow of liquid going from the bag, down the tube, through the needles in Arin's arms. She was so terrified for him. She had ceased to be afraid for herself if they discovered she was Dulcamara. She was well aware that if the drugs took Arin down the road they wanted him to travel, he would become like them. Judging by what they said, the concoction would leave him no choice. She managed to change the contents of the bag to water; just as he had shown her at the club. It went from a rich emerald to pure clear liquid. Aorcha didn't notice, he was so caught up in gloating over his victim. Sarah had no way of knowing how much of it had already entered his system but the level in the bag was still quite high, so hopefully it wasn't enough to be effective. She turned her attention to freeing herself from the bonds.

Arin opened his eyes to see Aorcha beside him laughing. His eyes changed colour and glowed red with the effect of the poison he had ingested. Burning rage rose up and fired his whole being with the desire to kill. He came to his feet breaking the metal that bound him, and tore off the tubes and paraphernalia. Blood poured down his arms from the tearing out of the needle, which partly helped to flush it out as it contained much of the green substance. This was something Aorcha hadn't thought of, but he should have done. Arin put both hands up in Aorcha's direction and before Aorcha realised the intent, both hands twisted and without touching him, he was lifted off his feet unable to breathe. He was writhing and twisting, his brain was being deprived of oxygen preventing him from thinking clearly.

"No", screamed Sarah and she ran between those two hands to clutch Arin round the wait, "Not this, not   for hate or revenge, let it go.   Don't leave me with them. Don't become one of them. "

His eyes now were two fiery burning coals and it was almost too late, but she caught his head down to her and standing on tiptoe kissed him and shut out everything else, hoping in registering her presence, he would turn to her defence. His hands went about her waist and he let Aorcha drop. He hit the floor unconscious, but not dead.

With all her being she willed him to see her. She couldn't eliminate the effect of the drug but she could try to get him to negate it.

"Sarah," he gasped. He saw her eyes bright with tears "Must protect Sarah," the thought rang through his brain.

"Yes," she said. "We have to get out of here."

He had to protect her from them. He held on to her, "Must keep you safe," he muttered. The Ferrishin doctor was frozen to the spot, but he pressed the alarm.

Enchanting Sarah by Morgan Fitzsimons

"Then we must leave *now*," she urged and he responded by moving through the door after her. Two Pitch Witches blocked his way, their rune sticks of death pointing his way, muttering their spells of sorcery, plunging the room into complete darkness, but they were unused to Enchanters who can see in the dark. Arin's response to their magic was swift and deadly and he left them lying on the floor, one with her neck broken. More of Aorcha's troops came on the run in response to the alarm but he just strode through the opposition as if on a walk in the park not looking back as they hit the floor, some with sparking circuits and mini explosions in the technical implants. Once outside they raced hand in hand into the deep wood. Where eventually he collapsed, his whole body was now a raging furnace and his mind seeing all manner of threats, though nowhere near as badly as Blackthorn had suffered all that time ago when Monkshood's potions were fed into him. She held his head against her and smoothed back his hair as he hallucinated, all the time whispering to him. Green leaves from the trailing branches enveloped them in a silent natural world and invaded their senses allowing a tranquillity to prevail. In between his mutterings he had a lucid moment.He began repeating a chant of just a few words in Dulcanara and she could see something forming around them. It began as a breath of the dragon. She caught the words and began to chant them   gently and quietly where he left off, his voice trailing to silence. Darkness was falling and they had started searching from the house but the enchantment wove easily around them as though spinning a bubble that shut out all reality. It was like sitting in the mouth of the dragon. Nothing could find them or come near them and Arin just slept for a time. He awoke almost in his right mind again and she was thankful. She told him what she had overheard.

"It is likely then it's Monkshood who is the master mind, and Aorcha and Hemlock who action it," said Arin.

"But what they were saying leads me to conclude Hemlock is Aorcha's son. If Monkshood can survive millennia so could they."

Enchanting Sarah by Morgan Fitzsimons

"You know I have to go back," he said quietly.

"I was afraid you would say that."

"He can't be allowed to damage any more lives, It is time for justice to prevail. Thank you Sarah." He raised her hand and kissed her fingertips.

"For what? I only used the enchantment you taught me."

"Maybe so, but you remembered it and used it."

He was a little shaky when he stood, but it passed. He called Yulir and raised up his hand and the great sword dropped into his hold.

"You are sure this is the right thing to do?"

"I am sure."

He ran his hand over the dragons carved on the sword and he spoke in the language of his people. "Today is your last Aorcha."

He strode back through the woods with Sarah behind him, walked boldly in through the pillared front entrance.

Enchanting Sarah by Morgan Fitzsimons

"Come down to me Aorcha, It is time to end it."

Aorcha stood on the stairs looking down at him.

"You think you can elfling?" Arin laughed.

"The sword waits for you. I may wield it, but it is their power dealing it, I am confident in that."

"It's just a piece of metal in the hands of a young upstart elfling who thinks he is a warrior" It was the same arrogance displayed by Kor-gat millennia ago when he had faced the young elf that was Blackthorn. Some of his followers appeared but he waved them back.

"You of all people should know how well the upstart was taught and who taught him. Doesn't that give you some cause for fear?"

Aorcha laughed but he was a little more wary. He remembered Alder well, he hated him so much.

"You are no Alder either!"

"But I am my mother's son," he said.

"The son she had with Alder," he almost spat at him."But you should have been my son, I loved her and she loved me."

"She never loved you Aorcha it was all in your evil mind and your partner Melusine murdered her for it, just as you murdered so many good people in your search for power over them."

Arin twirled the sword round and held it point to the ground and the dragons on the handle gleamed with a life of their own. The jewelled eyes reflected glittering shafts of light as Arin reversed it again.

"I will defeat you, Alder's son," he said almost as if wanting to shut out Arin's mother from the equation.

Aorcha held his staff in front of him and light began to shaft out from it and to weave about him in protective mode but Arin simply moved the sword from one side to the other like pulling back a curtain and the protection dissolved. He advanced to Aorcha up the staircase and Aorcha moved back to the top. Again he used the staff to direct a bolt of light at Arin but they deflected from the sword and set some curtains alight. Aorcha put out his hands and attempted to raise Arin from the ground. He succeeded for a few moments, but could not set him off balance. A|rin laughed and hurtled him u to the ceiling and twirled him round and round and he dropped to the floor with a thud. He began to mutter under his breath and coming to his feet he sent the same things that had poured from Jason's mouth pouring from him but these became huge and black and terrifying.

Arin laughed gain." They can't hurt me if I am in the right and I'm afraid your poisons didn't change that." The air was thick and black now and the Ferrishin and the Pitch witches converged toward him but he scythed the sword around him in a circular movement and they all went down like ninepins in a bowling alley.

Aorcha began to run now, beginning to see this was different. Arin threw the sword and it curved around the corner to race past him overhead and to curve round hitting him in the chest so hard it protruded at the back. He tried to speak but it was as though his throat was paralysed. The sword pulled itself out and remained point down in the wooden floor. The place cleared and the bodies lay were they had fallen and Arin bent over Aorcha.

"Justice is served, but it can't change what you did," he said sadly.

They could hear more people coming, so they went out of the window to roll to their feet. They were in a huge courtyard filled with Darg soldiers between them and the gateway.

"This is just too much," he groaned

"There are too many of them yet again," said Sarah. "Where have they been hiding them all."

"At least it's a clear field, "he said "We are agreed this time they are beasts who are bred to kill?"

She nodded.

"It's acceptable therefore to get them first?"

She nodded again.

Enchanting Sarah by Morgan Fitzsimons

"When Firedrake bonded with me, I received a rare gift, which the family discovered by accident, and they re named me Arin."

"What accident?"

"I set fire to several wheat fields," and with that he flashed his hands forward raising the palms slightly and a huge stream of fire gushed out over the oncoming Dargs. When he stopped they were just ashes.

"The name means flame of fire. It comes in some way from Firedrake."

He grabbed her hand and they raced through the gate. They didn't stop, tired though they were until they passed Drakeridge. Yulir took the sword and Firedrake appeared to take them back to her Egg. Ryder was still there playing Egg-maid. Sarah sank down in the dim light that permeated through several cracks in the terrain above them. Arin stayed by the entrance and contacted Darren.

"At last," Darren said, "where the hell have you been? "

"Unavoidably detained, but all is well at the moment. And the Egg is Firedrakes and may be about to hatch."

"Not fair," yelled Darren. Why am I missing it? Take pictures, you can video with that thing. Sarah can too."

He sent images over of the castle and some of its interior. It seemed to be in a remote place and in a position to see everything around it that approached. He had received the information from Colin, the FBI agent as requested by Arin. He had tracked down the connection between Hemlock and Jason. He found Jason and Kayla were the twins of Maura Carraway heiress to the Carraway fortune and she was divorced from Jefferson Hemlock. They shortened the name to Carr to protect them from the paparazzi. The castle was Carraway castle apparently Jason's from his mother's father.

Enchanting Sarah by Morgan Fitzsimons

"Great, Darren. We will see what we can do about pictures. Get yourself back home now and send Bogbean back to Blackthorn."

He joined Sarah and the anxious Firedrake, with the now proprietary Ryder fussing overhead. Firedrake allowed Sarah to touch it. It felt quite pliable under her fingers. Sarah and Arin sat and watched in awe and delight as the Egg cracked. Both of them took video with their phones recording every single second for Darren. First the head popped out and the rest of the body shook free of the shell. Its skin was both green and turquoise blue with a pale silvery underbelly. It was quite stunning. As it ejected from the shell it skidded forward and landed against Sarah who was knocked backwards clutching her arms round the baby dragon. It put out a red tongue and licked her.

"She likes you Sarah" said Arin. He reached out to Firedrake who was now hovering anxiously over her offspring.

Enchanting Sarah by Morgan Fitzsimons

Just at that moment Ryder chose to fly outside with a rush of wings causing Sarah's hair to fly up around her face. Startled they both looked up and Arin followed him to look down the mountain. Yulir was already restlessly swooping. He had spotted a whole body of males carrying weapons and leading blood beasts. These last were creatures bred to find almost anything living.

"Sarah, there's another lot of them down there. I must lead them away from here. As soon as it's clear, get Firedrake to take the little one to the top of the Ardreth Eryri. They will never pick up her scent that high up."

He promptly disappeared from her sight with Yulir beside him. He soon had the pack of them chasing after him. She ran to the edge and looked around before going back to Firedrake. The baby was staggering about now on four fat little legs and presented such a charming sight she watched in delight. She was alerted by the sound of small stones scattering over the rock face and to her horror the face of a Pitch dwarf peered at her from the entrance. Where the hell he had come from?

Enchanting Sarah by Morgan Fitzsimons

She made a chopping movement with her hands and his fingers lost their grip and he howled as he let go. She ran forward to see there were three or four of them clambering over the top. Ryder managed to dislodge one who rolled screaming down the rocks. It was all so fast yet to Sarah it was like slow motion. More of them appeared and Firedrake came to the opening destroying them as Sarah managed to send two more crashing to the valley below, but never saw the one now behind her as he hurtled his axe hitting her squarely in the back. She fell forward to the hard ground the axe still in her back the blood welling up around it. Firedrake destroyed the last of them but Ryder had already dealt with Sarah's attacker. He went straight for the evil yellow eyes with his claws and the creature staggered like some drunken doll, unable to see with blood streaming down his face. One last swish of wings and Ryder furiously pushed him over the edge. Firedrake bent her head to Sarah in distress but the little dragon was there first. She was walking reasonably well now and was almost crying over

Enchanting Sarah by Morgan Fitzsimons

Sarah, making strange little noises as she tried to push her up. Ryder seemed to know what Firedrake wanted him to do and he fixed his claws around the axe handle and pulled it. It came out with a jerk and more blood welled out. Firedrake reached out and the little one held up her front paws to receive the scratch over them. She whimpered a little but placed her paws on Sarah's back. The light that spread from the touch was a silvery blue that tinged Sara's flesh. An exhausted Arin hauled himself over the edge in time to see what was happening. His weariness for gotten he dropped on his knees beside her "What happened?" he asked listening intently to Firedrake.

The wound was already sealing and the bleeding had stopped. He waited until the light faded and the small one had ceased. He realised Firedrake had done the only thing possible to save her and his hope now was the blood of the baby was enough to do just that. He turned her over sitting against the cavern wall as he did so. He pillowed her head against his chest, his arms holding her securely. He knew from experience how hard it was going to be for the next hours. Her face was flushed, her eyes closed and her breathing sporadic, but at least she was still breathing. Her head threshed about and her skin began to burn. Her slim figure arched over his arm as the pain shot through her. But he patiently held her until the violent twisting ceased and her head subsided again on his chest. Her twisting and agonising was surprisingly short but now her body burned and her hair curled at the ends as it became soaked with perspiration. Her whole body was damp against his shirt but he laid her back against Firedrake so she acted as a pillow, not wanting his body heat to add to her temperature rise.

Firedrake shook her head and communicated. "She must burn it out, do you not remember?"

He thought back to his time of bonding and remembered the days of pain and the heat burning like a furnace. The dragon baby curled up against her on one side so Arin sat beside her on the other leaning back against Firedrake. He just waited and watched over her, but he didn't think the recovery would be anything like as long as his ordeal had been. In the first place, she was dying as he had been, but the period of agonising pain for her seemed so very short compared to that he had endured, possibly because it was a new born and perhaps was not yet as poisonous and corrosive as a full grown dragon would be.   He was proved right as Sarah opened her eyes within a few hours and smiled at him. Arin ruffled her hair and touched her face. She was cool and normal again. He was relieved her experience was so much easier than his had been.

"You look very seriously worried," she said, her voice almost a whisper.

"I feel seriously old," he said.

"What happened?"

"You almost died for a second time. Once was enough!"

"It was more than that wasn't it? It was the little one, I can feel her heart beat."

Enchanting Sarah by Morgan Fitzsimons

"She exchanged blood to heal you. I was bothered about the aftermath. Allowing the dragon's blood to enter your veins is a most painful experience. It can send you almost out of your mind for a time, and not everyone who tries survives either. Few are asked to sustain the event. The blood is both corrosive and poisonous. I was afraid for you."

He looked down at the young one. "It may perhaps be much easier to bond with a new born. I have not seen such a baby form an attachment before, and Firedrake wouldn't have had her do it if it wasn't right"

The little creature was alternating between licking Sarah and her mother.

"She will grow quite quickly." He said. "But she will take centuries to gain knowledge and wisdom and experience such as Firedrake has. Dragon Guardians bond with adult dragons and guard the heritage by using it wisely and sparingly."

"She and I can be babies together and grow together."

"A dragon bonds once only usually. The only thing to break that bond is death. It occurs to me if she is bonded to you no one else can bond with her," said Arin.

"You are saying if she falls into the hands of the Masters, they can't use her."

"They could control her with their vile practises, but the bonding would be a barrier to use in their revival of Tal-git and none of their number could bond with her either, they would likely die now if they tried."

He stood up and held out his hand to pull her to her feet.

"How do you feel?"

"Fantastic," she said.

"You must give her a name," said Arin. Sarah looked down at the beautiful creature, her eyes on the silver thread patterns etched so delicately into turquoise and blue scales.

Enchanting Sarah by Morgan Fitzsimons

"I wonder who your father was little one," she said softly. "I will name her Silvertrace," she said.

"Very apt" said Arin smiling.

"What is going to happen to my baby? She can't be carried out of here," said Sarah.

Firedrake urged Arin to get on her back. He did so pulling Sarah with him as she watched curiously. Firedrake rose above the baby gripping her in her claws. She went up through the crevasse and out into the air, soaring over Drakeridge and up to the top of the Ardreth Eryri. She let the baby down first and Sarah and Arin came down beside her. She rolled down the steps rather than walked and waddled into the room below finding a comfortable spot to curl up in.

Arin removed his hat and tossed it beside her.

"Look after the hat while you are playing Egg maid," he said to Ryder who completely ignored him, fussing over his charge.

The Ryder actually flew down into the room and perched on a rock watching her. He seemed to have quite a propriety interest. Sarah dropped a kiss on the baby's head and looked back at Ryder as she left. Arin had meanwhile communicated with Darren again assuring him the pics and videos were secure on the phones. He had sent copies back to his father anyway as a precaution. They had set that line up some time ago. He outlined a plan of action of sorts. They could stop the attempt to bring Tal-git back in several ways. They could steal the book and destroy it. They could destroy the bones. They could kill Hemlock. It was a question of playing it by ear and taking any opportunity available. Now for the castle and hopefully they had run Hemlock to ground at last. Leaving the Ryder in charge they soared upward. A group of eagles took up vigil from the top of the Ardreth and on down over Drakeridge as Yulir circled and flew after the dragon.

Chapter 21

Skeleton out of the closet

Arin fixed the image of Hemlock in his mind. Where he was so would the bones be. "Take us there," he said and they soared up to come down over a different set of mountains. The view was magnificent and any other time they would have been enthralled by it, but their minds were on other things. Below them they could see a castle set high on dark grey rock that swept almost vertically down to yet more rocks, and on down to a lake of rich blue water. These stark mountain ranges were the home of eagles and several came to join Yulir. Down below in the castle fortress people were scurrying to and fro. The radar system registered a huge blip which could only be a dragon.

"It has to be that infernal meddling Enchanter," rasped out Monkshood. He was huddled in his hoverchair, his twisted body of little use to him anymore. All the spells and magic in the world couldn't repair the damage he had inflicted upon himself by millennia of evil pursuits.

"If it is I haven't time to deal with him," said Hemlock impatiently. "The conditions we want are perfect right now but they may not last."

"Leave me to do it then," said Jason."It will be most satisfying."

"It would if you could do it," snapped his father, "but my father couldn't manage it and he was a hundred times the Elf you aspire to be and most certainly a brilliant Dragon Master. What chance have you got? An Enchanter War Lord is a formidable enemy. This one might be young but he is determined and by all accounts he has Domgeorn."

"I have the answer to that," said a voice from the doorway. Melusine emerged into the light of the room. She was beautiful but the dark aura of depravity oozed around her sinuous beauty like treacle. "If it is him, you can leave him to me."

"So mother, you would avenge my father? Perhaps you are strong enough at that," said Hemlock. "

"I can become invincible," she said, "if you feel the danger warrants it. Go do what you must!"

"At least let me come with you then father," said Jason eagerly.

"You will go to the island as planned and get everything ready for my arrival with Tal-git. Your great grandfather might have the inclination and the magic, but he isn't physically capable as you well know. You still have a way to go before you can handle being Dragon Master"

Enchanting Sarah by Morgan Fitzsimons

Hemlock went down by lift into the earth beneath the castle emerging into a tall corridor containing the start of a set of tracks with a carriage on it. A driver sat in the front and set the controls. They shot off at great speed through the tunnels in the mountain to emerge at a runway cut into the valley. There was a plane ready for His grandfather and his children. He boarded the helicopter ready to take off. The bones had already gone to their final destination and he was about to join them. In his hand he held the book. The final stages might prove a little difficult but he would just have to use what he had to hand.

Arin and Sarah had scaled the rock face to gain entrance to the castle, not yet knowing Hemlock was leaving. The outer castle walls and the main keep were still as they had been for centuries, but there were a lot of new building and technical additions. There was a huge inner courtyard and an even bigger outer one that ranged round on three sides and curved over the slopes. The fourth side was the steep drop and the middle one of the remaining three went on sloping down to a flat plain below in the valley bottom. The one to the right was flanked by an extensive ultra modern complexity of buildings. The information from their sources was rather scant on what they housed. They could only conjecture which Darren was busily doing, even as he travelled home, by considering the information he had gathered, particularly stuff on equipment delivered there. They had considered mind walking but thought it best to conserve their strength for any confrontation. Once over the battlements they looked around to see what they could recognise from the images sent to them by Darren. There were figures in the courtyards and others moving in and out of the buildings. They could make out Darg's Ferrishin and human beings as well as Pitch Elves.

"Wait here," he said briefly and swung down to enter through an open window below. A few moments later he emerged from the doorway out onto the battlements and tossed a Pitch Elf at her feet. Bending over him he administered a small shock to his system. His body jerked and he looked up at his captor. The deep red glow of Arin's eyes was reflected in the yellow eyes of the Elf. His ears quivered as Arin pulled his face towards him. He was immediately under his control.

"Where is Hemlock?" Arin asked.

"Lord Hemlock has just this moment departed," he replied obediently.

"Damn," said Arin, "thwarted yet again. "Where has he gone?"

"I don't know," he replied.

"Who does?" asked Arin.

"Lord Monkshood and his great grand children may still be here, but they were due to depart for the island. The Castle Senior Overseer would know and the Master at Arms, and probably the Duty Officer of the Day."

"Which one can you get to unobserved?"

"The easiest would be the Overseer. He will be in his office. The others are in areas full of workers."

"Take us to him." ordered Arin. He put up his hand and the faithful Yulir dropped the sword into it. As they descended the stairs he spoke to the elf again.

"Who are these great grandchildren?"

"Trainee Dragon masters, Jason and Kayla Hemlock."

"So it looks like we have managed to annoy several generations by killing Aorcha. I guess that really makes us targets!"

"That is definitely not good," said Sarah.

The Pitch Elf led them along corridors to an office in one of the towers. He obediently waited every time they encountered anyone so they would not be seen. Everything was , until they crossed from the ancient stone buildings into the huge modern complex. Instantly an intruder alert was triggered. In moments they were faced with TAB's pointing weapons. From the height and ear shape they were probably Pitch Elf with technical additions but there wasn't time to find out. Arin and Sarah used their athletic abilities to roll out of the way of the first blasts and run up the walls twisting and turning to avoid being hit. They were so fast, leaping down behind them to land on each side, knocking them inwards their touch overloading their circuits, and running as they exploded.

"In here," said Arin and he tapped the control box by the door market Senior Overseer. It crackled and died and the door slid back.

Sarah waved her fingers at the female who was sat in front of a bank of computer screens and Arin grabbed the male Overseer. He was a Pitch Elf of Ferrishin origin and not altered. Arin held him by the throat and forced him to meet his eyes. Once he entered a trance like state, Arin released him.

"Where did Hemlock go?" he demanded.

"He went to Darkenwald."

"But where is Darkenwald?"

"The new location is Iceland beneath one of its Volcanos."

Enchanting Sarah by Morgan Fitzsimons

"Has he the dragon bones with him?"

"They are already there."

"Back to Firedrake," he said, racing through the door leaving the Overseer still in the trance. Outside were more armed creatures and they had a battle on their hands, where they became separated, driving Sarah in the opposite direction. Arin had no choice but to force his way after her. He found the Sword was very effective at cleaving through the metal protection on the opposition. The magic of the sword of justice was seemingly more powerful than the supposed un-penetratable material of technology. They were now in the central area of the complex in which the power source for the whole place was based. They seemed to have emerged on a kind of mezzanine suspended out over the central area. Arin had dealt with those around him but was now faced with a tall female holding Sarah by the throat.

"We meet again Enchanter Lord!" The tones were mocking yet seductive at the same time.

Enchanting Sarah by Morgan Fitzsimons

"Melusine!" He exclaimed, warily moving nearer.

"If you will surrender to me, I promise not to drop her." Somehow Sarah was now hanging from Melusine's hand suspended over the drop down among the machinery.

"You know I will not do that," said Arin.

"Say goodbye then to your pretty little Golden bird," and she let go. Sarah felt the air whistling past as she fell. In the split seconds following she acted on instinct and raised her hands up willing herself back on the mezzanine.

Melusine had hoped to provoke Arin to rash rage but in that she was very mistaken. The serpents coiled around her breasts uncoiled to become reality and grew to tower over him. He set The Sword free to fly after the serpent heads and decapitate them. Melusine dropped to the floor crying over them.

"My babies, "she wailed and Arin turned to grab Sarah's hand and run to the nearest exit where they found themselves in the huge courtyard.

Enchanting Sarah by Morgan Fitzsimons

"You let her try to kill me," she gasped.

"I thought it a good learning experience," he said blandly.

"What if I'd failed?" she said crossly.

"I would have caught you."

"In the last two seconds," she said.

"It would have been close."

All the time they were talking they were moving across the courtyard, dealing with any opposition that met them. Yulir swooped down from time to come screeching and tearing at whoever was nearest. Several of the TAB's attempted to fire at him but he was adept at escaping the blasts.

Melusine had stopped wailing and began to chant. "The serpents are yours Lady Skuld, all yours and the Enchanter has taken them. I call you back among the living to avenge your own."

She followed outside and producing her stave of incantations ,she swiftly drew runes in the ground. She drew the black runes, necromantic characters to communicate with the dead. She called Nifl – hella the mistress of the veils to draw back the veil and allow Skuld passage. She drew Thurizaz, the troll rune, invoking demons from the netherworld   to bring Skuld from Irkalla.

Arin stopped dead in his tracks turning to look back.

"She is bringing Skuld into being. I should have known she would when I killed them. Sarah I need you to go as fast as to the far wall. Get yourself behind it."

"I am not leaving you alone."

"It will be easier for me if I don't have to consider your safety. You will go!" He was so decisive she obeyed but she didn't go down the other side but hid behind the crenulations on the battlements. "Yulir stay with Sarah, I need a clear line to Melusine." The great bird obeyed and flew to hover above Sarah's head.

Melusine rose to stand in the drifting shadows around her feet which grew around her, belching forth the black smoke and fiery flames of hell at the same time. She extended her arms which were instantly clad in the arm braces and metal of a warrior. Her body garments became armour and a helmet covered her face, the emblems of the skull and the serpent decorating body and helmet, serpents winding over the arm braces. Her fingers extended She was as tall as her opponent. Facing the transition of Skuld herself was bad enough but he knew it could get much worse. He had to do what was needed quickly and efficiently leaving her no time to invoke all her armies; for once they came they couldn't be stopped. When her armies fell she made them rise again and go on fighting. He ran at her, engaging her in immediate confrontation, giving her no respite or time in which to conjure up any support. The brief engagement was fierce and fast but Arin held, despite her use of magic to confuse, by moving herself to different areas of attack and shifting into different forms. She managed to gain a few moments in which she rapidly moved her fingers and cried out, in response to which a mass of small flying creatures came with the appearance of little metal serpents with wings, but he managed to knock her unconscious to the ground with the flat of the sword while she was briefly distracted. There were no more creatures but what there were, were sufficiently lethal. They ceased swirling and turned on him but he held his arms wide and closed them, sweeping them up as if tossing them away in the other direction. They descended on the castle buildings and moved through like scavengers. They devoured everything in their path but instead of flesh, Arin had changed their target to things of technology. As they passed everything powered by electricity was destroyed, eaten almost, and what was left collapsed. The whole of the modern building twisted and turned and collapsed on itself and destroyed the creatures within it. Dargs, Pitch Elves, and TAB's were fleeing from the buildings, but whatever technology on them, be it ear communicators to brain implants or body parts, they were imploding as they ran.

Enchanting Sarah by Morgan Fitzsimons

He made for the top of the far wall and raising his hands he sent flaming fire across the courtyards destroying what survived and adding to the confusion. When it reached the tiny serpents, they were full of static and the fire, with an added command from Arin, sent the whole place up into a huge explosion of sparks and flames. He rolled down the other side with Sarah racing after him. She helped him to his feet and they moved to Firedrake who bent as low as she could to allow Arin to climb up. Sarah got behind him to hold him steady.

"What about Monkshood and the Terrible twins," she asked.

"We have no way of knowing if they left before this started, or if they perished in it," he said. He tapped Firedrake, "Take us to Hemlock."

She obeyed flying up into the clouds with the ever faithful Yulir behind her, coming down again to beautiful stark mountain peaks, the rocks below them reflecting gorgeous colours in the light. This was the land of fire and ice the poets had sung about in his father's halls. It was a place of such powerful elemental presence, the existence of a supernatural creative force beyond the control of men, could not be denied, no matter how much they tried to harness it, they never would. High dark rocks reared up from the water smashing into it below, sending up clouds of white, billowing like smoke from a fire. For a brief time, she followed the wide path of a raging torrent, moving through dark grey rocks on either side with more water pouring down the face and adding to the rushing torrent below it. Yulir just loved it, spinning in the air over the water. Firedrake left the water to curve over the land of green grass and lava rock and the violent splash of red flowers.

She flew over a deep wide crevasse in between mountains. On either side was rich brown earth and mossy green grass with stones on the one side and waterfalls opposite. She flew down into it and travelled along it. They saw Yulir was still with them. It gave way to a very steep rise on the one hand, rich in purples and copper colours and the other sloped a little more, still with mossy green and the purple of wild flowers. It became starker and culminated in a curving end over which fell a huge powerful waterfall powering over the dark rocks. The sound of the water thundered and the cloud of spray was overpowering, creating a misty curtain concealing what lay behind it. She hovered before the magnificent sight and turned into an opening high up in the side of the mountain. The cave was dark as they flew well inside and she landed softly on the damp ground. The phosphorous gleam of the dragon skin gave some light as Sarah looked about in awe at the wonder of nature. The inside was dark grey stone with a blue cast giving an air of mysterious strength to it. The stone rose high taking on an even stronger blue, while the floor of the cave had a watery blue paleness. It narrowed toward the rear and disappeared tantalisingly into the dark. Sarah came down and Arin sort of rolled on to his back to lie in the pale blue dust. "Are you Ok," asked Sarah.

He sat up taking deep breaths. "It's nothing a few minutes respite won't cure."

Enchanting Sarah by Morgan Fitzsimons

He looked around at the stillness and quiet of the cave.

"You are sure this is the right place Firedrake?" he asked. Her reply was to toss her head disdainfully and puff out a little fire.

"Ok no need to choke us on smoke. I'm sorry if I offended you, but you must admit it is a little quiet."

"You need a moment to regain what you lost." said Sarah.

Firedrake nodded her head up and down.

"We haven't got any moments to spare."

"Maybe not! But you can't stop him at all without Enchantment."

He stood up and flexed his fingers. "We can move on. I am recovering all the time we are moving," he said. Yulir was restlessly moving about. "You can't go any deeper," said Arin. "Wait for us outside and keep vigilant."

Enchanting Sarah by Morgan Fitzsimons

Firedrake moved off to follow the winding trail through the caverns.

"Is it me or is it getting really warm in here," Sarah asked.

"Wherever Hemlock is, he must be near molten lava," said Arin. "He will need the same conditions in which Belladonna used the runes from the book. Sorrel said it was beneath Curithir where I understand was flowing lava"

Firedrake came to a halt and Arin squeezed past her. He emerged onto an outcrop overlooking the scene below. It was most daunting, layer upon layer of criss-crossing transparent walk ways all leading off somewhere and he couldn't see the bottom of it. Creatures carrying weapons, several units of huge Dargs and the like crossed while he watched. He observed lone Ferrishin officers and TAB's of human origin.

He ducked back out of sight. "How in hell are we going to find Hemlock?"

Enchanting Sarah by Morgan Fitzsimons

"You need to conserve strength, I will mind walk," said Sarah.

"But he is capable of sensing you, and you are still a novice. "

"And I'll always be a novice if you keep protecting me. I am a fast learner you know." And with that she was gone.

He fought the temptation to follow, but he knew she was right but it didn't make it any easier to let her go.

She fixed her mind on Hemlock as she had last seen him and her consciousness moved in his direction. Instinctively she kept away from the criss-crossed straight line walkways. They were linear intrusions, impositions of the Dragon Masters, and not where the Elf spirit should be. She moved through the air plunging down to an opening and followed it. It curved and twisted coming out into another large area. Below was a seething black mass of moving molten rock, the cracks showing the red hot glow of fiery lava. There were machines directed by Ferrishin TAB's accompanied by several Dragon Masters chanting and using some form of magic. She just caught the general gist of it, which seemed to be extracting the black lava rock while molten underneath, and creating some kind of monstrous thing within the tube. She didn't wait to find out how or what, her mind raced on to Hemlock. She saw the bones first. Tal-git had been recreated just as dinosaur bones were in a museum, each bone meticulously placed supported by a metal stand. Before the bones was Hemlock. He was on a tall structure bringing him level with the head. Beside him was a stone altar table. He wore his ceremonial long black coat heavily decorated with symbols. The black tattoo-like body patterns of the Masters were visible on his arms and completely covered his bared chest beneath the coat. On the stone alter table were bowls on braziers over molten lava and the book lay open beside him. He was already reading the runes from the open page. Several Pitch Witch spell weavers were chanting with him. Her horrified gaze took in the mezzanine overlooking the bones of Tal-git. On it were the corpses of several huge Dargs suspended over bowls into which had dripped their blood. It wasn't the pure amber colour of Dragon's blood, or even the black blood some had, but a mix of amber and green swirled in the bowls. There were several Ferrishin, one with each bowl. She could only assume in the absence of a dragon he was using Darg's to provide the flesh according to the spell. Her mind raced back at top speed to Arin who was impatiently waiting. She shared what she had seen.

"No time to lose," he said. "You will have to show me the way."

The trickiest bit was negotiating the open areas where there was a concentrated force but he couldn't deal with what he saw there, until he had stopped the releasing of Tal-git. With Tal-git Hemlock could destroy human technology in great sweeps and without consideration of right or wrong, just his own advancement. Arin had realised after the encounter with Melusine, it was something he as an Enchanter could accomplish,

Enchanting Sarah by Morgan Fitzsimons

but it would mean taking away the right to choose your own destiny and he could not do that without destroying himself. He could defend against the likes of Melusine and Hemlock, whereas Tal-git was already corrupted and could be used to destroy any technology. There was a fine line between positive and negative, which didn't always line up with right and wrong ways, good and evil, and Arin would never allow himself to cross it. When they got to where Hemlock was he had already finished the incantations and the head turned to look down at him. The bones had turned black and the eye socket was empty. The Ferrishin above the head tipped the bowl at a signal from Hemlock and it poured down over the head and chest of the dragon which before their eyes became the scaly flesh of Tal-git where the liquid had touched and a gleaming red eye now glared where the empty socket had been.

Hemlock saw Arin.

"Too late, Enchanter, too late," he cried.

Enchanting Sarah by Morgan Fitzsimons

Arin's hands went up and shot fire at the two Ferrishin standing beside the other bowls. They flew back burnt to a crisp. Sarah shot a power bolt at one of the bowls and succeeded in knocking it backwards spilling the contents back and down the wall. Hemlock screamed his rage and taking the flagon from the stone altar, he flicked his fingers and the head roared back and he poured the molten lava down the throat of Tal-git. As his body was incomplete it dripped from the back neck but some of poured down the front neck and throat and onto the inner chest area. The creature roared and moved off the stand crushing it underfoot. It was quite crazed as it was only partially restored and lashed out at anything, including the raised platform Hemlock was standing on It shattered, throwing Hemlock down to strike his head on the stone floor, blood seeping out from beneath him. Tal-git might be half crazed but he recognised Enchanter, the scent the power emanating from him, and the mark glowing deep and dark sending frissons of danger. His head hunted frantically along the ledges as

Enchanting Sarah by Morgan Fitzsimons

Arin and Sarah sought some temporary cover. But Tal-git caught the sense of something more than Enchanter; he felt the breeze of an air current and freedom beckoned. He actually flew up towards it as Firedrake flew into the space beneath him. Arin and Sarah immediately leapt on Firedrake's back to follow.

The air current followed the lava flow out onto the side of the mountain to pour down in a long narrow fall. Tal-git rose until he was above the whole mountain area and drifting back over the crater at the top. Yulir appeared from nowhere to hover over Firedrake.

"I know what you are thinking Firedrake," said Arin. "Hold me as tight as you can Sarah," he said "Do it!" he commanded Firedrake.

Without hesitation she charged full tilt at the whirling black creature and hit it with a hard crunch at top speed. Yulir followed to slash his claws ripping out the eye of the beast. Tal-git twisted the head, searing teeth and sparks along Firedrake's side before shattering into thousands of bone fragments at the impact. The parts fell down into the crater sending a flash of fiery sparks into the sky , causing all the artificial channels to overflow with magma and rise up to overflow the top of the crater. Firedrake also plummeted down and landed with a thud against the dark rock of the mountain. Sarah had been thrown, but Yulir had managed to soften the impact by catching his claws in her shirt which ripped free, but not before she landed. Arin staggered to his feet looking up in horror as the trails of lava began to flow down the mountain directly toward them. The air was filled with acrid smoke and dark dust clouds billowing up. He turned Sarah over and she was limp in his hold. Firedrake was stirring and he urged her to waken and rise. She staggered to her feet and to Arin's relief Sarah began to cough. He helped her up to climb onto Firedrake who soared up ahead of the cloudy billows, albeit a little wobbly in her flight. This time Yulir was ahead of them. Sarah looked down at the flowing black sea broken up with trails of red fire. It was amazing, primeval, and powerful. Inside, the creatures who survived the first blast up, were being overcome with the smoke and the lava. There was no sign of Hemlock who must have perished with the rest. Fortunately there were no dwellings in the area and the flow was already ceasing and the smoke receding.

"My father was right," Arin said. "Evil has a way of destroying itself. It sets in motion the very thing that will eventually destroy it."

"Back to Silvertrace," said Sarah.

They arrived at The Ardreth to be greeted by the Ryder. Silvertrace was walking around and being fussed over by Ryder.

"We need to take Sarah home," Arin pointed out.

"She is still small enough for me to carry in my claws," Firedrake communicated. "Ryder and Yulir can fly beneath just to be sure."

"Let's try it," said Arin. He retrieved his hat from where he had left it.

Enchanting Sarah by Morgan Fitzsimons

The little cavalcade took to the air with the anxious birds flying beneath. They made it with no incident and Firedrake lowered the little one onto the grass in the little wood behind Sarah's garden. Her parents were still at work and it was still light and they had been lucky not to have been spotted

"I must shower and grab a clean shirt," she said.

"I rather think your parents will panic if they see you looking like that," he grinned. She was covered in sooty smudges and her hair was filthy.

"You can clean up as soon as I've done." He followed her into the garden and sat under the oak tree.

What seemed like only moments later Paul shook him awake.

"Bogbean and Frogbit went home and Darren should be here shortly to hear what went down." He took him into the house to the shower, tossing him one of Charlie's sleeveless black t shirts when he emerged. Sarah had made a drink to refresh her throat. It was tea with lemon and lashings of honey. She passed a mug to Arin.

"Drink it. It is soothing and it has lots of honey."

He did just that and was impressed for once.

"I like it. You must show me how you make it." They went down to the bottom garden where Darren and Chrissie were already waiting.

.

.

Chapter 22

Comedy (or tragedy) of errors

They heard the cars arriving as mum came first then dad. Dad slammed his car door as usual and they went in through the side door. Sarah knew it was time to acquaint her parents with what had happened. She couldn't put it off any longer. She left the others in the garden and went inside alone. She sat down with them in the kitchen, and began to explain from the beginning when she had found the twilight star. As she went on, they just sat there throwing in the odd comment, like 'pull the other one Sarah,' and 'it's a great fantasy but no one in their right mind would fall for it.' She didn't tell them about what they had gone through; there was no point in alarming them now it was over, for the time being anyway. When they actually caught on to the fact she was serious, they began to worry about her sanity, but Sarah demonstrated a few things which had them sitting up in shock.

"I can really convince you if you come out side with me."

"Ok we might as well give her joke full reign," said mum and they went into the garden where she promptly took a run at the wall straight up to the roof to somersault down landing on her feet.

Sarah's dad just stood with his mouth open.

"I can't believe it," said her mum.

"It is true," said Darren.

"I guess you need to give them all the shocks at once," said Chrissie. "Tell them about Arin."

So she did. He came from the shadows and took off his hat, and they saw his ears like Sarah's.

Enchanting Sarah by Morgan Fitzsimons

"I would like you to meet my greatest friend and companion," he said. "I hope it isn't too much of a shock to you."

"You mean there are more shocks," said her dad.

"How do you feel about dragons?" asked Arin.

"Dragons, I love them. Haven't you seen my collection of all things dragon in the house."

"I meant real ones," said Arin.

"You mean living and breathing?"

Arin nodded.

"Your'e not serious, a live one," he almost stammered. "Oh boy, oh man you are kidding me."

Arin beckoned a finger and Firedrake came from the shadow of the trees. Sarah's dad was speechless.

"She will let you touch her," Arin said smiling a little at his reaction. He was like a child in a sweet shop; he was so awed and excited at the same time.

"The other one is my friend, but she is still a baby," said Sarah and the beautiful Silvertrace came shyly from behind the tree.

"Oh," said Sarah's mother. "She is beautiful, so small and delicate, just like you Sarah."

"You mean my daughter actually owns one?" said dad.

"We don't own them, they are our friends and if anything, they own us," said Sarah. "You understand it's something we can't ever tell people outside this group. We would become something to study under a microscope,"

"But how do you keep these magnificent creatures hidden?" asked her dad.

"My foster father keeps Firedrake in the woods behind his ranch. Silvertrace is newly born, but I will take her home soon," said Arin.

Enchanting Sarah by Morgan Fitzsimons

They all sat on the grass and talked for a while and Sara's mum and Chrissie brought sandwiches and apple juice and they sat talking well into the small hours. As they grasped the extent of Enchanter skills, they saw why she had to keep it to herself. They sensed the friendship between Sarah and Arin could be a little more than that and they were a little wary. The more they talked with him the more they were made aware of his integrity in his dealings with Sarah, and sometimes he seemed no different than Charlie and Mike, but they knew he was different and it wasn't really what they wanted at present for their daughter.

"Would you like to ride Firedrake," he asked Sarah's father.

"Is that possible?"

Arin helped him up on to the dragon's back. "You need not do anything. She will not let you fall. Do exactly as Sarah says and you will be fine."

Me ?" said Sarah "You will trust me,"

Enchanting Sarah by Morgan Fitzsimons

"With my life," he said and tossed her up to join her father.

That set alarm bells ringing madly in Sarah's mother's head. Her dad was ecstatic at the experience and went to bed talking of nothing else. Darren went home and Chrissie went to bed in Sarah's room. It was so late, Arin thought he would sleep under the oak tree one more time, at least that's the excuse he gave himself, and the animals disappeared into the little wood. Next morning he was sitting quietly when he heard voices and he moved to indicate he was there, but saw Sarah and her mother carrying their breakfast to the garden table. He just watched her, but then her mother began to talk and he hesitated.

"But this hasn't changed anything has it. I mean you still want all the things we talked of and your ambitions are still the same? You are so different from any other student. Everyone says you're special. The top universities are bombarding me with literature as are your sixth form tutors. They all know you could have passed the exams two years ago for entrance to any one of them."

Enchanting Sarah by Morgan Fitzsimons

"I know all that and I haven't changed my goals I want all the things I always wanted, but..."

"No buts are necessary. If you keep this standard up and don't slip, you can achieve anything you want, do anything and everything. You don't want any more distractions, just keep your eyes on the goal It's lucky you haven't a boyfriend or anything like that, you can leave all that until you get where you need to be. Get a secure future first. Boyfriends are all very well but girls your age have some silly ideas. I am glad you're not one of them."

Sarah didn't know what to say to her and decided not to say anything. Her mother had enough shocks last night and needed to adjust. Once she had assimilated events, maybe she could talk to her properly and say what she really felt. She went inside as her Dad appeared. Arin sat down again under the oak tree to think, but he couldn't shut out the voices.

"I'm relieved Sarah won't let any of this affect her future," said Sara's mother.

Enchanting Sarah by Morgan Fitzsimons

"She has a brilliant future ahead," agreed dad. "We've always known that. You're bothered about this guy I suppose. I quite like him."

"You do?" said mum, "most fathers take a dislike to males their daughter likes."

"Oh I'm not worried. She's a sensible girl. Most of them have a crush on someone or other at this age, but it doesn't last. It's the love of their life one day and the next they are talking about someone else. That's the fun of being young; it's all part of the game, part of growing up. It's just a lot of words really. "

"But for Sarah it could mess up her career, she need to concentrate on that for the next few years at least with no distractions," said her mum.

"Maybe she does like him but you know Sarah, she's soft hearted enough to be affected by his circumstances," he said," anyway she hasn't said she likes him more than as a friend has she? She would have said something when you chatted."

"I suppose so, she is a staunch friend and even I feel moved by the loneliness he must be experiencing," she said.

"Well let's just give her some space to become who she is meant to be," said dad. Both of them went into the house to refill their coffee cups and get ready for work.

Darren arrived to collect Chrissie and he came down to the bottom of the garden surprised to find a silent Arin with his hat tipped down over his eyes.

"What are you thinking about so deeply?" said Darren.

"Tell me," said Arin "What is expected of girls in your circle Darren?"

"I haven't thought about it," said Darren," but I suppose anything goes. There are no limits on what they can do these days, other than having children and that's not a restriction if you can afford child care. Girls succeed in all walks of life on the job front. I suppose it was different in the time you came from."

"The opportunities have advanced beyond Sorrels understanding anyway. I think in a way he was relieved to go back despite his curiosity. Is the role of Centre of the Home one that isn't any longer prized? There are women in top positions at the Foundation but I have had no opportunity for real contact with families."

"A lot of females do prize their freedom to make their own choices without the hindrance of family and have relationships that are meaningful or not as they please, but there are those who run a career and a family."

"Where do you fit into Chrissie's life?"

"Chrissie? She and I grew up next door to each other. I have known her all my life. I suppose you could say we have a mutual understanding. She knows I'm nuts about her, and I think she feels the same way, but she wants to enjoy being a student, so I just coast along until she decides she wants to make a commitment."

"I would find that very difficult Darren, coasting along as you put it, might be possible for an elf like Sorrel, but the Dulcamara nature is a bit more volatile."

"It can get precarious," Darren admitted. "But she isn't that hell bent on some super job career. She is one for whom being the centre of the home is all she wants, but not just yet. I don't think I'll have to wait that long."

"Sarah is different though,"

"Sarah is different from most girls I know. She is special, anyone will tell you that. Boys follow her like sheep and both the boys and the girls envy her abilities. She is an enigma to guys like me. She has always loved learning, it's natural to her. She can hold her own in any academic circle and always knew where she was going and what she wanted."

"And do you know what that is?"

"She has this tremendous imagination within all that academia that is capable of extra – ordinary leaps of new paradigm thinking. She wants to use that to make a difference to humanity and she can choose from a variety of fields. Everyone has expectations for her so I understand the pressure she is under. I get enough of that from my father let alone anyone else. I sometimes wish they would all stand back and leave me alone and give me space to do my own thing. That's why I enjoyed this last episode. It gave me a new set of parameters, or perhaps a better use of the old ones, and my father had nothing to do with it."

"I think perhaps my understanding is clearer," said Arin.

"She had all this before she discovered her genetic origin, but I do wonder if it hasn't something to with it. I have noticed the speed at which you acquire knowledge, and I think you are probably as capable of the same kind of thinking. Maybe sometime I could study it."

They were interrupted by the two girls in question joining them.

"Are you still here Arin," said Chrissie.

Enchanting Sarah by Morgan Fitzsimons

"If you can see me I must be."

They were interrupted yet again and this time the interruption was a great surprise to all of them Sorrel strolled from the direction of the portal. With him was the gorgeous Solandra, the Dulcamara companion of Blackthorn's wife and a long standing friend of Sorrel and Aeshna. She was carrying a small bundle in her arms.

"Aeshna insisted I brought my daughter to meet you. She wouldn't come herself, she is such a creature of nature, she can't relate to the world I described."

Sarah was delighted at his next words.

"She is Sarah Rose in honour of our friendship," said Sorrel "She entrusted her to Solandra clearly thinking I was too new to it to take proper care."

Solandra was a stunningly beautiful Elf with long dark hair, who was as ageless as they all seemed to be. She passed the baby Elf to Sarah who was fascinated with the tiny hands and pointed little ears. Chrissie too was taken with her. They didn't notice as Arin whispered to Sorrel who looked at him as though he were mad. Solandra joined them and Sarah looked up to see him laughing and talking with her, so at ease with his own kind.

"I have decided to go back with Sorrel. It is time I was with the Dulcamara again and who knows, I may find some old friends among them."

She almost dropped the baby so great was the shock.

"But I thought we were friends now after all we have been through," said Darren. "It's more likely you won't know *any* of them."

"But I could at least be myself. The real me can't ever be public here."

"But you are real to us, "said Chrissie.

"We will still be friends Chrissie, I just won't be here for a while," he said.

Sarah couldn't bring herself to say anything that wouldn't betray how she really felt. "What about Greg and Mitsouko?" she said finally.

Enchanting Sarah by Morgan Fitzsimons

"They are fine with whatever I choose to do," he replied but he didn't actually look at her as he said it. It appeared he had made the right decision for she said nothing about wanting him to stay.

"We must go back now with the baby," said Solandra, cheerfully holding her arms out. Sarah put the child into them.

"Things should be quiet now," said Arin. "I doubt this Jason survived, but even if by some chance he did, he would have a long way to go to replace Aorcha and Hemlock, but he probably didn't make it. You can get back to your own life for some time to come.

Sarah turned to hug Sorrel.

"I will miss you so much," she said to him what she couldn't say to Arin.

"We will see each other again," he said. He had felt her hurting when he hugged her goodbye and for the life of him couldn't grasp what Arin thought he was doing.

Enchanting Sarah by Morgan Fitzsimons

The hardest thing was to make her goodbyes to Silvertrace. She wept over her and the little one kept turning back, but her mother pushed her on and out of sight. Firedrake belonged with Arin and the baby needed her mother.

"Are you coming Arin?" Solandra called.

He did look at her then for a brief moment. "Goodbye Sarah, I hope all the things you want happen for you," he turned abruptly and walked away.

Sarah watched Arin go with Solandra. She wanted to call him back. She wanted to say, I am falling in love with you please don't go. It was there on the tip of her tongue but her mouth was frozen and no sound came out. Like most teenagers she could be forthright but when it really mattered she was afraid to put it to the test, particularly if she may have made a mistake and there were so many others present. Panic raced through her, she didn't know how to stop him and at the back of her mind was the idea he probably didn't want her to anyway. He suddenly seemed much more the adult and she felt totally immature and couldn't for the life of her, see anything to attract him in the immature sixth former she really was. Although Sorrel turned to wave, Arin didn't look back. She was devastated. She felt like someone had kicked her in the stomach. It hadn't occurred to her seeking out anyone from his past still with Blackthorn, was an option She realised she should have expected it. It didn't make it any easier to bear. Right until the last minute she thought he cared for Gary and Mitsouko too much to put himself first. To her it was simple. If he really cared for her, he would stay here, so he obviously had decided he didn't. He had made a choice that didn't include her. The garden was empty now but for Darren and Chrissie who didn't know what to do and had to accept there really wasn't anything except be there for her when she was ready. They wondered what had gone wrong but the obvious didn't occur to them. For Sarah and Arin just a few straight truthful words with each other would have set them straight, but they were words thought, but not spoken and other people's opinions made the decisions. Sarah just ran past them and up the stairs to slam the door to her room tight shut.

Chapter 23

Disaster

She wept on her own for hours emerging only for the occasional meal, then when she had no more tears left, she reappeared to resolutely set herself to sort out her future. She was an A student in everything and had been before she discovered her origins. She threw herself into her studies gaining the highest passes in all subjects. She could get through this. She was courted by several top universities as her mother had pointed out. Her parents were thrilled with her results but perversely now were worried about this totally workaholic Sarah. She had no interest in boys though she went to the odd movie or disco with

Enchanting Sarah by Morgan Fitzsimons

Chrissie and Darren. It was every parents dream teenager in fact but despite that her parents were dissatisfied. She was working harder and eating less. It was rather like a light inside had been switched off. Her mum's best friend told her she didn't know how lucky she was to have a daughter like her; she was constantly worrying what hers were up to.

Chrissie ducked any questions put to her though she wasn't clueless, but Sarah's mum was anxious. Maybe she had misjudged the extent of Sarah's feelings for Arin, but she was still sure in their opinion, she was way too young to make a commitment and really her future and what she could make of herself would matter most for several years to come. They couldn't really see a future with someone who could have no status and would have to continually dodge the authorities, fascinating though his background was. Sarah now, was already rooted in who she was and had a direction. It was so easy to make mistakes when you were so young, the evidence of that was all around. All her relatives and friends had made bad choices in their teens and suffered for it before finding life partners. In most cases they would perhaps be right in their assumptions. Unfortunately they had forgotten two important things. The first was the most fundamental; whatever happened in Sarah's life wasn't their choice to make She was the only one who should be making life choices for herself, particularly as she was of an age that allows the freedom to choose. She had to make her own mistakes and learn from them however hard. The other was she might just be different from the rest, one for whom the attraction was permanent and the one and only time she would fall in love. It could be so with her and only time would reveal the truth of it. Destroying that possibility could prove a heavy responsibility to bear, and they had, as many do, based their assessment of Arin's situation on assumption without actually finding out or asking him. If they had, they would have known he could have a better future than any one envisaged, for Darren was right, the Elf heritage was the same for Arin as for Sarah.

Enchanting Sarah by Morgan Fitzsimons

Sarah sat at the bottom of the garden with Ryder and often read her essays and things she was studying to him. He just sat in silent support, believing she would overcome her sadness in time. He was ever watchful for he knew the Dragon Masters were still out there. It was just a matter of time before they surfaced again. Given her origins, she developed a passion for the things of nature and her affinity with wildlife of all kinds, fuelled her studies of the biology of plants and animals and the ongoing development and preservation of nature alongside technology. Eco biology also interested her as did the exploration of woods and nature reserves. Creatures she encountered trusted her and came to her naturally. She also had an interest in genetics given her own life changing discovery and all the machinations of the Dragon Masters.

She liked to run in the twilight and sometimes at dawn light. She just ran and ran with Ryder swooping over head and would return home before people were about to notice her. In time however Ryder grew restless and longed for

Enchanting Sarah by Morgan Fitzsimons

Blackthorn and Sarah knew she must let him go but she didn't know how she could bear it without him too. He disappeared one morning and she had two days of loneliness that had her weeping in her pillow again but eventually he reappeared with a companion.

"I brought you a new friend. Blackthorn says she will bond with you and remain with you always. She is offspring of one of Asphodel's hounds and has belonged to no one personally. She wanted to be the chosen, and she is wholly yours."

The animal was a beautiful silver and white wolf wearing a deep decorated collar of intricate Elven silver, and a saddle shape protection on her back. Her eyes were deep green and even as she looked into them she heard Blackthorn communicating through her. "I hope you will treasure your gift she has all the intuition of the Ryder and will remain devoted to you always. She has been part of the group with Amaryllis, the minder of the hounds. Trust her She has battle ways and will defend you to the death if needs be. "

Enchanting Sarah by Morgan Fitzsimons

She put her arms about her neck and wept out her frustration, before curling up together under the oak tree. The wolf seemed to understand her loneliness and grief, but she in turn knew she would be loved. Sarah didn't think she would need defending as all was quiet on the dragon master front, but for the wolf it was instant devotion. They became inseparable companions when Sarah was at home and she waited patiently for her return from college. Sarah named her Treasure remembering Blackthorn's words.

Darren was impressed with Treasure too but the amusing part was her attitude to males who came near Sarah. It was obviously her duty to defend her mistress, but she seemed to think she should protect her against everybody, friends as well She treated Sarah as her child and growled against any young male who came too close, even her brothers. Sarah's dad approved entirely of course. Darren and Sarah still had the videos of the birth of Silvertrace and often watched them when he was home. The ones she herself had taken had glimpses of Arin and they brought brief solace when she actually watched them but after a while she couldn't bear to anymore. A birthday came and went and she got into the habit of spending time in the dark of night under the oak tree in the garden and on one such occasion she felt something there. Turning her head her eyes fell on the most beautiful of creatures. At first she thought she was dreaming, she was seeing what she wanted to see, and the vision would vanish. But she wasn't going anywhere. She was almost the size of an adult dragon though was still only about a year old. She had beautiful patterns and scales of blue and green and turquoise and everywhere, were the trace patterns of delicate silver. It really was Silvertrace and she fell against her laughing and crying.

"I should not be here," she communicated "But we are one and I was drawn."

"You have grown so fast in the time we have been apart," said Sarah.

"I will still grow a little more," she said. "I am not yet the size of my mother."

Enchanting Sarah by Morgan Fitzsimons

"How is Firedrake?" said Sarah.

"She teaches me many things."

"And Arin? What of him?" She asked holding her breath.

Silvertrace was silent, "Will you ride with me," she said.

"Can we ride together? Sarah said, her excitement at the prospect overriding everything else.

"It is why I came."

Sarah climbed on her back and Silvertrace rose on the night air. High into the clouds and back again round and round they went, the air whistling past, blowing her hair out in a stream behind them, and as they turned she flung her arms out wide confident that Silvertrace would keep her steady. Silvertrace floated twisting and turning rhythmically.

"She is dancing, we are dancing," they were joyful in their coming together as one creature, bonded forever in time and space.

Enchanting Sarah by Morgan Fitzsimons

"I am truly dancing with a living Dragon," All too soon Silvertrace brought her down and Sarah slid to the grass.

"I must go before I am missed but I will come back," she said.

Just before she disappeared into the trees, she met Sarah's eyes. "He is well, but very lonely," she said and was gone.

 Sarah was startled, "How could he be lonely?"

She pondered the thought but it brought her no comfort.Time passed a little faster and another birthday came and went and the University of her Dreams became a reality. Chrissie was still her best friend and she turned up one evening wearing the ring Darren gave her. Sarah was delighted for her and if she felt any tug at the heartstrings it wasn't apparent, but Chrissie was always in tune with her moods and had become used to the sadness in her eyes behind the still enchanting elfin smile. Darren had acquired honours degrees in his chosen subjects and had been offered some dream job when he had completed this extra course required of him, though he seemed a little reticent about where.

She had lots of friends at university and there were quite a few boys who would like to be more but she didn't encourage any of them. The sadness added to her mystery and none of them knew what she really was about. Her elven abilities were still part of her, and she used them, where it could be unobtrusive. Her skills as Enchanter however were a different thing and there seemed no place for them in the realities of the day and she would never use them to cheat or to gain advancement or to dominate others. Arin had shown her the folly of that and even if she never saw him again, she wouldn't break faith with the code he had taught her. One evening, she went out to the oak tree as she did everyday and found a package. Puzzled she looked around, but there was no one there. Inside she found data sticks. She raced indoors and put them into the computer one by one. She found them to contain all sorts of teaching about Elf. They contained things about their beliefs, their commitment to nature, their way of life, all manner of things. One contained teaching of the language itself and how words and poetry were used in Enchantment and much more. The voice on them was Arin's. It must have been part of teh work he had mentioned doing at the Foundation.

Why had he done this? Someone must have left it through the portal. His voice made her weep again but she was inevitable fascinated by the wealth of information. She learned a lot more about herself and the Enchantment and had found the stuff Arin had committed to the USB sticks was invaluable. She learned many of the chants used in Enchantment. The items with his voice speaking the words and teaching the language brought both pleasure and pain in equal measure. His statement he made before he left, about never being able to be yourself, struck home. She couldn't even be that with her parents anymore. There was no one to understand the meaning of being elf in today's culture, just Arin and he was no longer here. She lived at home still. The train journey to and from uni was only half an hour and the faithful Treasure would be waiting impatiently. Today was Friday and it was half term. When they went back it would just a short time to the holidays. She took a taxi from the station which was her bit of end of term extravagance. Paul was in the kitchen when she arrived home. He had developed great athletic abilities and one or two little Elf traits but none of the Dulcamara magic, but he did have Elf intuition and understood Sarah better than most and was sensitive to her moods. Treasure bounded in to join her. She switched on the TV to hear the news as she made her coffee, and was about to sit down with it when she caught what the reporter was actually saying. Paul came behind her to hear it all.

"It could prove to be a second tragedy for Greg O Neill, the multi billionaire from California who tragically lost his son today for the second time. No one really knows what caused the disaster. There were reports of an underground tremor causing the buildings to collapse. IGR was called in and almost as soon as they got here there was a series of what seems to be rapid explosions, the last underground, causing a whole section of the damaged buildings to slide into the earth itself."

They showed a panorama of the terrain with horrific looking devastation. The screen flashed back to the newsroom and a picture of Arin in the dark green jacket and jeans of the O Neill Foundation sitting in the dirt with a group of kids all enthralled with the eagle, and still wearing the hat she bought him. The newscaster continued the dialogue and the images changed to suit the words.

"Inazo Global Rescue was founded by Gregory Inazo O Neill after his son was caught up in an earthquake on a visit to Japan. It is funded by The O Neill Foundation one of today's staunch bastions of Ecology and Nature preservation and of course Everybody's Child, caring for children everywhere."

There was a flash to a picture of Arin among a group of homeless kids in the city streets.

"Mr. Oneill's son, Arin Inazo was eventually found alive on the previous occasion. Since then he has worked with both the Foundation and IGR becoming one of its most valuable team members and is known for his uncanny ability to find and rescue people when hope is gone, but this time it seems his own luck has run out. No one appears to be able to find him."

The words hammered into her brain. Paul was horrified but his sister was ashen faced. She didn't even register the fact he wasn't with Sorrel as she thought. She just registered the words of the reporter. She couldn't get past that to wonder how it was he wasn't with Sorrel. Paul picked up her feelings immediately.

"Paul I need you to watch over me with Treasure while I mind walk."

She didn't hesitate but was gone in moments concentrating her whole being on where he was. She flew through the space between them coming to the piles of rubble and wreckage and desperately circling around searching for contact. She tried to infiltrate it but there were blockages everywhere she went, and there would be no way to get him out that way. She was conscious of a presence of something dark and evil and shapes loomed toward her. She twisted her fingers in her mind just as Ain had shown her, and the creatures ceased to be. She moved back from it again and saw Yulir. Her mind followed after him to the far side of the mountain. She was still searching with all her being for Arin. Normally she wouldn't have had a chance to find him in an unconscious state, but she was aided by knowing he was actually here somewhere. It was just a matter of systematically searching and using the Elf instinct. She was drawn to what seemed a steep rock face but eventually she felt the presence of the dragon and found a way into the darkness. She moved inside the mountain through caves, still drawn by the dragon. She found Firedrake and made contact. The Dragon was too large to go further. There was no sign of Silvertrace. She knew it was Sarah mind walking so she watched and waited pointing Sarah into smaller caves. Eventually she came to a deep dark drop that looked like a hole into hell. She floated down trying to estimate its depth. So far it seemed a very small opening down, but very, very deep. She came to the bottom where the presence of something really bad permeated her senses. She stopped briefly to concentrate totally on Arin. She was aware of her own heart beating fast and along with it, his heart beat. She moved quickly to where it was and found a whole area of what had been empty space now filled with metal bars concrete and the rubble of buildings and wrecked vehicles. There were other heartbeats, very faint, maybe two or three even.

She came to the source of those first and in the misty darkness she registered be two children, one of them clutching a baby. How they had survived she didn't know but maybe Arin had something to do with it. She saw his hat first and he was under a whole lot of wreckage and quite unconscious. She also felt the menacing presence was moving nearer. Whatever it was it didn't really know where they were, but was searching blindly. She had to come back in the flesh to save him. She was the only one who could. She tried to contact him but knew she had to be flesh and blood to do it. She raced back to Firedrake. She moved into her mind convincing her she could help him best by fetching her in the flesh. There was no other way to get there fast enough. She rushed back to Paul, everything flashing past like lines of colour ever changing. She opened her eyes and told him what she planned. She grabbed some boots and pulled them on. She was wearing jeans already and she quickly pulled on a t shirt and grabbed her anorak and slammed her Stetson over the ears.

"What do I tell mum and dad?! Paul asked.

"That I have to go, I owe it to him many times over anyway, but even without that I would do it. Tell her they need my research, just wing it, and don't panic them with what I will really be doing."

She went out into the garden and there was Silvertrace waiting, not Firedrake Treasure was there before Sarah, lying across the back of the dragon. She looked fiercely down at Sarah who picked up her communication. In no way was

Enchanting Sarah by Morgan Fitzsimons

Treasure allowing her to be in danger without her. Once she was on her back they rose high into the clouds and Sarah didn't need to concentrate of their destination. Silvertrace was just going where her mother was. She went up and came down again at the scene. She deposited Sarah and Treasure out of sight and joined her mother in the cavern vigil. Sarah raced at elf speed round to the base camp of the rescuers making straight for Greg. The police tried to stop her progress at the barriers, but she somersaulted over their heads so fast they didn't see where she went and she was with Greg grasping his arms. Treasure followed her and curled about her legs daring anyone to approach.

"I know where he is and he is still alive," she gasped.

"Sarah, how did you get here?"

"Never mind that, I have to go down there, no one else can do it. It will take my small size and my Elf skills to reach him. I have mind walked and I know."

Enchanting Sarah by Morgan Fitzsimons

"But I can't let you. He wouldn't want his life at the price of yours. And what about your parents what would I tell them if it went wrong.

"Just that it is not an impulse of valour misspent, but a cause worthy of it." She used words she had heard from Arin in Gregory's garden.

Greg understood her inference she would pay any price to save him and it was a conscious decision.

"There is something bad searching for him and I need to get back to wake him before it finds him. He will find a way back."

"What will you need?"

"Do any of your people know about him? Is there anyone to trust?"

"His immediate team, there are five of them. Only Sam knows his true origin, the others believe he is a genetic throwback like you. I didn't want too many people knowing he was adopted."

"Take me to them," she said.

Enchanting Sarah by Morgan Fitzsimons

He rushed her to the HQ tent and there were three males and two females all kitted up preparing to go out and search again.

"This is Sarah," he said.

She threw of the Stetson and they saw her ears.

"Another one," exclaimed the Japanese female team member.

"I know where he is and time is of the essence. I will have to go the last bit alone but I need you to come as far as you can get," she said

"You are just a child and inexperienced to boot," said Sam, the leader of the group.

"Don't let my looks fool you. I'm an adult and at University. I have the same origins as Arin. I have the abilities he has. I need one of your jackets to protect my arms and one of your communication systems."

The Japanese girl being the thinnest gave her a jacket and turned the sleeves back. As she worked she said "I am Kiko," and Sarah nodded. The jacket was still rather wide and dropped at the shoulders. She was given a helmet with the headset and speaker attached and set on their frequency.

"If you have any weapons Greg, the team will need to be armed just in case. I think the creatures we battle with are still targeting him. I could feel them."

Greg nodded.

"Is the scabbard here for the dragon sword? He did usually have it somewhere with him. "

Without a word Greg dived into a box and produced it, helping her strap it on.

"Don't worry, I don't intend trying to use it, but he will need it,"

"You are so sure he will live," said Gregory.

"I cannot believe anything else," she said firmly.

He hugged her, "bless you and thank you for this," he said.

Enchanting Sarah by Morgan Fitzsimons

"I am doing it for me just as much as for you," she said simply. "He may not be coming back to me, but bring him back I will."

He was very impressed with this grown up Sarah and was content to let his hope rest with her. Once armed, the little group followed her to the far side with Treasure at her heels. As soon as they were out of sight of cameras and people, she stopped.

"I am going to run ahead. He has little time left. Follow the eagle and just move through the caverns to Firedrake. You will be able to go further, just follow the passage ways but when you come to the very steep drop down, wait. We will come to you. Have ropes and harness ready to toss down to me when I call. Oh and there are two children and a baby alive with him so make some preparation for that."

"Maintain contact with us," said Sam.

"I will but once I help them I will be weaker just as Arin is after using his skills and I don't know how strong he will be yet either."

Enchanting Sarah by Morgan Fitzsimons

She snapped out orders with all the conviction of Arin who was born to be a leader, and they responded. The powerful presence innate in the Dulcamara had come to maturity in what still looked like a slip of a girl, and probably would for a long time to come.

She turned her face up to Yulir.

She held up her hand and Yulir dropped the sword into her hand, which she got Sam to put in the sheath on her back. She was thankful it wasn't as heavy as she thought it would be, but it was Elven made after all. She raced off with Treasure, leaving them way behind.

Chapter 24

Light in the Dark

Once she reached Firedrake, she told her what was happening.

Firedrake communicated back. "Lady Sarah have a care. I can feel them too. I am helpless until he is out of danger. I could harm him more by breaking through. Hurry!"

Sarah touched Silvertrace "Stay here," she said feeling the dragon's desire to follow. But she too would get stuck or cause rock fall. She slipped through the opening and raced as quickly as she could. She didn't need the light on the helmet as like Arin and Blackthorn she could see in the dark. Some of the passages were narrow but she thought them passable enough for the team following her. Once she reached the hole into hell, she stopped to drop a rock down it. It was a long time before she heard a thud and in fact probably wouldn't have without the elf ears. She couldn't run down, she would have to jump in and trust she would land on her feet. She had never faced such a jump. She had no idea if she would break bones or not.

"Treasure you will have to stay here. I won't be able to get you back up this drop and it is too tight for you to go down."

The hound looked across at her, her eyes glowing amber as she communicated.

"I will find a way." She raced off back the way they came. She shot round to the wreckage above ground and after sniffing here and there she suddenly disappeared under a pile of rubble.

Sarah fixed her mind on her goal and dropped into the hole. The air whistled past her ears as she fell for what seemed forever, and her feet touched the bottom with a tremendous jolt. Her legs seemed like jelly when she stood up and she staggered as she walked. She just followed the heartbeat and came back to where he was. She checked the children first who were still not conscious. The baby was just lying there held against the girl, not crying but definitely awake. She unstrapped the sword sheath and laid it down before moving through into the area where he was. She dropped beside him, reaching out to touch his face. She got the hat and dusted it off then reached for his shoulders. She needed to use the enchantment now to pull him out, but before she could, there was a scrabbling noise and the hound came carefully through the wreckage. She grabbed Arins jacket with her teeth. The metal girders curving over him were actually protecting him from what was above. He didn't appear to be caught on anything so she willed him to move and the girders to hold, and pulled in unison with Treasure. He slid out so fast and easily she fell backwards, but not before willing something in there to replace the body. One of the girders slipped across but still held the structure. If it all came down it would fill the area and crush all of them under it.

Scrambling to him she looked down at the mess. She could see signs of his head being struck, possibly by flying debris. Her heart almost gave out when she saw the bloody mess that was his chest and rib cage. She peeled back the jacket. There was too much area for her little hands. She saw the knife still in his belt and drew it from the sheath. The blood from the handle covered her hand. She gingerly attempted to cut the shirt open at the front having the sense to preserve her strength for healing. She peeled back the shirt and wished she hadn't but it was crucial to get the healing power directly to him. She didn't see how it could possibly work, then pulled herself together. Negativity wasn't good. She pulled Kiko's jacket open, throwing it to one side and she hastily pulled her t shirt over her head and placed her body over his. It was the first time she had ever attempted this and she was going by the book as it were. She was terrified she would do something to jeopardise the process and had to make herself concentrate. She whispered in the Dulcamaran language as she touched his arms knowing they were broken. The healing glow grew around her covering her skin and moved from her to him enveloping them, but as she grew weaker he grew stronger, the glow fading about her. He suddenly coughed and his eyes flew open.

"Sarah?" his fingers moved up to touch her as if to reassure himself she was real. He caught her hand and held it to his face. He turned his head and realization of events hit him.

"You have put yourself in danger?"

"There's no time to explain. Can you feel them?"

She raised herself up and he saw the blood all over her from neck to waist.

"Sarah?" he felt suddenly dizzy. "You are hurt?"

"It was all yours, but you seem to have stopped bleeding." She moved back from him and he touched his ribs. The gaping wounds and jagged edges had sealed together as had the bones but the blood was dried and matted into his torn shirt.

"It was bad I take it."

"It was," she said briefly He may have residual weakness from any enchantment he used to save those children but she could not replace that, it had to come from within.

He sat up and gripped her hand. "I can feel them now, and the first of them are almost here."

"Did they cause all this?"

"No they just took advantage of the natural event and enhanced it with some more explosions well placed. They meant to kill me"

She pointed to the sword lying next to her hat in the opening to the smaller caves He pulled her to her feet. "I thought it would save your energy."

" Good thinking, and the children?"

"Still live," she said.

Enchanting Sarah by Morgan Fitzsimons

She staggered now, the healing having taken its toll. She looked a mess with her bra and body covered in his blood and smudges from her hands on her face mingled with tear streaks. He grabbed her jacket and put it on, catching her close.

"Sarah, I must deal with the threat. Have you enough strength to reach the children and get them moving?"

She took his hat in her hand and she reached up and put it on his head at the familiar angle. He moved her with him intending to pick up the sword. Treasure raced past them and the whole structure beyond them moved and collapsed inward in a cloud of dust and debris.

Sarah was shaking uncontrollably. "If I had taken a few minutes longer," it didn't bear thinking about.

"But you are always ahead of yourself, impulsive girl. How could you ever be too late!"

She answered his previous question.

Enchanting Sarah by Morgan Fitzsimons

"I can get them to the bottom of the long drop I came down. I am hoping your team will be there at the top, but it is probably too narrow to negotiate. It's one time my size is useful."

They could hear stirring sounds in the darkness beyond.

"I will be back soon," he said.

She turned to Treasure. "Go with Arin,"

"You look as if a breath of wind will blow you over, take care little one," he dropped a kiss on top of her head and reached for the scabbard swiftly strapping it on his back.

"I am not anyone's little one," she said. "I'm all grown up and an adult with exceptional reasoning so they say."

"Which is why you were daft enough to come down here to get me, that exceptional brain telling you it would be a walk in the park." he said. He swiftly kissed her leaving her in shock, and gripping the sword he moved toward that which came to them in the darkness. Treasure bounded alongside eager to reach the enemy threatening her much loved Sarah. Sarah quickly touched the faces of the children and they opened their eyes as she strengthened them. One had a broken arm and she healed it, deeming it would be easier for him to move up that drop, but she left all the surface cuts and bruises for later.

She stuck the helmet back on. "We need to go this way," she said and switched on the light for their benefit.

She moved them through the small caves carrying the baby. It was fortunate they were small and the baby was light, but she was labouring somewhat as she had not recovered her strength at all. She felt the battle behind her. More than anything she wanted to go back but she knew the children came first. In her present state she would only be a burden anyway. She heard rapid fire briefly which indicated at least some of them were the TAB creatures. Whatever they were Arin cut them to pieces, whirling and slashing at such rapid speed they didn't see it coming until the moment of death. The sound of Treasure's snarls carried then all went quiet as Arin came after Sarah reaching her just as she looked up into the dark hole. She spoke to Sam who responded instantly.

"Arin is with me," she said, and she felt his overwhelming relief.

"There are more in the vicinity," said Arin as he joined her."We must be quick."

"Treasure, go and delay them then make your own way out again. We will join you as soon as we can."

Treasure licked her fingers then bounded off into the dark towards the oncoming danger.

"I think it will be too tight for you at least," Sarah said.

"I know it will, but we can fix it. Tell Sam to stand away from the top."

She spoke into the microphone.

"I will have to use Enchantment which means I will be as weak as you are. Sam will have to pull the kids up in the old fashioned way," Arin told her.

She passed on that information to Sam.

Arin put his hands out on either side of his body and began to spin and in moments was spinning so fast he couldn't prevent the fire flashing from his hands. He shot up into the hole as though he were a drill, the sparks flying as it widened though he himself didn't actually touch the rock walls. When he reached the top, he was exhausted but he grabbed the rope and harness.

"Someone, give me a jacket," he said and one of the men took his off and tossed it to him.

He leapt back into the hole taking the items with him. When he reached the bottom again he collapsed in a heap.

"Sarah, put the coat around the girl and then the harness. The coat will protect her from the wall."

She did as he said and told Sam to haul her up. Arin sat with his head in his hands.

"Reason and adult behaviour had nothing to do with it anyway," she said looking up to see if the harness was coming down again.

"Had nothing to do with what," he asked.

"With my coming to get you, though why I should when you didn't even tell me you were back is beyond me."

"Impulse! Perhaps it was the first emotional response taking over?"

She glared at him. "I did stop for at least a second to consider the consequences," she snapped.

At that point harness came down again; the coat was tied to it. She swiftly wrapped it round the boy and sent him up. Arin had sensed something moving close by and went to confront it. He disappeared from view but came back swiftly though the confrontation left him breathing heavily now, the weakness showing. He may have the injuries healed, but he had been so near death his body was still not recovered.

Enchanting Sarah by Morgan Fitzsimons

"They have Ochra and are sending fire through the caves. We can't wait to climb a rope." They were frustrated at not finding their quarry and sought to destroy whatever survived the quick way.

"Do you have the girl," she asked Sam.

"We do,"

"Forget the ropes!   Move back!"

He obeyed without question.

Arin slammed the sword   into the scabbard on his back.

"Hold tight to the baby," he said and wrapped his arms about Sarah.

"You will need to help me. Concentrate on reaching Sam,"

He muttered words into her hair he was so close. It took all his remaining strength to sustain the rise into the vertical tunnel. Sarah mustered what she had left and added to it. A rush of fire reached through the caves on the bottom just as they shot upward with the flames following, rushing and billowing behind them. Arin curved them backwards over the rim and the three who had stayed to wait pulled them away from the edge as the flames shot up in the air. Sarah gasped for breath and realisation flooded in.

"Treasure," she moaned. "I sent her to hold them back. She can't have survived the flames." She was devastated at the thought.

Arin tried to get up, but had to content himself with reaching to grasp her hand. "Don't grieve yet Sarah, she's a battle hound from Asphodel's stock. They are bred to survive against worse things." He was out of breath again.

They couldn't move for a while and the baby was rushed away by Kiko. Sam and Gary stayed with them until they could stand.

"Once we reach the wide cave we can stretcher you out," said Gary.

"Over my dead body," said Arin.

Enchanting Sarah by Morgan Fitzsimons

He staggered up and held out his hand to Sarah and they moved out to where the anxious Firedrake and Silvertrace waited. Gary and Sam gave them support on either side. Firedrake nuzzled at Arin's head and Yulir came down to touch his arm with his claws as though wanting to perch there.

"You've got no chance Yulir," he said with a laugh. "I can't hold myself up, never mind you."

Sarah watched, just content at the moment to know he was alive, but her heart ached unbearably for Treasure who was nowhere to be seen.

"Wait until dark Firedrake then take Silvertrace back to the Ranch. We will see you there."

Firedrake was content to do whatever he wanted now he was safe. Arin felt Sara's distress over Treasure and supported her in the curve of his arm. They stumbled out onto the mountain side but the media had caught on to where the action was and were waiting. They were calling questions at them but they just kept going to reach Greg.

Enchanting Sarah by Morgan Fitzsimons

"Who is the girl, what happened down there?"

A host of voices hammered at them and cameras sent images to TV screens. It suddenly hit home to Sarah that Arin was here, he wasn't with Sorrel and those from his own time, he was here and he hadn't made any attempt to contact her. What did that mean? She began to feel very shaky, but he knew and tightened his grip again She was crushed against his side and she could feel his heart beat or was it her own, it was going rather fast. Her legs were jelly and she knew she was going to fall.

"Don't let go Arin, I can't stand up. I can't feel my feet."

"Don't worry about it. I have no intention of letting you go again,"

"Then why did you walk away?"

"A lot of reasons that seemed the right at the time,"

"But you didn't ask me what I thought?"

Enchanting Sarah by Morgan Fitzsimons

"If I had, I wouldn't have been able to go at all. You didn't say anything to make me think I was wrong. Why didn't you stop me?"

"Could I have done?"

"Most definitely."

"I thought you were gone forever, when did you come back?"

"Almost as soon as I left." He admitted. "I didn't really go. I wanted at least to be in the same hemisphere."

She stopped walking and glared up at him. "You mean you have been here all this time and didn't contact me? How could you? Do you have any idea what you put me through? Her anger sent adrenalin flowing fast, which gave support to her weakness.

"Don't kick my shins again," he warned.

Her mouth curved in that mischievous elfin smile. "Maybe I should hurt you a little. You deserve it."

Enchanting Sarah by Morgan Fitzsimons

He hugged her close again "You couldn't hurt me anymore than I already hurt myself," he replied, "but I'm wearing boots Sorrel gave me. They are Darg claw proof and will break those pretty little elf toes."

They were in the tent now and she pulled off the helmet and threw it at him. He deftly caught it and passed it to Kiko.

"We might as well get it all over with in one go," he said."I should tell you Darren has just started working for The O Neill Foundation, but I did pressure him not to tell you"

"Next you will be telling me Chrissie knew you were here too?" She was angry again.

"Yes, but she only just found out, and to be fair she gave me an absolute beating verbally insisting I was, and I quote, "truly gutless, stupid and not who she thought I was for walking away. At the very least she said I should have talked about it with you.   But for this event I would have been sitting on your doorstep."

Enchanting Sarah by Morgan Fitzsimons

"My parents will have seen the news programmes by now and will be worried. They can't fail to recognise me. I have no idea what Paul will have told them .I will go home now if you will arrange it Greg," she said.

Arin's reaction was to grab her with both hands and pull her into his arms. "Don't push it Sarah! I told you I wasn't letting you go this time and I am still wearing the boots."

She stamped her foot instead, which set her off shaking and tears welled up and spilled over, her emotions taking over altogether. Arin let her weep but he was concerned when she didn't stop."Please don't do this Sarah, Its killing me."

"Delayed shock, "said Kiko. "It's just hitting home what she did."

"I don't think so," said Arin "Elf abilities are a way of life and the enchantment leaves you weary, not in shock." He held his hands away from her. "The choice will always be yours Sarah,"

Enchanting Sarah by Morgan Fitzsimons

She didn't move away from him. "They almost killed you this time and they are not going to stop trying are they. We don't even know which of them it was who set this in motion." she said into his shoulder.

Her words gave him hope she had forgiven him, but then again she was just as distressed for Treasure.

"Aorcha's hatred of me ran very deep, but after the Hemlock episode I suppose his grandchildren will eventually make a comeback, but there have been no signs of Dragon Masters and Monkshood may have the inclination but he lacks the physical strength."

"Then why where those creatures down there? Who sent them? Why can I still feel Dragon Master presence? Since I have been back near you why do I keep getting this suffocating panic? I don't know how else to describe it."

Greg had her parents on the phone by this time. He held the phone out to her. Arin still didn't let her go even when she talked to them.

Enchanting Sarah by Morgan Fitzsimons

"I'm perfectly fine mum, "she said but they found it hard to believe she was as fine as she claimed.

They had seen the news and recognised Arin and saw the mystery female was Sarah. They wanted to know why she had done what she did and she patiently explained because she was the only person who could. She didn't tell them she had been physically involved.

"I could see things they needed to know if he was to be rescued."

"There's more to it than that. From what I can see you dropped everything to be there, does he mean so much to you? Would you give it all up just like that?"

"Yes and Yes I would, but I really don't have to you know."

"We wanted the best for you," said her mother tearfully.

"I know," she said gently," but I'm all grown up now and I can work it out for myself. I admit I'm a little stressed right now so I am going   to

Enchanting Sarah by Morgan Fitzsimons

Greg's ranch to calm down. In case I didn't tell you, he is Arin's foster father. Greg will explain. He and Mitsouko will take as much care of me as you would. I love you both."

She passed the phone back to him, her eyes entreating and he smiled and moved away still talking to her mum and dad. He was an expert at handling people and would probably make more sense to them right now than she would, A moment later the tent flap moved and a battered animal appeared in the doorway. She was covered in dust and debris and her fur was streaked with dark smoke. She had a fierce bloody slash on one side below the silver patterned saddle. Sarah sank down to the floor and hugged her, tears streaking through the sooty dust. She put up her hand to brush them away and added the dust to the bloodstains.

"Oh Treasure," she said.

Arin came down beside her to check the wound. "Allow me," he said gently and ran his hand over it and the wound healed.

Enchanting Sarah by Morgan Fitzsimons

"Will it be so hard to stay," Arin asked, as he ministered to Treasure.

"Not really, my parents would bombard me with questions I don't want to answer. I want to visit with Silvertrace, I love her madly."

"Could that extend to me by any chance?"

"That would take a lot more work, at least a couple of years."

Greg called across to her and she turned her head.

"I've arranged to fly your family out here for a couple of weeks, a change of scene can change ones perspective."

She broke free of Arin to hug Greg, "Thank you for that," she said. "They haven't quite got used to the idea of letting me go to make my own decisions, but they will."

"They just love you Sarah," said Greg. "By the way Mitsouko doesn't know about all this. The staff managed to keep the news from her. I don't know what I would have done but for your intervention. Now thanks to you, Arin can tell her himself and make light of it."

Sam stuck his head into the tent. "The helicopters are here to fly us out," he said, "Great to know you Sarah, I was most impressed. You are much more capable than you look. Maybe Arin can persuade you to join the team."

"Particularly the dog," said Gary.

"She is a wolf," Sarah said laughing.

"Wolf, dog, she is fantastic," said Gary.

"I agree with that, "replied Sarah.

"So are you Sarah" Arin said. He could feel there was a change in her. Now he had time to look he had noticed the hair. She had allowed it to grow like Sorrel's long and flowing down her back. It was like a gleaming shaft of moonlight.

"You look just like Queen Lilia now," he said.

"I don't think I have the stature of a queen," she said.

Enchanting Sarah by Morgan Fitzsimons

"It isn't height, its presence and charisma."

"I'm sure the O Neill Foundation could make use of all that research stuff as well. Think about it," called Kiko, still continuing with Sam's theme.

"I should think you would have enough of the British peculiarities with Darren," she called back. "You know It just came to me, Treasure doesn't normally allow any male to get as close as you are. Why isn't she growling at you?" Sarah said.

"I am Dulcamara, she is responding to what she knows and is familiar," Arin spoke quietly. "Can I persuade you Sarah?" His voice gave no indication of how much the answer would mean.

"Persuade me to what?"

"Can I persuade you to work with the Foundation, and maybe join the team?"

"Why would you want to? Tell me exactly what you want from me Arin?"

Enchanting Sarah by Morgan Fitzsimons

"I want to keep you near me, It isn't dealing with the Dragon Masters that provides me with purpose, its being with you."

His grip was firm but gentle as he raised her hands to his lips. "All I ever wanted to be is here within my hold, don't take that away from me, it's all I have left." and she remembered his words to her about Asphodel and Lilia. "If it takes a few years to convince you, then so be it, but spend them near me please."

"Is that what I am to you, a queen you are duty bound to protect and watch over, the fragile lady and the chivalrous warrior knight together."

"We are flesh and blood Sarah and bleed like anyone else; you should know that, you have enough of mine all over you."

"Truthfully the elf in me would love to be Lilia to your Asphodel but there is something I would love even more."

"Tell me what it is and I will give it to you."

Enchanting Sarah by Morgan Fitzsimons

"I am Sarah, part of the human race as well as an Enchantress of the Dulcamara. I am not something fragile that will break and fly away like a leaf on the wind. I want you to love *me*, not someone's idea of what I should be. I may look like Lilia and aspire to follow her example, but inside you and I are the same, we may have to hide who we are from the rest of them but not from each other."

She lifted her face, still a little tear stained but her eyes sparkled like the grass after rain and that glorious elfin mouth curved and his resolve to let her set the pace went out of the window and he kissed her breathless.

"Now why didn't you try that argument in the first place," she said, "though I may need a little more convincing,"

He laughed and kissed her again, "Oh I do love you Sarah," he said.

 His father tapped him on the shoulder and Arin swept Sarah out into the sunlight, followed by the prancing Treasure at her heels, to board the helicopter and for a brief time they concentrated on the moment and left the threat of the Dragon Masters until another day, as Chrissie said what seemed a long time ago, they would cross that bridge when they came to it.

Several hours later, in the magical twilight hours two figures hand in hand could be seen leaving the old hacienda and racing across the lawns to the wild wood beyond the garden. They stopped briefly to exchange a kiss and the girl ran on, dancing round the oak tree and lingering at the ancient group of Alders, moving on to where their friends waited. Moments later the dragons climbed up in the night sky twirling and swirling on the wind, their riders content to allow them free reign. Down below sat the wolf gazing up at the madness of two legged beings. For the moment they hadn't a care in the world for they had found each other again, but how long the enemy would leave it that way is anybody's guess......, but maybe mine to know.

www.ingramcontent.com/pod-product-compliance
Lightning Source LLC
Chambersburg PA
CBHW050019030726
47506CB00001B/20